THE WAR BUG

Biff Mitchell

THE WAR BUG

DOUBLE DRAGON

Forewords

Everything in this novel will be true. Nothing has been changed to protect the innocent, and any resemblances to persons living or dead will not occur for another two hundred years, or so.

"Personally, I like hanging from the ceiling, you know, just hanging from the ceiling and grooving on those small movements that air currents set in motion. Unlike you, I don't spend my days worrying about the string suspending me from the ceiling. I never give it a thought."
~*Betts, the paper mache fish*

"Being human is a lot easier when you're dead."
~A dead guy

"You will settle."
~*A Reality Law*

"Why is there an ant on the cover?"
~*Biff Mitchell*

Chapter 1 - Cripes

"If God truly is in the details, then DNA must be God."

When Jared Friedman, the biocomputist who invented the DNA bubble computer said this, he failed to understand that it meant the details *reflected God's work,* not that God was just a bunch of details.

So much for details.

Maybe it was a tiny mishap in the sequencing of Jared's own DNA that caused him to misunderstand Goethe, or maybe he was just blinded by the boggling enormity of his invention: a computer that used simulated DNA structures to store information and to perform computing operations, though "computing" was not what it did in the traditional sense. Jared's computer used strings of programming, similar to DNA codes, riding on waves of bubbles smaller than atoms, to simultaneously access enormous data warehouses and spit out results trillions of times faster than any computer before it.

Jared's computer was based on a biological entity that could replicate life, which on second thought, might make him right and Goethe wrong after all. But who really cares? They're both dead; Goethe for centuries and Jared, for, oh, about ten minutes. The details were just too much for him, so he jumped off his balcony—about an eight-foot drop—but landed on his head and broke his neck.

Details.

What drove Jared over the railing was the realization that this new computer of his—a computer that could fit into this period, but could store all the information currently contained on earth a billion trillion times over—was beyond anything he could ever hope to comprehend. Its implications were more staggering than his mind could handle.

Cripes, he thought, and jumped.

It would be a couple of hundred years before a young Virtual Code Geneticist would crack the encryption on Jared's work and actually build a working DNA computer. And when that happened, he wouldn't go crazy like Jared. He would keep his wits and neck intact because he would build his DNA computer for something far larger than eternity. He would build it for love.

Chapter 2
A Hundred and Fifty Years Later...

Viennese Lead Crystal

"Call me the Four Horsemen of the Apocalypse." Yang Yin giggled. "I am Armageddon!"

He chuckled as he clicked icons and files, copying and pasting furiously. Around him, an unsteady breeze trudged through the park, bumping into sparse trees. There were no birds in the sky.

"Nobody screws the Scourge of the Earth."

He dumped file after file into the same folder, its contents growing by tetrabytes each second.

"I am the Revelations of my Age."

He burst out laughing hard enough to skew the glasses on his nose. He reached a heavily veined hand up and righted them. With his other hand, he clicked and dumped.

"That which I have builded, so shall I tear asunder."

It would be a vast understatement to say that fire leaped in his eyes. It was more like his eyes were balls of fire spinning inside the furnace of his head, casting a baleful glow on the screen of his laptop, which many would consider an artifact of an ancient past. "An antique," the polite would say, even though the machine had been upgraded beyond anything on the market. The exterior, though, was exactly the kind of idiosyncrasy that distinguished Yang from most other humans; for he was a creator, a builder of worlds, a maker of destinies, and a juggler of the pins of fate. He was a god of sorts. And at this moment, an angry god of sorts with bursts of lightning flashing through the ramparts of his lofty self- esteem.

"They screwed me! They screwed me and my creation!"

Twenty feet in front of his park bench, a dark motionless pond struggled to be water-like. Whatever microscopic life it once supported had fled in terror from whatever the pond water had become.

"Financial Philistines! Turned my perfect world, all my beautifully programmed modules of CityWare, into a temple of false gods, a Mecca of Marketing, a corporate corruption of beauty." He didn't always talk like this, but he'd just learned he'd been royally screwed up the butt and tossed out of bed without so much as a cigarette.

"Time to unleash my Angel of Death."

He chuckled as he clicked, copied and pasted, dumping file after file into the folder, which would have appeared to bloat and burp if he had been doing this in VR. But Yang Yin, for all his claim to being a millennium ahead of his time, loved his ancient laptop with its lifeless icons.

The folder grew with files whose extensions were unlike any ever used before. These were components in Yang's personal language, a language that only he, in all the world, understood.

This was the one thing they'd overlooked. They'd forgotten to consider that maybe he didn't completely trust them, that maybe he'd built a little surprise feature into all those millions of lines of programming, and that maybe he'd built in a little door, a hole in the wall of the mighty citadels he'd created. Something only he knew about. Something he hoped he'd never have to use, but having at least one iota of his own godly self-absorption connected to reality, always suspected that someday he might have to use. And that little surprise was the folder into which he now dumped a staggering magnitude of information.

"Not even their best will ever find it." He laughed insanely. He tilted his sharp- nosed face up from the laptop screen and looked through metallic gray eyes at the lifeless pond liquid. "And that's what it'll all look like in time." The water was so thick it resisted waving in the wind. A pebble dropped on its serene plateau would likely bounce back without a single ripple. "But it will be slow...painful and slow."

He clicked and clicked, and copied and copied, and pasted file after file into the folder and the folder grew not just with size—but also with life.

"Fly now my Angel of Death and bring the walls crumbling down." And he dropped the last of the files into the folder called War_Bug.

***

Definitely does not taste like chicken, he thought as he sipped again from the crystal stemware wine glass with a delicate snowflake motif cut razor-sharp into its shiny circular surface. *Only the best Viennese lead crystal when you drink a cyanide cocktail.*

That was the last thing Yang Yin thought before the death pain wrestled him into his next level of being. Whatever that turned out to be.

Chapter 3
Another Fifty Years Later...

The Trouble with Kids

"I love my daughter. But she's going to get us killed." The Zen-rhythm sameness of four large fan blades inscribing a monotonous circle on the kitchen ceiling captured Abner Hayes' attention. He felt like his mind was whirling with the blades, the argument going around and around, going nowhere. "They'll delete her. They'll delete you and I'll be Included," he heard himself say.

"So what are you going to do? Lock her program?" Claire sat perfectly erect in a loose white sweater and baggy gray slacks, her hands folded neatly in her lap, legs crossed at the ankles, composed, a study in defiant patience. "Maybe you could recode her behavior modules? Treat her like another piece of software…"

"Stop it! You know I wouldn't do that." Abner's avatar shifted a fraction of a minipixel, a miniscule blur of anger expressed by his entire presence; what 'liners called emotional shakin'.

Aside from the shift, he appeared calm, staring at Claire, his wide face and droopy eyes and mouth emanating serenity as always. He leaned against the counter and looked again at the rotating blades, mesmerized as a point of light winked rhythmically from the edge of one blade each time it arced in his direction. *That should happen on every blade*, he thought. "I just want my little girl to be safe. I don't want to lose her."

Claire looked at him with dark brown eyes floating in a white corneal lake surrounded by black eye shadow shores. It was this intense black and white of her eyes, contrasted with her pale skin that had first attracted Abner to her.

Even with the stark contrast, her eyes were soft when she turned them toward him. "I know you want her to be safe. So do I. But she's not a little girl anymore, and she needs you to reach out to her like you would to a human sixteen-year- old girl. You can't just keep on throwing her into one new domain after another. She has your DNA, Abner. Simulated or physical, what you were, she'll repeat."

Abner turned his gaze to the scene outside the window, a comfortable neighborhood with neat houses, careful lawns and exact shrubbery. The street stretched into a perfect horizon of early evening summer blue and suburban starched green lawn. Across the street, he watched a shrub keel over and the earth crack where the shrub's skinny little trunk uprooted itself. *It's all falling so fast now*.

"I was a teenager *out there*." His arm moved in an arc through the air, indicating the world they both understood to lay beyond the bandwidth. "It was different. Children weren't tracked, at least, not as much as here."

He looked back at Claire, at her wide mouth with its rich redness contrasting with her pale skin. There was something so irresistibly sensual in those flat, lazy red lips. "Out there, they don't delete you."

14

Claire stood up, a relaxed, easy movement. Her straw-blond hair shifted in a slow rhythmic wave over her shoulders. Her walk was a smooth glide toward him, her wide Mondrian eyes and wide red lips filled him with her presence as though she were a red, black and gold panorama stretching across the horizons of Abner's being. She draped her arms loosely over his shoulders, her hands flopping down in the air behind him. He could actually feel her lips as she brushed his mouth lightly with hers. She wrapped her arms around his back and pressed herself against him.

"I love you, Abner Hayes. I've loved you ever since I met you, before I could even feel love for what it is, before you gave me this gift, and before you gave me Cassie.

"But lately, you've been far away from us, even when you're right here, and we don't do the things we used to do. It's always…"

"It's what I have to do now." Abner pulled his face away from hers. Her arms were still around his neck, and his long brown ponytail, sprouting from the bottom of an otherwise hairless head, draped over them. "I have to make the bubble safe for you and Cass. This is all collapsing and I don't know when that's going to happen. We have to be ready to get you and Cass into the bubble or you'll both go down with it."

"But, we can pull into the bubble computer from…"

"No, Claire. There're no 'buts' anymore. Atlantiscity and the other citystates can't last much longer. God, it'll likely be the entire Net."

"Then we'll be safe in the chaos."

15

"Nobody will be safe! I don't even know if you'll be safe in the bubble. I don't know if that's going to cut off essential parts of your sentience, or not. That's why I don't want all of yours and Cassie's components in there until it's absolutely necessary. And that's what makes it important we not draw attention to ourselves, not this close. If I lose my Net access now, you and Cass will die!"

"But we can just make our own way to the bubble computer, store ourselves."

"No, Claire, it's more complicated than that. Cassie has to start acting more responsibly. No more boyfriends! Especially human boyfriends. What was she thinking!"

Claire pulled away from him. Her arms flopped by her sides. "She was thinking what any other teenage girl was thinking, a good looking boy, and a harmless date."

"A date that could have gotten her killed! She tried to pass herself off as an avatar. She could have been traced!"

"Abner..."

"I'm going to be late."

Claire looked at the Cheshire cat clock on the wall and sighed. "What about Cass? Aren't you going to talk to her before you leave?"

"I'll talk to her when I get back. I have to leave now."

***

Abner opened his eyes.

He faced a dirty cracked ceiling. He wore a breathable blue Net-suit. Its chip- embedded

16

material covered every inch of his body surface for complete Net immersion. A chip implanted in his brain linked his central nervous system to the suit and re-created him online exactly as he was offline. With the suit on, and the chip set to 'lining, the real world was illusion and the online world was reality, complete with everything but smell and taste. And this only because the Reality Laws outlawed simulated feeding online.

Within seconds of being offline, Abner missed Claire. He could still feel her arms around his neck. He wished he could have stayed longer so he could talk to Cassie and try to smooth things over…if that were possible. He flexed the muscles in his arms and legs, rotated his head gently, and felt the sensations of the real world return slowly. Making contact with his real body was always a drag, a process of accepting cramped muscles and aching joints. He hated coming back to the real world. He hated the real world.

He sat up on his 'liner's lounger. He forced himself to not look around the squalor that was his real world. For Abner Hayes, the real world was on the Net in the biggest of the online citystates, Atlantiscity, where he worked as a Virtual

Code Geneticist. He studied DNA from plants and animals, and then simulated its biological code with programming code, which was used to make products in the real world. Like billions of other 'liners, he not only worked online, he played and lived online. He had an online home that was more real to him than the barren room in which he lay. He had an online family who were more real to him than anyone in the real world.

But now it was time to venture out there, into the real world, the world he hated more than anything he could think of.

Chapter 4

Hair Day

A dozen vipers, strawberry-blond eyes ablaze with empathetic anger, snapped at the air around Cassie's head.

"Cool," said a teenage girl's face on the wall screen. "I think I'm going to get a Medusa 'do just like yours."

"Well, watch out. Hair or not, they can really bite, even though they're supposed to reflect your own moods." She squeezed her hazel eyes and wrinkled her pug nose. "Sometimes they really hurt."

The face in the screen looked puzzled. "Hurt? You can hurt?"

Cassie rolled her eyes. *Careful now*, she thought. "I meant that figuratively." The face in the screen stared, expressionless. Cassie looked around her room.

Clothing, stuffed animals, magazines, books, combs, brushes, dolls; everything was strewn, tossed, tangled and twisted into a meticulously constructed masterpiece of disorganization. Cassie had long ago turned off the auto-pack, auto-hang, and auto-tidy features in every object in her room. When she threw a shirt on her bed, she expected it to stay there until she was damn well ready to move it or wear it. It was just the way she felt about things, and the orderly rooms of her virtual friends seemed spooky to her. The vipers curled up against her scalp, creating a tubular style hairdo, with just

19

the occasional tiny blond eye peeping out of the strawberry strands.

"I dunno, Celina," she said to the face on the screen. "Sometimes I think my father hates me."

"Oh, Cassie…"

"I mean it. Every time I meet a boy or make any close friends, he subscribes me to a new school or shifts me to a whole new social domain. I'm always making new friends and as soon as I get to really know them…POW…new girl on the block again."

"He must have his reasons, Cassie. You and I are friends, aren't we?"

God, what kind of freakin' random comment selector is this one running?

"Yeah, Celina, we're friends…until my father says different." An idea crossed her mind then she looked at the face on the screen. "By the way, just how long have we known each other?"

The head on the screen cocked to the left, put a finger to its cheek, and mouthed, "Why, all our lives. We've been friends all our lives, Cassie."

"Would you believe one day? Would you believe that you're part of the new domain my father just shoved me into?"

"Whatever you say, Cassie. I just want to be your friend."

Three vipers struck from the folds of Cassie's hair toward the face.

"That wasn't meant for me, was it, Cassie? I would be disappointed if it were." Cassie, vipers writhing around her head, gawked at the face a moment then walked toward her bed. She wore pink briefs and a black bra. Her figure was lean and muscular, like a rubber pipe bulging with air pressure. She touched a red t- shirt on her bed, and she was wearing it.

"No, Celina. It wasn't really meant for you…just for…things…things in general, I guess." *And now I'm condescending to a piece of software, concerned about feelings that it doesn't even have.* "So you think I shouldn't be mad at my father?"

The face in the mirror smiled. "Yes, Cassie. You should be understanding of your parents. You have a right to freely express your anger with this unfortunate situation, but your parents love you and they want what's best for you. I know this to be true."

Yeah, sure, and what database did you just dig into for that knowledge? She touched a mini-skirt with an ancient Grecian motif, then heavy black knee-high socks and black hiking boots. She looked at herself in the mirror. "What do you think, Celina? Greco-Grunge, or what?"

"Very self-expressive, Cassie. I think you'll make the desired impact."

"Yeah, sure. Thanks Celina. But I'm just going somewhere to be alone, somewhere where nobody can find me or bug me."

"But, Cassie, you know that you're not supposed to…"

"Screen off and lock for three hours," said Cassie, and the face disappeared.

Time for some clouds.

My Baby, She Dumped Me

A crystal tube, tinted rose, stretched from the floor to the ceiling. Inside the tube, on an amethyst platform, stood a naked man, muscles still wet with lovemaking. His blue eyes emanated adoration as he watched Bella across the room. She leaned seductively in the quartz doorway, her nipples flaring hard pink against the smooth gold of her breasts. He smiled shyly, even though they'd been intimate for days. That was the way she liked them, muscular and shy, right to the end.

She smiled and pressed the button. It happened instantly.

The amethyst platform disappeared and he fell.

***

It was suddenly breezy and hot. He was moving downward. The shadow over his head was moving away from him. No. No, he was moving away from it. He was falling, falling into an immense green and blue surface far below. His arms flew away from his body. He looked up. Acres of polished green crystal reflected the roiling mass of water into which he was descending. His hair fluttered crazily as his body accelerated toward the mass of water that stretched from one horizon to the other, a thousand feet below.

Then he knew.

A scream wrapped and wrapped around the small brown object plummeting from under the five acres of synthetic emerald that was Bella Bjork's floating palace in the center of the Pacific Ocean.

***

22

A circular screen in the tourmaline wall flickered. "And none of them ever suspects?" asked a dry voice. A mass of gray flesh and white robe appeared on the screen. Something like the end of a German sausage with a face etched into its center. Orange spikes protruded from the top of the mass. Microchips in the spikes caused them to curl and twist to reflect Jeemo's excitement.

"You watched?" asked Bella. Her voice was deep and disinterested. "How could I not," said the thick pink lips in the center of the sausage.

Bella stood straight and strolled slowly into the room as the amethyst platform reappeared. "They think it's an ion bath, something to relax them and prepare them for more sex."

Around the pink mouth, rolls of gray flesh curled upward into a strange smiling shape and Jeemo Roosenvelt laughed. "Your sexclone bill must be in the millions."

Bella stared at the sausage face. Bio-chips transformed her hair into a dazzling waterfall of chestnut water splashing over the tops of her breasts.

Jeemo's narrow black eyes squinted as he stared directly at her engorged nipples. "Killing them turns you on, doesn't it?"

Bella smiled coldly then dropped it in an instant. "From now on you stay out of viewing mode until I say that you can watch me. What I do with my clones is my business. Now, have you finished working out your trail of smell, or whatever it is?"

23

"Digital scent trail." His voice was flat and sluggish. "It's called a digital scent trail, and yes, it's finished."

"I still don't see the need." Bella sat down on a quartz pedestal. Her back and legs formed a perfect ninety-degree angle as she crossed one long golden leg over the other.

Jeemo's eyes followed the movement of her legs. "With normal VPs, it's not an issue. With sentient VPs, it's different. Their programs interact with the programs and code around them, like a human brain emanates waves that interact with the surrounding air. That interaction lingers after the sentient VP leaves, like perfume, only longer. Our targets are cloaked to hide the interaction from the City Central detectors, but when I spring the capture program, the cloak will crash.

That's why it has to be done quickly—so that City Central won't be able to track them. But there will still be some residual interactivity traces. To this end, I've…"

"But it's all finished now?"

"It would take years for anyone to trace the paths I've programmed into the capture application. And even then, the physical location of the server would stop them cold."

"The server is ready as well?"

Jeemo sighed. "Yes, it's ready. It's been ready for weeks."

Bella recrossed her legs, exposing a patch of fiery pubic hair that sent a flush of pale red across Jeemo's face. "You're sure that you'll capture both of them? All the modules and links?"

"Yes. Yes, I've worked out every …"

"I'm sure you have, but I've heard programmers say they've worked it all out and everything's going to be just fine before. But look around Atlantiscity. It's crashing, just like the other citystates. Everything is not just fine. Everything is falling apart and it's the programmers who made it that way!"

"It wasn't the programmers who went to war…"

"It was the programmers who designed the war tools and…oh damn it…let's not get into this again. I want every line of programming from both of them to be captured. It has to be both of them. There may be code links between them and breaking those links would make the girl useless by herself."

"I've set up the capture for both of them." Sections of flesh drooped from the lower part of his face as though his chin were melting into the air around him. "We'll have both of them within minutes of each other."

Bella looked suspiciously at the massive figure on the screen. "I need them. I need both of them. This is important. Now, one last time, can you really pull this off?"

Jeemo's small black eyes stared at Bella's breasts. "Yes. I can do it. You don't need to worry."

"I'm not the one who needs to worry about this not coming off right." Bella glared into the folds around Jeemo's eyes.

Jeemo looked at something off screen. "Time to do it."

Bella uncrossed her legs and stood up slowly, bringing Jeemo's gaze back to the screen.

"And yes, Jeemo. It does. Very much."

Jeemo spoke calmly, refusing to show his confusion. "I beg your…"

"It turns me on. Killing them. It's the best part."

Jeemo flushed deeply.

Bella narrowed her eyes on him. "And will it turn you on, Jeemo, darling, when I have *you* in the tube?"

A thin line of drool slid out of Jeemo's fish-like mouth and was about to drip onto his pudgy chin when the screen flickered and his face disappeared.

The Great Nano Canyon

"Cold murdering bitch. Damn, just one night with her, one hour!" muttered Jeemo, as he wiped drool from his chin and took off the white robe. The orange spikes on his head stood straight up like sharp erections.

Jeemo Roosenvelt would gladly have taken the sexclone's place if he could have fallen to *his* death with his brain fresh full of sex with Bella and the smell of her cruelty seeping into his gray flesh.

He stared at his naked body in the wall length mirror. "Perfection!"

Vast folds of flesh rolled over thick layers of fat. Seven feet, seven hundred pounds. Jeemo loved the symmetry of the numbers. Somewhere under that mass his penis twitched crazily. He could feel it. "Yes. Throb my hidden toy, throb for the goddess Bella, psycho lust kitten of the emerald palace."

He turned sideways, looking up and down the bulk of his body, at the gray face bulging out of his shoulders, and the fan of orange hair spikes forming a line from one ear to the other. His hands and feet were small and delicate; his movement as he turned before the mirror, fluid and graceful. He loved to watch himself move. He loved to watch himself standing still. He loved to watch himself eat, sit, lying down. Every wall of every room in his mansion, except one, was a mirror. Through the mirrors he could watch his enormous girth stretch into an infinity of reflected images.

A tuxedoed serverclone—one of the lower orders of clones, bred without legs, but equipped with anti-gravity boots so that their footsteps would not irritate their owners—floated to his side with a glass of red wine on a silver tray. It was reflected thousands of times over in the walls. "Dinner will be ready in ten minutes, Mr. Roosenvelt."

Jeemo whisked the wine glass to his lips with a single motion and the serverclone floated away. Sipping wine, Jeemo bounced lightly, mounds of skin shaking like sickly jelly, to an arched window. The glass in the window could withstand the force of an F7 tornado—and it had.

Outside, the moon spilled over a Mid-west gutted like a war zone, spreading into the darkness, deep into the New Tornado Alley leading right up to the edge of the Great Nano Canyon. In the distance, strange light played in the air over sections of the canyon, dancing in bursts of blue and orange. This was normal.

The canyon wasn't.

27

Less than a hundred years into the new millennium, the human race came close to becoming cheese soup. It started with the world's smallest computer, a computer so small, it could only be seen with an electron microscope. It was the first assembler nanobot, a concoction of seven atoms that had been circuited, programmed and instructed to build—though what the nanobot was supposed to build was never known. In the process of building, it killed ten million people, including the people who had programmed it, and the last communication with them had been from the project's lead Nano-applications Specialist, Milton Nadd. His pallid face had filled the phone monitor as he whispered, "My god, it's cheese soup..."

Then the screen had gone blank.

No one will ever know why it was cheese soup, but here's how the nanobot was supposed to work: it was supposed to visit neighboring atoms and nudge them around until it had built another nanobot exactly like itself. Then the two nanobots were to visit neighboring atoms and nudge them around until they had built two more nanobots exactly like themselves. Then the four nanobots...

It was much like E-bola, only faster. In fact, it was so fast that, by the time Milton Nadd had said "cheese soup", he *was* cheese soup. And his videophone was cheese soup. The other researchers and scientists and administrators and computer technicians in the room with Milton Nadd were all cheese soup. Desks, computers, chairs, paper clips, Far Side calendars, pencils and papers and books were all cheese soup. A million dollar electron microscope shook twice then collapsed into a splash of cheese soup that turned most of the floor into cheese soup. The walls literally flowed into the floor and the ceiling fell and bubbled into the yellow-orange liquid. Within minutes, the entire underground high-security maximum-containment, fool-proof, fail-safe, absolutely accident free and "Senator-Jonz-you-won't-ever-have-to-worry-about-anything-escaping-from-   this-place-or-my-name-isn't-Doctor-Milton-Nadd" facility was cheese soup, and it was working its way up through the ground, turning layers of red granite, quartz schist and an elevator containing junior research assistant, Jaqui Wright, who, strangely, had always wanted to be cheese soup, into cheese soup.

Now the assemblers were in gear, revved up and ready to rock, rarin' to chew into the atoms of igneous and metamorphic rock, bite into the neutrons of trees and grass and asphalt and spit out cheese soup. Highways, lakes and towns, swimming pools and rivers, airports and trains, canoes full of frothy cold beer, and entire cities all churned into cheese soup. Hundreds of square miles of North Dakota were cheese soup by the time the news began to spread. Around the world, people panicked and rioted while others prepared quietly to become cheese soup. Jerry Springer was thawed from cryostasis and hosted a special on people who had sex in vats of cheese soup. Leaders of the Unified Global Village pondered and debated over international chat forums and concluded that it was time to try something new, and soup was always

OK. Just when the world was ready to accept cheese soupness, the assemblers stopped.

Just stopped.

There was no apparent reason. They just stopped, after having created a mass of cheese soup that stretched from Winnipeg to Fargo and from Williston to Duluth. The whole planet held its breath in unison, as the ocean of cheese soup trembled like gunky jello without advancing a single atom in any direction. It stayed like that for three days. Then the giant mass of cheese soup went "ping"— not a loud ping, but a barely audible "ping", like two expensive champagne glasses toasted by ladybugs. By the time the "ping" had "inged", the cheese soup was gone. In its place was a perfectly round bowl in the earth, its walls polished and smooth. Millions of people who had flocked to the edges of the cheese soup stared quietly, their faces a wall of open-eyed non-expression around the massive hole left by the cheese soup.

Nobody knew why it disappeared. Nobody knew why it stopped. Only the handful of Nanotechnologists Milton Nadd had called just before he became cheese soup knew why or how it had started, and they later restricted all nanoresearch to space stations far from the Earth's orbit until the research was proved safe. Or at least somewhat reasonably safe.

Of course, there were those who thought a giant empty bowl was a big improvement over the former landscape.

***

For the briefest flicker of time, Jeemo's mind drew him back to the failure of nano-treatments to change his body, rejecting him like a bad odor. Then the rejection by his parents, as though he were an insult to their DNA, and then his childhood spent with serverclones and software. Other than his parents, he'd never been in the same room as a real human, never touched real flesh other than his own. But that was all he'd needed, to feel himself real and nano- resistant, so perfect even the bots couldn't improve him. He was the new standard of human perfection, and he loved every cubic inch of space he occupied.

But he'd gladly die for just a brush of Bella's cold touch.

"Hot damn! That crazy woman's going to fuck my brains out and flush me into the ocean." The throbbing between his huge legs went into hyper drive at the thought of plunging into the ocean with Bella's acid love fluids burning into his body. All he had to do was get the woman and the girl for her.

He sipped his wine as he stared into the sky over the Great Nano Canyon. The pink hole that was his mouth curved into something like a smile. *And there's the key to it all*, he thought, *why didn't I think of that sooner? I'll move it later. He'll never find them now.*

A sweet aroma curled into his nostrils. *Mmm, honey glazed ham.* There would be Poinsettia Eggs en Gelee. Potatoes Savonnette and watercress soup. And none of it would taste like chicken. Oh, it might hint of chicken on the aftertaste— chicken

31

was inescapable these days—but the glazed ham would taste like glazed ham on the first few chews.

Patterns

The wall-size screen display at City Central was the most sophisticated information gathering, report generating and data synthesizing chunk of technology on Earth: it had 3D charts and graphs, pie charts, cross-sectional multidimensional interactional cross-platform integrated technology information rendering units with squiggly lines and bobbing graphics, and charts and graphs for transportation usage on the main land trunk bandwidth and others for secondary trunk bandwidth and others for local trunk bandwidth and others for regional, area and local line bandwidth and others for virtual backup emergency bandwidth and others for main wireless trunk bandwidth. That was where most of the traffic had migrated in the last hundred years, especially since the colonization of Mars and the opening of research and mining operations on the moon and Jupiter, not to mention the deep space nanotechnology research ships which tended to disappear on a regular basis. Everything and anything in the millions of CityWare modules that made up Atlantiscity showed up on the City Central display. In fact, most of what was going on all across the Net showed up.

Including disaster.

"Jest lookit dat." Abu Spitz scratched his head, a gesture that was not lost on his physical body lying outside the bandwidth. As a Connecting

Balances Infoflow Integrator, Abu could afford the best, and the new Bodystate Enhancer module was the best ever, allowing his physical body to experience the sensual pleasure of his online scratching. He'd been to multisensory sex chats every night since he'd bought the module, but now, as the ominous patterns of shape and color shifted across the wall-size screen before him, tiny pellets of fear speckled the corners of his eyes. An undertone of gray flushed every visible surface of his small brown body, an empathetic reaction from his physical body.

He pointed at a section of the screen where swatches of bright red exploded across a field of pale blue. "We got us big trouble here."

Karthymelon nodded and pressed a button on the arm of her control chair. The area Abu pointed at filled the screen. Brilliant red patterns wrapped aggressively around layers of blue streaked with white. It seemed the white streaks retreated into the blue away from the encroaching red.

"Muz be somethin' wrong go on here, Abu. Iz not the possible of dis, no way!" She lifted her arms and clenched her fingers together on top of her hairless head. The motion caused her breasts to rise prominently under her tight orange t-shirt. Abu felt stirrings both off and online.

Damn, this feels so good, he thought.

Abu wrenched his gaze away from Karthymelon's breasts and scanned the snaking rhythms of color and movement on the screen. It looked bad.

"Am thinking Atlantiscity gonna go down real soon enough," he said. Karthymelon nodded. "Them bandwidth are not gonna hold if this iz true.

Maybe we run diagnostics onna flow program?"

"Flow program workin' jest fine, Karthymelon. An' look!" He pointed a stubby brown finger to one of several smaller screens embedded in the large screen.

The small screen was a miniature reenactment of the larger screen, same colors, same rhythm, same pattern. "Troycity gonna go down too." He pointed to still another small screen. "Pompeiicity gettin' all ready enough too!"

Karthymelon nodded again. "Shit."

"Bandwidth all gone crazy. Ain't no fixin' dis, too far gone."

"How much longer?"

"Couple days. Maybe."

Karthymelon studied the screen, her blue eyes wide under thick blue brows. She squeezed her blue lips together. "Yeah. I think thaz right. You right, Abu. What you think has caused dis?"

Abu turned his round brown head toward Karthymelon. "Is War, Karthymelon. War is done this. What you thinkin' of that?"

"Am thinkin'…" Her fingers parted and one hand floated down to the collar of her t-shirt. She reached under the collar and brought out a thin white paper tube. "Am thinkin' thaz time to fry our brains some more."

And maybe toss off a little multisensory office sex, thought Abu as his eyes rolled from the joint to

the protruding nipples under Karthymelon's t-shirt.
Love this new module.

Chapter 5

Funny Old People

"It would even have wrenched the heart out of a work of granite like yourself, son."

What the hell, thought Abner, *me a work of granite? Just because I don't bend my back on top of a building five days a week, gardening?* Abner glared into the deep vacant blue of his father's eyes, those eyes that once burned into the truth of things, questioning and probing into everything that crossed their powerful gaze.

But not now.

Now as his father talked, those eyes stared dully out the wall-sized picture window at the high-rises of Towercity soaring thousands of feet into the sky like a forest of monumental gray trees, each flaring out at the top with acres of green enviroplatform. Abner flicked strands of sandy brown ponytail off the shoulder of his sweater.

"It was so sick, you know," said his mother as she rambled into the room wearing the same brilliant white sports shoes as his father. Abner had to admit they added a peculiar balance to his parents' white hair and white-toothed smiles.

"We thought for sure that it was going to die." She placed a tray of glasses and a pitcher on a glass-topped coffee table. "But we're not ones to give up on life, are we, Dolan, dear?" She looked lovingly at Abner's father.

He smiled and looked at Abner as he answered, "No, Ata, where there is life, there is hope."

God, thought Abner. *This from the man who once said, never let your life become a cliché? And I haven't given up on life; I've created it...just not in your world, Dad.*

On the wall opposite the picture windows, Niagara Falls dumped millions of gallons of water across a wall-length nanoscreen, filling the long wide spaces of his parents' apartment with a low rumbling sound and the smell of wild water from sensorchips embedded in the ceiling.

"We nursed it for nearly a week, you know," said his mother as she poured lemonade from the electric blue pitcher into tall blue glasses. "Your father and I. Without any direction whatsoever. It was one of the new breed, you know."

"New breed?" asked Abner.

His father answered, nodding thanks, as he accepted a glass of lemonade from his wife. "One of the bio-enhanced atmosphere mix plants, designed to rebalance the gases in the atmosphere...undoes global warming." His father's lips nudged his mouth into a smile. "Rightful work, son. In the real world."

"We're putting the planet back together, Abner, dear," said his mother as she handed him a glass of lemonade. His parents stood before him, blue glasses in hand, white hair, white smiles, white sports shoes, ridiculously happy eyes.

What funny old people my parents have become. When did that happen? But he knew exactly when it had happened. *God, I wish they'd just killed the both of you. And maybe that's what they did.* Abner immediately hated himself for the thought. He loved his parents, even after they had been Included, even wearing the ludicrous white sports shoes simply because their profiles said they valued comfortable feet. He could picture the interstitial searing across the wall-length nanoscreen, erasing Niagara Falls or Victoria Falls or whatever falls his parents were playing, with happy people bouncing around in bright white sports shoes, singing: "Our feet are so comfy and cool in Nikiaka Nano-fit Sports Shoes…" Then the message: This important update brought to your attention at YOUR request through your Towercity personal profile.

Once, they would have axed the screen, literally. But now his mother just smiled and said, "Don't you just love our new shoes." She gestured down with her glass. "They're Nikiaka Nano-fits. They're us, you know. Everything we ever wanted in a sports shoe."

Abner's father nodded agreement. "One of the benefits of living in the real world, son." He swept a disapproving glance over Abner's sweatshirt, jeans and sandals. His parents wore the latest black cotton pants and white Grecian half- togas with cotton belts, and every stitch of clothing loaded with invisible microchips to repel dirt, control temperature and ensure a perfect fit.

If only you knew how pathetic the two of you look, Dad. If you only knew how goddamned silly you look.

Outside the window, a green dirigible floated slowly over the green tops of the tall gray buildings. Members of the People's Environmental Army, called PEA for short, looked up from their work in the rooftop gardens and jungles, just like the ones his parents worked in at the top of this building. They waved to the smiling faces inside the cabins under the huge craft.

"I live in the real world, Dad. Probably more real than this one." He swept his gaze around the huge room, filled with the miniature water gardens that gurgled and bubbled in the homes of all PEA members, supposedly to calm them, but Abner figured they just made his parents all the more receptive to the interstitials that played across the nanoscreen. "I get to pick my work, pick where I live. Decide for myself if I want to raise a family and even have as many children as I can afford. I get to…"

His father smiled and pointed out the window. "But it's not real out there, that's where the real world is. Real air. Real buildings. Real plants and animals. Real people."

God, Dad, if you only knew about Claire and Cassie. If you could only meet them; then you would understand what's real. "No, Dad, that's all just an elaborate illusion. You think it's real, but it's not..."

Abner caught his breath. What was that flicker in his father's eyes; some lost remnant of the real Dolan Hayes winking out from under the calm void of those blue irises? There even seemed to be a small trace of it in his father's voice. "Your virtual cities are the illusion, Abner, constructed out of electrical current by software designers and programmers. And how can you believe that virtual families are real? They're just programs!"

Abner frowned. His mother put a hand on his father's arm. They looked into each other's eyes and smiled. "We gave him a name, you know."

Abner just stared at her. "Abner," she said. "What?"

"We called him Abner. After you, dear."

"Called who Abner?"

"The plant," said his father. "But not until we were sure he was going to live. Wouldn't want to name it Abner and then watch it die, now would we, son?"

"You have a plant named after you, dear," said his mother as she took his arm and led him toward a glass table with three dinner settings. "And it's a whole new breed of bio-enhanced plant. They call it the Hope plant, you know."

Abner breathed deeply as his eyes filled with fluid. Visiting his parents always made him miss them.

Atlantiscity Mall

Just once I'd like to do something normal on a weekend with my husband and child, thought Claire. *But here I am, strolling through Atlantiscity Mall all by myself, just like every other Saturday evening, while my husband is off to supper with his parents. With my in-laws. The in-laws I've never met. The in-laws who don't even know I exist. The in-laws who don't even know they have a granddaughter.*

It was the biggest mall in Atlantiscity. It had everything. Pet stores with designer species, book stores with every poem, story, novel, biography, text book, travelogue and other word-encoded manifestation of human thought ever printed (all cross-referenced and hyper linked), family stores for buying families and VR gyms for VR people and real people. Here were VR chat bars for art lovers, mercenaries, stamp collectors, lonely people, sociable people, game players, racists, racist haters, freedom of expression repression haters, business people, runners, charity organizers, small business owners, baby sitters, teachers, parents, grandparents, prisoners, ex-prisoners, crime victims, white people, black people, and blue and green people with orange hair. Here were chat rooms, chat theaters, chat football games, chat worlds…all of them peopled by voices, avatars, VPs and, at some level or another, the War. Atlantiscity Mall had over ten million outlets spread through servers around the world and linked to over a billion households.

Claire saw herself in stunning gowns and ensembles in the windows of Blushing Women, each of the emulation bio-mannequins having assumed her features and pose. One of them even winked at her.

If he would spend just one Saturday with us. If he would just say no to his parents once and yes to his wife and daughter —just once. But even as she thought this, she knew Abner couldn't cancel a single Saturday visit to his parents. Not ever. It would be noticed. *Damn the Reality Laws! And damn the fools who made them!*

She walked by Shaped For Comfort on her left, its windows displaying the latest in shape-shift furniture—beds that agreed with your opinions. On her right, KITCHEN filled its windows with icons of pots and pans and other cooking utensils, all of them codeless graphic objects, decorative only, to fulfill the psychological needs of 'liners.

41

Reality Laws.

But he loves us. He created us. He gave me life and then gave me a daughter with life, and risked everything in doing it. But what's this life worth if we can't express it, if we always have to hide what we are?

A kiosk called A Picture To Remember offered single license and one-use runtime art that deleted itself after making its statement. Better not blink.

But maybe it will all be different after the Net crashes and they build a new one. Maybe the death of the online citystates will change things outside the bandwidth as well. And now her thoughts turned to the server preparations Abner had been making, the coding he'd been working on every spare moment for the past six months. It was their only hope when the crash came. There were still no guarantees that she and her daughter would live through it.

All I want is for my family to be safe and together. I don't want to...

A bio-mannequin in the Blushing You interactive display window took Claire's form and looked straight at her. Its face contorted into startled eyes and wide- open mouth. *What kind of display is this?* It winked, smiled and stepped right through the glass window and walked toward her. It was as though she were being approached by herself, except Abner would never have been able to afford the gown the bio-mannequin was wearing.

It stopped a few feet from her, winked again, and said, "Glad to see that you're right on schedule."

This better not be some dumb marketing scheme to get me to buy clothes I can't afford, thought Claire.

It wasn't.

Choices

"Shit onna chip!" Abu jumped up and pointed at a section of screen where a trail of small white bursts faded into the blue. "Lookit, Karthymelon!"

A green spot on the side of Karthymelon's hairless blue head flicked off, indicating that she had just turned off the music channel. She looked at Abu lazily. "What you on about now, Abu? Wazzit so dam important..." Karthymelon squinted her eyes at the last remnants of the bursts of white as they disappeared completely into the blue. "Wazzat?"

"Don't know dis, but am thinkin' I've seen dis shit before, just sorta 'round the edge of the flow patterns. Kinda shit you seein' with big surge, but bigger 'an anything we got us, or anybody else got. So it shouldn't be there."

Karthymelon pushed herself erect in her chair. A sad dog-like face settled over Abu as he stared wistfully at Karthymelon's lithe figure. Abu had turned off the Bodystate module for fear he would have raped his co-worker after smoking the virtual pot, but even in normal mode, Karthymelon was a knockout. She turned her head to him and shrugged. "Then, Abu, we are say it jest not there. An' no problem."

43

"But it wuz there. Streakin' white across dat pattern."

"But you sayin' it there, and you sayin' in can't be there. You choose one. Choose...it can't be there." She stood up and turned her back on Abu.

His eyes clung to the curves of her butt packed into the tightest pair of virtual body pants he'd ever seen. *And this what she like in real life?* He wished desperately that the Reality Laws would allow 'liners to meet each other outside the bandwidth.

She turned around and thrust her hand out toward him. In her palm, Abu saw a small red pill. *Oh shit*, he thought. She put her other hand to her mouth and Abu saw a dart of red. He took the pill that she offered him.

"Soon, we be the pattern. That maybe help you choose," said Karthymelon. Abu swallowed the pill and turned his Bodystate module back on. He wouldn't have to worry about raping anybody in a few minutes. He eased back in his control chair and stared into the patterns of the Net bandwidth as they danced and tumbled on the screen before him.

A Floaty Kinda Feeling

It was a feeling like the word "pluck", or maybe "poof" just before the "f" has a chance to sound, but you know it's coming. Then she saw an endless string of pearls in a straight line right through the heart of the bandwidth. She was riding the pearls into the distance. Or was *she* the pearls? It didn't seem to matter. She was vaguely aware of every part of herself, every thought she'd ever had, and every feeling she'd ever felt, all floating in a tiny space that stretched into infinity—both inward and outward. That's when she knew she was there, or here, wherever either would be, like being there was to realize here, and both were just a second that became all time since a beginning that never was and an ending that never would be.

Guess it wasn't just another marketing pitch, thought Claire.

The Woman Who Loved Power

Bella Bjork loved Power. She craved Power. She was addicted to Power. If she could, she would have fucked Power's brains out. She would have made Eggs Benedict and served them in bed to Power in the morning. Then she would have washed Power's feet, and washed Power's socks and underwear. She would have walked Power's dog; given Power the side of the bed with the nightstand and lamp. She would have waited up late and greeted Power with a smile and a cold beer in the small rooms of the night. She would have listened to all of Power's stories and agreed with all of Power's opinions. She would have fought for Power, shielded Power from the painful truth, pressed Power to her bosom and said, "Everything's going to be just fine."

But even with all her obsession with Power, it was just a means to an end, or in Bella's case, a means to not ending.

Bella wanted to live forever. She wanted to hold her hands over the eyes of time so that time would not see her—and maybe even forget her.

She eased off the cushion of nano-air that had been massaging her back. In the center of her body, a carefully sculpted patch of pubic hair flickered red and gold like soft psychedelic seaweed. She wore a see-through body suit with invisible massage units that kept her nipples continuously erect.

She ran a long slender finger over a perfect copper brown outer thigh that had cost Bella ten million dollars. She had two of them. Twenty million bucks.

She walked around her desk on shapely nano-enhanced legs that had cost fifteen million dollars each. Thirty million bucks for legs. She lowered the world's most expensive ass onto a quartz chair. Twenty-five million a cheek for a total fifty million dollar ass. But what an ass, curved like the end of a golden egg, but spread and parted like two scoops of peach ice cream.

"I can feel it now," she whispered. "So close, I can feel it. I know those two virtual bitches hold the secret to breaking the termination factor." Her jade-green eyes were hard and cruel. "And when I have it, eternity will be my playground."

Her eyes hardened even more and her face darkened as she leaned back and allowed the nano-enhancements in the chair to massage her back. Her entire body had been reengineered for beauty and longevity, and she wasn't a bad looker for a one hundred and thirty-nine year old woman.

I should just stay here for good and never go back home, thought Cassie. She floated in a cloud about two thousand feet above a sparkling turquoise ocean, and all around her billowing mountains of bright white climbed into an endless blue sky. This was Cassie's secret spot. It resided in a corner of the Net so far away from the main trunk bandwidths nobody would ever find it, especially these days of War-wrought havoc.

I can't believe he made me stop seeing Takei. It's so stupid, as if every avatar and VP on the whole Net is some kind of spy for the Powers. She rolled over onto her stomach with a light splash of cloud and pushed a chunk of cloud-mist under her chest to form a pillow. *I'm so sick of having to make all new stupid friends all the time. I miss Andrea and Seneena and Caroline. I shared secrets with them. They were becoming part of my life and I was becoming part of their lives. I was important to them. I was important to Takei. He took me on my first date.*

She boosted herself up on one elbow. Her hazel-green eyes flashed over a freckled pug nose and dimpled cheeks. *Then he smashed everything. Why won't he trust me? I didn't say anything to Takei to give myself away. He was sure that I was somebody's avatar.*

She watched three large Mallard ducks flap by overhead. One of them quacked. Another croaked froglike. *Jeez, even the programming for* this *place is starting to screw up.* She scooped up a handful of cloud and tossed it into the air where it forked

47

upwards into several white streaks that exploded into silver and gold starbursts high over her head.

"Cool," and as soon as the word left her mouth, she felt alone. There was no one with whom she could share her secret place, no one with whom she would ever be allowed to get that close. Sixteen, and the closest people in her life were her parents, grown-ups worlds away from her. She watched the last sparkles of silver and gold flick out.

She knew she had grandparents somewhere outside the bandwidth. She didn't know anything about them, and knew they didn't know anything about her, not even that she existed. She wondered about them. She wondered what they were like. She wondered what they would think of her if they knew about her. She wished she could experience their world, the world outside the bandwidth. She wished she could learn what air tasted like and she wished she could feel the wetness of rain. And to swim in water, ah yes, to swim. These were things she was not allowed to know about, but Abner had told her mother and her mother had told her. He could have been Included for telling her mother these things, and Cassie could be deleted just for knowing about them.

In the distance, four vast yellow balloons floated into a rainbow horizon and each in turn popped noiselessly as it nudged against the digitized sun. She wished she had someone with her to share the sight.

A movement to her left caught her eye. She turned her head and saw an ancient red and blue biplane puttering noisily toward her. There was something in the cockpit…like an opening or a hole in the windshield. She squinted her eyes.

A rush of horror swept through all the modules of her being as she felt herself being sucked into the cockpit of the shambling air machine.

Strange Bandwidth

"There!" yelled Abu, pointing at the white bursts shooting through the blue. "There! You see it dat time!"

Karthymelon gawked at the screen. "Holy shittin' spurs an' leather! Eeeeeehaa! Lookit dat go!"

The small bursts exploded into white spears of light streaking across the lower half of the screen.

"Told ja! Told ja! Woooo! It flyin'! It workin' somethin' real big!" Abu was out of his control chair, standing and waving his arms. "Ain't seen them bandwidth play like dat ever! You got a fix on dat, Karthymelon?"

Karthymelon's fingers danced crazily over the buttons on the arms of her control chair. She was half sitting, half standing. Her eyes were like large white coins. White teeth glittered from her gaping smile. "Nothin' there to trace, Abu. I'm gettin' nothin'! Like it don't be there!"

Abu crashed into his chair. His fingers scrambled across the buttons. "What the…?"

"See what I tell ya?" yelled Karthymelon. "Iz not possible but it there!"

Then the white seeped into the blue in a hundred places and disappeared. "Where it go!"

screamed Abu. "No bandwidth ever jest knock out like dat! No way!"

Abu slumped into his chair. Karthymelon slumped into hers. They both stared at the huge screen, at the patterns of color mixing and swirling like a liquid kaleidoscope.

"That really happen?" asked Abu, still staring at the screen. "Yep, Abu, it happen. What you thinkin' it be?"

"Dunno."

"War anomaly?"

"Dunno."

"Some fuck rogue alien bandwidth spawned outta lightnin' or somethin'? It gotta be somethin'. Can't no fuck be nothin'. We saw us somethin'!"

"Iz War, Karthymelon. Iz the War again." Abu sank deeper into his chair and sighed.

"Maybe the pills? This stuff pritty strong, Abu."

Abu looked at Karthymelon. In spite of the red pill, he felt a stirring in his loins both on and offline, enhanced even further by the Bodystate module. "No, Karthymelon, definitely not dem pills. Gotta be War. Whole damn thing goin' ta shit inna basket."

"We call da bitch now?"

Abu glanced at the screen and looked back at Karthymelon. His desire was growing, even though, after taking the red pill, he shouldn't have been aware of even the minimal simulated physical sensation 'liners felt through their avatars on the Net. He thought about turning the Bodystate module off, but said, "I guess so. We call da bitch. But first …" His eyes were on Karthymelon's tight t-shirt.

"What dat look in your eye, Abu? You thinkin' some cybersex junk or somethin'?" Karthymelon bent her head to the side.

"Net all fallin'. Maybe as well enjoy what we can in meantime." Abu smiled shyly.

"We call da bitch later." Karthymelon shrugged then touched a spot on the right shoulder of her t-shirt and suddenly Abu was facing the firmest, most well-nippled blue avatar breasts he'd ever seen.

"Yeah, we call da bitch later," he whispered as he pushed himself out of his control chair.

Neither of them saw the light pink implosion in the lower far end of the screen. An anomaly that, if they'd seen it, would have prompted a call to the bitch immediately.

***

It was like a little window into forever and, suddenly, forever was vacant. It was squatter time, and this particular squatter had been eyeing the property for a long time; in fact, ever since it became apparent that this computer was exactly what was needed to escape death.

The squatter felt around. *Yep, empty. Nothing left in here of the woman and the girl. And not that hard getting in, but then, nothing makes a better hacker than a chunk of pure code. Now, if I can get the owner to disconnect at the right time...well, then I might just live to destroy again. How am I going to get him to do that?*

The squatter settled in.

***

The pink implosion on the Atlantiscity City Central control screen melted into the surrounding colors and disappeared.

Sidewalks

To Abner, the real world was like a skin rash on his inner thighs. He hated the feel of the cement sidewalk under his feet. He hated the emanations of power generated by the mighty skyscrapers as he walked by their smart material, disaster-proof foundations. He hated the cool sensation of late evening breeze brushing up his baggy pant leg. He hunched his shoulders and plied through the real world as though it were a bowl of sour milk.

This was the world of his parents, a world teeming with too much detail and too much texture, a world with too many senses, a world of smell and taste. A world where air replaced bandwidth. A world of disease and sunburn. A world where weather was still for the most part out of control. A world with far too many variables for Abner's liking. A world he would be trapped in after the Net crashed. A world he would have to suffer through, until the next Net was finished. They were already working on it. Totally optical, they were saying. That would be fine with him. That's what he'd foreseen and that's what he'd built into Claire's and Cassie's programs.

A security camera mounted under the filament in a night lamp whirred as it followed Abner's movements. Every inch of pavement, stone and steel in Towercity was monitored day and night; every inch of cityscape was subject to minute scrutiny day after day from cameras concealed in lamps, buildings, trees and satellites. And crime was still on the rise. Crime would always be on the rise.

But soon he would be online again, exactly how a 'liner should be. He would be with his family again. *I'll talk to Cassie and smooth things over. There must be some way I can get her to understand the danger all around us.* Under Abner's feet, the walkway vibrated with the movement of thousands of vehicles speeding through the vast maze of underground freeways. Around him, the city's walkways spread into traffic-free darkness on every side.

Maybe the next Net will be different. Maybe my parents will be able to drop in and visit with me and Claire and Cassie. Maybe someone will get rid of the Reality Laws and they'll finally meet their daughter-in-law and granddaughter, and maybe they'll finally understand. But even as the thoughts formed in his brain, he knew these things would never happen.

Leaning against the steel railing of a traffic well, a hooded man faced him. He couldn't make out the face inside the hood; in fact, it appeared that the coarse brown material was wrapped around nothing. *Using a laser hood to obscure his face*, thought Abner and averted his eyes, and his course, to make a wide arc around the ominous figure. As he passed the other man, he heard a hacking noise and saw the hooded figure spit on the sidewalk in his direction. The dark glob of sputum sank into the sidewalk as though it were tar dissolving into turpentine.

A string of images flashed across Abner's mind as he remembered the news reports a few years earlier. When the first smart sidewalks were installed, pigeons were swallowed by the smooth hungry surfaces. Dogs and cats disappeared. Before they managed to work out the bugs, large chunks of the city's squirrel population were decimated. Surprisingly, the carnivore sidewalks had no appetite for insects. Cockroaches thrived as the sidewalks devoured their predators.

As crazy as things could become on the Net, they could never be as crazy as life outside the bandwidth. Abner quickened his pace. He wanted to get home to his 'lining suit and get back to where he belonged.

Poor Little Rich Bitch

Abu's round hairless head flicked off the tourmaline screen on Bella's wall. *That little bastard's been fucking the blue one,* she thought. *And on 'liner drugs, as well.* But Bella knew it didn't matter how stoned the technicians running Atlantiscity were while they were working. The whole thing was falling on its ass anyway. *Let them puff and fuck all they want, just as long as they don't interfere with my plans.*

She walked through an arched portico and outside onto an egg-shaped quartz balcony. *Jeemo was right. The capture program was picked up at Central. He was right on the second count; those*

54

dumbass stoneheads at Central couldn't make any sense of it. Bella looked down on a low-hanging cloud. Above her, bright clouds billowed for miles. *Maybe I shouldn't flush him. Maybe I should keep that tub of fat around after I let him lick my toes. If only he weren't so resistant to the nano-treatments. I could use a good-looking genius around here.*

***

Bella hadn't always been a heartless bitch. There was a time when she was a heartless little brat. She was born on a jet right in the center of the Pacific Ocean, in the exact location where her jewel palace floated a thousand feet in the air. She'd been born higher than that, but she didn't want to wear an oxygen mask whenever she went to her balcony to enjoy the view. The jet she was born on was a private jet and it belonged to the richest man in the world, Jaffanu Hynus Abba Bjork, Jaff to his friends. Bella's mother, Panuit, was number twenty-nine of Jaff's three hundred and sixty-four lovers. Jaff was with Bella's mother one day each year, January 29. On one of those January 29 copulations, he impregnated her with Bella, and Bella become his four hundred and fortieth child, born while her mother was traveling from a shopping spree in Kyoto to a shopping spree in New York.

As the four hundred and fortieth child of the richest man in the world, Bella had everything she wanted: private schooling with some of the greatest educators in the world, a wardrobe of designer clothing so big she never wore the same article twice, her own mansion-sized playhouse (complete

55

with tennis courts and Olympic-sized swimming pool) attached to the main mansion in Switzerland, cloned pets to torment and servants to treat like shit. She had it all. At least, until one night, when Jaff, in one of the drunken stupors that characterized his later years, came knocking at the door accompanied by a recent acquaintance (from a night club in Copenhagen the night before) and demanded that his twenty-ninth wife have sex with his friend.

Panuit had protested, "How can you possibly do this to me? It's not January 29!" Whereupon, Jaff and his new friend, a burly misshapen man named Ghunnnnar, dragged her into her bedroom and raped her. The following day, after Jaff had sobered up, he apologized for the inconvenience, dragged Ghunnnnar off his screeching wife number twenty-nine, and left.

It turned out that Ghunnnnar was infected with one of the new millions-of-years- old viruses released in the waters flowing out of the melting polar cap. There was no cure. Nanobots just bounced off the virus. Traditional antiviral treatments just pissed the virus off and accelerated its progress. It took the virus a year to kill Panuit and her death was painful and ugly. Puss-bloated sores broke out all over her body. She puked green fluids even when she went for days without food or drink. She screamed and she cried. She had sudden fits of anger and sudden fits of remorse. She developed a morbid taste for twentieth century country music. Moments before she died, the servants (who all thought the same thing: *Soon, the mother will be dead and we can throw the child over the side of the mountain*) dragged Bella from her mini-zoo, where she was setting fire to monkeys' tails, and took her, screaming bloody blue murder, to her mother.

"What!" screamed Bella at her ashen-faced mother. "I'm dying," she whispered.

"You've been dying for a year now, mother, and it's getting to be a bit of an imposition, you know."

"I'm dying today."

The young Bella quieted down and thought.

"Does that mean that I get the rest of the week off schooling?"

Bella's mother sighed, and died. The servants smiled at each other. A screen over the bed that was attached to Bella's mother by remote electrodes flickered on and played a videocam of Panuit's last will and testament. It went like this: "I own nothing. It all belongs to Jaff, that filthy Arab scumbag. Bella, I fear that the servants are likely going to throw you over the side of the mountain. But that's OK, dear…you probably deserve it." And that was it. The screen flicked off. Bella, wide-eyed by now, looked around at the servants she'd been treating like shit for twelve years. They were all smiling brightly.

But fate had other things in store for Bella Bjork. Just as the servants began to move toward her, the door opened and Jaff staggered in. He was covered all over with puss-bloated sores. He puked green fluid. However, in his case, he'd been drinking. In fact, he'd been on a liquid diet for weeks, alternating between Scotch and Vodka. He looked at his dead twenty-ninth wife and wailed, "If not for my lechery! If not for my perversion!" He pulled out his videophone, called his lawyers, and right there on the spot, he changed his will, leaving everything to Bella, then he died.

Suddenly, Bella was the richest person in the world. Suddenly, the servants were no longer smiling. Bella was smiling. Within a week, the entire mansion had been re-staffed with serverclones and the bodies of the former human staff lay strewn and broken about the base of the mountain.

Before she was even a teenager, Bella Bjork was one of the most powerful people on the planet.

***

A serverclone floated up to within ten feet behind Bella as she stood gazing over the Pacific Ocean and announced that Jeemo was onscreen with important news.

And now for the most potent of all power, she thought, *the power of immortality.*

Chapter 6

A Crowded Place for Dying

She was trapped tight as air in a beach ball. The bandwidth here was rich and pure, the stuff of light, but it flowed strangely, like a river flowing downward into a lake from which it had just emerged. She came upon herself as she floated around herself and through herself and then she was far beyond herself in a strange new landscape full of strange new things that were all parts of herself floating through and around the parts of herself. And it was crowded.

"Jeez, Mom, you're taking up all the room!" said Cassie.

"Well, I'm sorry, your Imperial Majesty, but it's just a little crowded in here, if you haven't noticed," said Claire.

"How can I not notice? You're standing on my Pain Regulator module."

"Oh, sorry about that, dear."

Cassie sensed a realignment of the space around her. "There, is that all right?" asked Claire.

"Yeah, better. Jeez, where is this place?"

"I don't know, but I think we're in trouble."

"Duh …"

"Drop the attitude, dear, my left foot is still close to your Pain module." The two drifted in a petulant silence that was not unlike runny glue.

"It's kinda like Dad's server, but it's not. There's something missing. All the space is here, but it's not. It's like this space goes on forever, but it ends right here," said Cassie after a minute.

59

This is really screwed up, she thought, and the thought might have come from that part of her program that rendered the big toe of her left foot in perfect detail through any conceivable movement whether the toe could be seen or not. Or it might have come from her Brain module, from where it was supposed to come. She sensed worry in her mother's presence. "Mom?"

Silence.

"Mom. You're starting to freak me. Say something."

Cassie felt her mother's coding brush against her own as she shifted her coordinates in the dense bandwidth of wherever they were.

"I don't think we can live in here, dear."

"You got that right, Mom. I don't think I can ever get used to this. I mean..."

"I mean, if we don't get out of here, we're both going to die."

Cassie probed the clear muck of bandwidth around her and knew her mother was right. "Bummer."

Home Again, Home Again

Abner's apartment was a dump. It was a basement apartment in a section of Towercity where there were no towers, where the streets were narrow and the vandalized security cameras were replaced every morning. The walls in Abner's apartment had long since stopped pretending to be walls and had resigned themselves to being nothing more than cracked and sagging stacks of former building

60

materials. Abner's apartment smelled of rat death and the victory of roaches over humankind.

But it was home. At least for as long as Abner was in the real world, which wasn't long. Less than a minute after flushing the toilet in a washroom where the tiles were cemented in place by fungus, Abner was into his 'lining suit, lying on his 'liner's lounger, and his mind and body were tumbling, tumbling, tumbling and he was *really* home.

But something was wrong.

It was more than just the décor in his virtual abode, the bloated chairs and ottomans, the fat couch, the clutter of family pictures in gilded frames over the fireplace, the green Victorian lampshades, the ponderous burgundy and gold curtains, and the rustic wagon wheel wallpaper. Abner's online home was a study in mis-coordinated kitsch. But there was something more than bad taste vibrating in the bandwidth here.

He went to the kitchen. Claire should have been there, but wasn't. He went upstairs. Cassie was still grounded. She should have been in her bedroom, but wasn't. He went to his and Claire's bedroom. Empty. He was alone.

Something was definitely wrong.

Thoughts tumbled over thoughts in Abner's mind. Could they have been victims of one of the War viruses? Could they be so pissed off that they left him? But where would they go? Then a frightening thought occurred to him.

The bubble!

Back in the recliner, where Abner's body lay in the 'lining suit, the baby finger on his left hand bent slightly and Abner opened his eyes. He sat up quickly, shook his head, and stood up. A gray filth-caked carpet creaked under his footfall. He touched the right sleeve of his 'liner suit and it peeled off his body and stored itself by the lounger. He pulled up his sweatshirt and dug his baby finger into his belly button. He scooped out a tiny bubble-like object on the tip of his finger. This was the computer he'd built for Claire and Cassie. The tiny object on the tip of his smallest finger was the most powerful computer on earth, its power immeasurable by any conceivable standards or metrics. It was also highly illegal. Just being within a hundred feet of it would likely be enough to have him included, let alone having the damn thing on the tip of his little finger, not to mention that he'd built it.

It was a long shot. He'd stored some of their core programs in the bubble, and didn't really believe Claire would ignore his concerns and store herself and Cassie in the bubble before he said the time was right. But there was nothing of them in his online home. Nothing.

He walked across the room and stopped in front of a wall that might have been the grandfather of all walls. It was beyond peeling and cracking; it had entered a stage of slow evaporation into the surrounding air. Abner stuck his finger, the tiny button-size computer still stuck to its tip, into a hole in the wall and a slat of wall sizzled into a plastic screen. Abner touched buttons on the screen and read information displayed in dialog boxes, and within minutes the terrible truth was apparent.

His wife and daughter were gone. They hadn't been deleted; someone had captured their programs. Someone had taken the core programs out of the bubble and transferred them to another computer like his, or something at least powerful enough to take the full transfer of two infinite programs. That person had also taken all instances of their programs from wherever they had been on the Net.

Then he saw something strange in his computer, something that shouldn't have been there. He would have to go back online immediately to find out what the hell this peculiar thing was.

Attention Getters

Jeemo's face beamed with self-satisfaction on a screen framed in fire opal. The orange spikes in his hair curled around each other in a dance of self-approval. His eyes slid magnetically over the smooth chestnut curves of Bella's body. It was difficult to say whether her form blended into the e-chair or whether the empathy chips caused the e-chair to blend around Bella's form. In theory, it was a mixture of both. In reality, it looked like she lounged lazily in a remarkably comfortable chunk of smoky quartz.

Look at his eyes, she thought. *He can't wait for me to kill him.* Bella was accustomed to men obsessing on her beauty—she'd spent millions of dollars perfecting that beauty in the last century—but the thought of allowing this repugnant mass of lard to touch her made her thirteen million dollar stomach contract as though it were going to eject something poisonous. *If I can just get him to die without touching me.*

"Central picked up the capture," she said. "But they didn't know what to make of it, and it got away from them."

"Just as I knew they would," said Jeemo. "They don't have the equipment to…"

"Are they alive?"

"Yes. Of course…"

"Both of them?"

"Both of them."

"And you've run the diagnostics? Their programs are intact?"

The thick lips around Jeemo's mouth puckered slightly. "Yes, of course, it was the first thing I did. Everything's there, every module, every executable file, every…"

He's lying, thought Bella. "How soon?"

"I…?"

"How soon can you break into the modules and recreate the code?"

Jeemo sighed. "I can't say for sure, but…"

With a quick stealthy movement, Bella stood and stepped toward the lustrous red screen with the ugly mound of flesh in its center. Her nipples, caressed by the see-through top, were stiff and pointing. "No buts, Jeemo. How long?"

Jeemo looked directly at Bella's right nipple as he spoke. "A day or two, maybe…"

"One day."

The gray washed slowly out of Jeemo's face, leaving a bleached white mass of folded flesh. He spoke directly to the large brown nipple. "One. Yes, yes, of course. One day."

"You can do it?"

"Yes."

Bella smiled, raised her hand, touched the nipple that held Jeemo's eyes like a steel trap, and began to stroke it with her index finger. "Don't fail me, Jeemo. Don't you dare fail me."

Jeemo's face disappeared from the screen. *Something's wrong*, she thought.

If Whales Could Dance

If whales could dress as sausages and dance like ballerinas; if hippopotami could shimmy into wiener skins and pirouette like prima donnas; if a towering mound of nearly shapeless grease could spin gracefully like a Tai Chi China doll, then there might be a precedent for visualizing Jeemo Roosenvelt's enormous mass spinning and bouncing lightly, almost daintily, and certainly gracefully, around his mirrored room. But even serverclones stumbling upon Jeemo's dance had been known to blow DNA circuits and just stop floating, dropping trays and crashing to the floor with their eyes wide, as though they'd just seen a dancing whale dressed like a sausage. Probably best to just think of him as a walrus with a black belt in ballet, wearing orange candles on its head.

Mirrors in the walls, ceilings, and floors multiplied the image of Jeemo dancing thousands and thousands of times and cast the images into infinities emanating in every direction around him.

And he sang, "Dying in the rain. I'm dying in the rain."

He landed gracefully on the mirrored floor. Layers of flesh and fat sloshed downwards like a ponderous wave screeching to a halt in slow motion. The orifice in the sausage folds of his face was bent into something akin to a fat-faced chipmunk smile. "Oh how it feels…to be dying in the rain!"

And while he sang, he thought, *Soon, soon, soon, I'll be at her feet, at her cold feet with her beautiful hateful eyes burning the life out of me, consuming my soul. She'll walk me to the flushing tubes, haughty and heartless. Just another lover down the tubes.* He looked out the portico. *And now the server is definitely safe.*

He stopped moving. He stopped singing. He stopped breathing. He'd lied to the object of his love and lust. He'd looked her directly in the tit and lied. He'd been so excited about capturing the two VPs that he'd flipped immediately into the screens to tell Bella.

He hadn't run the diagnostics. For all he knew, the two VPs might be dead. He walked heavily across the reflecting floor. As his body approached his mirrored image, the section of wall directly in front of him slid open and Jeemo walked into an exact replica of the room where Bella flushed her clones into the ocean. In the center stood an exact copy of the tube into which she placed her doomed lovers. A dozen times each day, Jeemo walked slowly, his hidden genitalia throbbing under his drooping stomach and massive thighs, his mind recreating Bella beside him smiling wickedly as she walked him to his death. Then he just stood inside the tube until he exploded and felt the hot cream, slippery and trapped tight between his thighs.

The tube also contained the interface for his prison server, and even though he was here on business of a sort, he still felt the pangs of lust, the loss of breath, and the quickening of pulse. He opened the tube door and climbed in. He touched a spot on the side of the tube wall. There was nothing there, but as soon as his finger made contact, a screen slid into view on the wall directly in front of his face. He gazed at the patterns of color. He touched the screen. The patterns changed. The colors changed. Jeemo's face changed. His eyes widened. His mouth bent downward. He touched the screen again. The patterns and colors changed again. Jeemo's face changed again, slowly, fold by fold. His eyes bulged at the screen. He touched it once more, quickly. His eyes continued to bulge. He touched the screen again, hard. He grimaced.

Imagine a sausage squeezed hard in the center and what that does to both ends just before they burst. Imagine eyes wide with terror in the wrinkles at the bloated ends of the sausage.

They're dying.

My Baby's Growing Up

"How's it going, dear," said Claire. "Oh. Ok. I guess," said Cassie.

They floated quietly, bumping occasionally into each other's modules, crossing each other's thoughts, delving into each other's fear.

We're going to die in here, thought Claire. *And we don't even know where* here *is.*

Shit, thought Cassie, *now for sure I'm never going to see Takei again.* "So, Mom…?" Cassie floated around her thought, the thought of what she was just about to say, examining the coding in molecular pockets of executables stored in billions of double helix strands used to put the thought into words, and the thought unraveled before her consciousness, then evaporated into the past.

"Yes, dear?"

"Didn't I...?"

"Dear?"

"Oh shit, Mom, I think we're gonna go crazy before we die."

"Language, dear." *My god, my baby's growing up. What a time for my baby to grow up.* As this thought crossed Claire's awareness, she too glimpsed the double helix strands of her being. *It's starting to happen. We're coming apart.* "It'll be OK, dear. Your father will be searching for us by now. He'll find us. He'll take us away from this place. Your father will find us and take us home."

As one, they felt it. A new presence in the bandwidth. Something cold and probing. Something not of DNA. Something uncaring and unfriendly. Something that did not belong in the mash of programming in this place.

It's going to kill us, thought Claire.

The Mallway

He tumbled and tumbled again, but this time he plopped into the main trunk wireless bandwidth, a beamed information path that tentacled around the planet and into space. It presented itself as a subway, a subway that looked like somebody had jacked up the roof, widened it enough to insert a row of stores on each side and still have room in the center for benches and kiosks. It was a high bandwidth mall, capable of travel at the speed of light, but set to move slow enough to capture its travelers' need to shop in its thousands of stores and see its countless advertisements. They called it the mallway.

Abner worried. His Stomach module squirmed. His real stomach squirmed. His mind was chaos. He wasn't thinking straight. His vigilance lapsed. He looked for more than three seconds at an interactive ad. It was a picture of a woman on a billboard over a kiosk. The picture registered Abner's three seconds of eye contact and the woman transformed into Abner, bald head, pony tail, thick lips, pug nose, dark eyes, thick body—blue taffeta dress. He was trapped.

Damn it, he thought. *It's not supposed to do this*. As the applications and operating systems that fueled the virtual world of the Net crumbled from the effects of the War, life online had become increasingly frustrating. The ad failed to notice Abner was a man. Or maybe it just didn't give a damn. It locked on him. A holographic image of himself in a blue taffeta dress floated toward him. Abner watched the image smiling seductively as it applied blue lipstick. He looked away, but the holograph was still in front of him, still smiling, still applying lipstick. He frowned and walked toward an exit portal wall. Its windows looked out into the slashing darkness of the bandwidth outside the mallway. It looked very much like the tunnel on the other side of a subway window. An area of the darkness cleared and the holograph was back.

Abner watched his image press blue lips together and smile as the head of a handsome dark-haired man came onto the screen and kissed him.

"Oh shit!" he said out loud. "I don't need this."

Abner in the blue taffeta dress watched as the head of the handsome man drifted off the screen, then locked eyes with Abner's avatar eyes. In a deep, sensual woman's voice, the image told him, "No man can resist the lips of Aphrodite."

Abner in the blue taffeta dress blipped off the screen to be replaced by the words:

Aphrodite Lipstick. Who can resist?

Then it disappeared.

He saw the flash of a transfer node as the mallway rushed by it. These were the junctures at which virtual travelers could switch directions on the bandwidth and travel anywhere on earth, and anywhere in the solar system where there were mining operations or connected research and exploration ships. He turned back to the mallway's interior, careful to keep his eyes off the ads.

A family of five, dressed in thatched, EnviroStatement clothing from the twenty- first century, passed by Abner and hurried toward the exit portal. From their eyes, Abner knew the woman and all three children were avatars of real people. The husband, a tall man with a placid face and soothing voice who urged the children gently toward the portal, was a VP. The family joined hands, the mother touched the bright green panel beside the portal, and all five disappeared.

Minutes later, a sign above the exit portal announced: GRID A2E4: ARRIVAL 10

SECONDS. Abner walked to the portal and touched the green panel.

He tumbled into a secondary trunk, blistered through a series of minor transmission lines, blipping from node to node, then through a series of pass- protected lines and bandwidth streams, and finally, he arrived at his bubble computer, which was embedded in his own belly button in the real world.

One Day in the Park

Pompeiicity Park was packed. Avatars and VPs played Frisbee and catch over the wide green spaces where the grass sparkled like dense slivers of paper emeralds. Serverclones walked virtual dogs along crushed stone paths and scooped up droppings of virtual doggy-doo. Avatars lay half naked in the invisible shower of virtual sun beams, their white 'liner bodies darkening slowly, almost imperceptibly, with no concern for cancer or burn. Everywhere, on benches and grass and blankets, the citizens of Pompeiicity read books, picnicked, scampered and ran, slept, held hands, and watched virtual babies take their first steps chasing after perfectly rendered butterflies.

Fountains dripped and sprayed water alongside verdant gardens as figures garbed in clothing from a thousand eras, from ancient Greek to post-information age angst, strolled under a cloudless blue sky. A red marble statue of Cupid with his bow taut, arrow readied, mischievous eyes focused on trouble, tilted slightly as a patch of philodendrons

71

sprouted out of the statue's serpentine base. A passing avatar dressed in khaki shorts and plaid bowler hat noticed the plants growing out of solid rock. She looked around quickly, fearfully. *Something was wrong. Seriously wrong,* she thought. *Viral attack*? Her eyes settled on the sun. Beside her, a hedge shuddered and its leaves turned into blobs of black. The hedge began to spin, catapulting the deadly blobs all around it. But her eyes stayed on the sun.

In the digital distance, across the green grid of parks and paths and pedestrians, the sun was sinking convincingly into a horizon with just enough irregularity to make it a perfect rendition of twilight. Soft tones of orange and red bled into the darkening blue, the warm colors intensifying and compacting around the disappearing yellow blaze. But something strange was happening in the sun's yellow umbra. Suddenly the sun shook violently. It ripped open and liquid blackness seeped out of the hole it exposed. The pitch splashed across the parklands, engulfing grass and shrubs and fountains. And people, both real and virtual. VPs screeched as the blackness spread over them like an oily shadow, infecting their programs and deleting their files, replacing virtual life with virtual death. The screams of human minds melting into comatose trauma blared through the mouths of avatars in the Pompeiicity twilight.

The woman beside the fountain melted in the shower of black blobs from the spinning hedge. The last thing she saw before the brain in her body lying on the 'liner's lounger clicked off, was the sight of thousands of hedges along the path she was walking, showering black death over every life form in the park.

Then the rip in the sun widened and lengthened and the ground and the sky ripped apart and all that had been Pompeiicity Park disappeared. Seconds later, the entire online city disappeared.

***

"Holy backward fucked dog spikes!" yelled Karthymelon. "You seein' dis?"

Abu pried his avatar head from between Karthymelon's legs and looked at the screen. His jaw fell. His eyes bulged. He gazed, shocked. The entire wall had gone into auto-focus on the Pompeiicity bandwidth. In sound, it would have been like two orchestras playing Beethoven's Ninth Symphony Choral Movement, one of them backwards. Then the dividing wall between the two would be lifted and the crash of over a hundred musicians would have been the site that riveted the eyes of Abu and Karthymelon. Abu's mouth moved as though to say something, but he was stumped for words.

The wall throbbed. It breathed and panted and hacked. Blinding shards of yellow twisted murderously into floating islands of vermilion as hundreds of millions of human minds went suddenly insane. Homes, business buildings and malls melted into sizzling masses of muck. Thousands of schools disintegrated into pixellated oblivion, frying the brains of millions of children in VR suits around the world. Streets and mallways disappeared from the main trunk bandwidth,

73

deleting billions of VP travelers and erasing the minds behind avatars.

Then the screen was black.

And still.

Like a pool of petrified ink. "Fuckin' cool," said Karthymelon.

Abu nodded. "Jest make sure we not here when dis place go to hell like dat."

"You right on dat," agreed Karthymelon. "Call da bitch?"

Abu thought a moment and stared directly at Karthymelon's crotch. "Smoke another joint and finish dis first?"

"Don't be needin' more dope, Abu. Jest munch." She chuckled and spread her legs.

Abu turned up the juice on his Bodystate module and slid his head up Karthymelon's blue thighs.

Chapter 7

The Pig in the Machine

Abner immediately sensed the presence in his server. As a smell, it would have been something like a mix of old socks and stale Twinkies; as a taste, it would have been aniseed tea and raccoon adrenalin just before it became road kill; as a feeling, it would have been a vial of the pure madness of King George and a tank full of Attila's revenge; as a sound, it would have been the scream of a fly becoming splatter and Dark Side of the Moon played at double speed. Now, if he could just see what the damn thing looked like.

He drifted around in the pure bright bandwidth of the computer he'd invented, the only computer in the universe he knew of, that would sustain sentient life, unless of course, you viewed, as Abner liked to entertain in flights of fancy, that the entire universe was one giant computer, the macro of Abner's micro. The presence was all around him. It seemed almost to be snickering. He sensed it was backing away from him just far enough, a neutron or two, to stay away from him. He could feel its ubiquity. It was like no other presence he'd experienced online or offline. Some might say it was close to godliness. Some might say it was a wrapper of insanity ready to fold around the unwary. Some might say …

There it was.

Against a background of solid white. Pink and plump and naked.

A short, fat cartoon-like pig. It stood with its legs crossed, its chubby arms in front, hands covering its exposed genitals. Its face was red and it smiled modestly, as if to say, "Oh goodness, you caught me with my pants down." It put one finger up to its mouth and smiled all around it, careful to keep the other hand covering its parts. It blushed deeper and fluttered its wide, white eyes with their tiny black irises.

"Please tell me that you don't really look like this," said Abner.

The pig's face changed another shade of red. Blood-engorged veins spiked into the blank whiteness of its eyes, and the eyebrows curved angrily inward. The pig clenched both hands into little pink fists, raised both shoulders, and put its fists on its hips. It tapped its right foot peckishly. A tiny knob with foreskin pointed from its midsection. It opened its mouth and screeched, "Well, whatcha expect, Myrna Loidy for cryin' out loud?"

Abner stared.

The pig tapped its foot faster. "Who are you?" asked Abner.

The pig stopped tapping. "What? You're not gonna ask who Myrna Loidy is?"

"I…"

"Only the sexiest vixen ever to adorn the silver screen, you dumbolt!"

"Silver screen?"

The pig shot Abner a withering look and shook its head. "Never mind. Never mind. So you really don't know who I am, smart cookie like you. Invented this fancy little computer and you ain't got a clue who I am?"

Irritation at the pig's insulting tone began to replace Abner's initial shock. "No," he said acidly.

"Haven't got a clue. Who the hell are you and what are you doing here?"

The pig banged both fists against its head, squashing it so that the head looked like a pink hourglass with eyes. It threw its arms up and its head rushed outward into a wide oval, then snapped back into place, round, pink and scowling. "Whoa! Listen to him! Attitude! Lotta attitude for a man who knows diddly squat!"

Now Abner's face flushed red just as did his face back on the 'liner's lounger. He yelled angrily, "My wife's gone! My daughter's gone! And you're here! Who the hell are you and what the hell is going on? Where are my wife and daughter?" A red leather chair appeared beside the pig. The pig jumped up and sat on the back of the chair, plump legs dangling over the red leather like pink sausages. It stuck its nose straight up and huffed, "Well, if you're going to take that tone..."

Abner squeezed his eyes shut, breathed three times, and opened his eyes. Calm now, he asked, "Do you know what happened to my family?"

"Gone."

"Gone?"

The pig exploded, literally. All its pink parts flew away from its center, stopped a few feet out, hung in the air, vibrating—head, legs and arms all disembodied. The mouth detached from the face and screamed, "GONE!" Then the entire body shot back in together with a *whoomp*. The pig looked nonchalantly at Abner. "In case ya haven't noticed boyo, they're...gone."

Abner stayed calm. "Do you know where they are?"

77

The pig shrugged its nose and studied one of its hands. "Maybe."

"Maybe you do, or maybe you don't?"

"Maybe. Maybe I…"

"Yes?"

"Do." The pig looked up from its hand. "At least, I did know."

"What's that supposed to mean, for Christ sake…?"

The pig wagged a bubbly pink finger at him. "Now, now, remember the tone." Abner breathed deeply. "Sorry. You said that you knew where they were?"

"Yes."

"And where would that have been?"

The pig shrugged its shoulders and rolled its eyes around the blank whiteness. "In a place a lot like this. At least, that's where the girl went. From her cloud place. I figure your wife's there too. I mean, if she's not here and all."

"That's impossible."

The pig frowned at Abner. A cowboy hat grew out of its head and it suddenly had a six-gun in each hand. "You callin' me a liar, pardner?"

"I'm not calling you anything. I'm just saying that they couldn't be in a place like this. This is the only place like this in existence."

"Nope. 'Nother place just like it." The hat and guns vanished. "You've seen it?"

"Been inside it." The pig dropped off the back of the chair and onto the cushion. It rested its pink arms on the red leather arms of the chair and crossed its legs. "Been scouting this place for a while and then I found the other place. Saw your daughter get pumped into that place, but when I tried to go there, it was gone, probably went offline. Wasn't exactly like this place. Close though."

"Close, my ass," said Abner. "It has to be exact, or they'll die! And you— whatever you are—you have to get out of here!"

The pig's eyes flashed. From where he stood, Abner peered into the eyes, into a world of death and madness. He stepped back. "Who…who, or what are you?" The pig smiled. "They call me the War Bug." The pig smiled wider. "Oops. Now I have to kill you."

Getting to Know You

Cassie's fear was lump of acid in Claire's Stomach module. Claire was just as frightened. Whatever the presence was, it was cloaked. If human, it showed no avatar. If code, it showed no Net presence. It was invisible and moved all around them. It moved between their lines of DNA coding, snaked through the millions of rows of virtual personality module components and the neural objects that formed their basic programming, and poked and prodded everywhere it went.

"Ouch!" yelled Cassie. "Mom, what is this pain-in-the-ass thing anyway?"

"I don't know, dear," she answered as she focused her floating awareness on the area where she knew the pain had originated in her daughter. But there was nothing. It was gone. Then Claire felt it tearing painfully into her Logic module, and just

79

as it was about to compromise the module, it backed away.

It's talented, she thought. *It knows programs, where to probe, when to stop, how to move around in the code.* She knew what it was. It was a human. A programmer. A programmer every bit as good as her husband. And if that were the case, then maybe Abner wouldn't find them. Maybe this programmer who held her and her daughter in this place was good enough to hide them from Abner until they perished.

A faraway tickling sensation told her the programmer was in her Spatial Concept module. It would have been a pleasant sensation if the situation weren't so terrifying.

Where, O, Where Is Life?

Where is it? Jeemo was getting desperate. *Where's that damn code?* The two sentient programs were getting weaker. *It's got to be in here. This is all of them! I have all of them!* He feared the mother and daughter VPs would become too unstable to be of any use. They might even crash. Then he'd have nothing. *Where is it?* He darted into a cluster of behavioral objects and pried into numbers, letters and strange characters, but everything in the cluster was normal, nothing unusual enough to create life. He heard the daughter VP swear and backed away from the cluster. He guessed they would sense his presence, but he was certain they were unable to identify him. Not that they would be able to stop him, but he feared

80

coming face-to-face with something he knew he was killing.

He was looking for the essence of life, for the coding that made them sentient. This was what Bella wanted. It would give her eternal life. It would give Jeemo death most erotic. Bella would kill his ass as he stared at her hard brown nipples and he would love every second of it. He would go out coming.

But the two VPs weren't cooperating. They weren't showing the secret of their sentience. On top of that, they were dying. *Damn you for being so weak! Just give me your little secret and you can die all you want!*

***

Jeemo hadn't always been a suicidal bastard. When he was a kid, he was just a young bastard. He'd never known his father—or his mother for that matter. He'd been born a blob and his condition had been completely resistant to nanobot treatments before and after birth. His parents had regarded him as an insult to their DNA and would have given him up for adoption, but nobody would have wanted the living balloon that needed adult diapers to cover its mass.

His parents had been the last of one of the planet's oldest and wealthiest families—if not wealthier, then certainly older than Bella's. They could have tried to have more children to keep the family blood flowing, but after Jeemo, they'd decided it was time to call it quits.

"Not all paths lead to the jelly dessert," Jeemo's father had said, and once they'd accepted this, driving into each other in matching his and hers Porsche Ferrets was easy. *Yip...* Jeemo's mother had thought a quarter second before the crash. All their money, all the billions accrued by the family in over a thousand years through business dealings, arranged marriages, exploitation of the masses, avoidance of taxes, mergers and takeovers, and strategic alliances, all of it had gone to Jeemo. He'd been even younger than Bella when he hit the jackpot by way of his parents kicking the bucket. There had been one stipulation in the will— nobody human was to see Jeemo until he was an adult. He'd been raised by serverclones and computers in one of the most godforsaken places on earth— the prairie lands on the doorstep of the Great Nano Canyon. Pictures of other human beings had been withheld from him until he'd reached puberty. The serverclones had encouraged him to roam the mirror-strewn premises naked, to get used to his body, to grow to accept it as normal, maybe even as beautiful. When he'd finally been exposed to humans through the Net monitors, they'd looked at first like little more than serverclones with legs.

Until he'd started 'lining, and discovered porno.

He'd mixed schooling with porno. Those were the only two things in his life, besides self-adulation. He'd studied bio-programming and genetic-based information systems in the daytime and at night, he'd 'lined the world of virtual sex, using the first prototype Bodystate modules to magnify the experience a hundred-fold. Then he'd stumbled into an online world of snuff porno, where submissive avatars drooled as they were killed slowly and cruelly by beautiful women who snarled and sneered as they squeezed every ounce of life out of them. To Jeemo, these women had not looked like serverclones with nylon- sheathed legs, as they killed one Jeemo avatar after another. He'd come to see them as goddesses. He worshipped them as they killed him, and then sent in new avatars to lick their feet and beg again for pitiless death.

Being one of the richest men on earth had its benefits—you could have all the avatars you wanted. Being one of the smartest men in the world also had advantages—you could program the avatars so your mind didn't burn out when the avatar died, and you could program it so you could savor every microsecond of the death. He was hooked.

Then he was sunk. He'd seen Bella. She'd contacted him through closed Net. She knew all about him: his brains, his work, his sexual proclivities. She wanted a bio-programmer to help her to become immortal.

DNA could be modified to prolong life, but then for no apparent reason, it just pooped out and died after a couple hundred years, in all the computer simulations. It was called the termination factor and nobody had an explanation for it.

But Bella had had a theory.

Computer simulations showed simulated human DNA introduced into VPs outlived the termination factor seemingly forever. Digital DNA was eternal, but once the DNA was digitized, there was no way to extract the coding and reintroduce it into the original, or any other life form. Just as soon as the nanobots began restructuring at the molecular level, the recipient died. Instantly. The theory was that sentience was present at the sub-cellular level. DNA could be simulated, but its sentience could not, and introducing non-sentient DNA contaminated and killed the entire organism.

Bella's theory was that if she could create sentient software, it would live forever. Its DNA would be eternal, as would its nano-reconstructions in biological life forms. If she had her DNA modified, based on the DNA of a sentient software personality, then she would break through the termination factor and live forever. She needed Jeemo to create sentient software.

Jeemo had listened carefully to her theory, staring straight at her nipples, then he'd laughed and told her she was crazy. She'd immediately widened the screen and let him watch her fuck a young dark-haired sexclone. Then she'd let him watch her kill the clone. Death by Bella. That was all he'd been able to think of since. He'd wanted to touch her perfect skin, to smell the evil in her pores, to shiver in the coldness of her voice then watch her mean smile as she flushed him to his death.

His studies had long since been completed, and now he studied Bella, over and over, as she went through one sexclone after another. Her appetite for sex was voracious, her appetite for murder, unrelenting. When he wasn't watching her fuck and kill, he was coding and researching, trying to find the codes to immortality.

Then he'd come across an anomaly on the Net. A slight fluctuation. An irregularity. A teenage virtual personality who was unlike any other VP of the billions on the Net. She was sentient. She was software. She was immortal. He'd told Bella about the girl.

And she had promised to kill him if he made her immortal

***

Now they were dying. Dying before he'd learned their secret. *Selfish ingrates*, he thought. He probed hard into a cluster of objects and heard another virtual "ouch" from the younger VP. But he also sensed the diminishment of objects within the cluster and understood that, if he didn't back away for a while, then he would crash their programs. He'd kill them. Then Bella wouldn't kill him. He backed away and went offline.

And just in time. Bella was calling.

My Baby, She Bin Foolin' Around

"How close are you?" The massage chips in Bella's transparent orange dress were working overtime to keep her nipples erect. Her normally cruel features were mellowed by something akin to addled. "We don't have much time."

"I can't rush this," said Jeemo. "Pompeiicity just crashed."

"What part?"

"All of it." Bella's eyes roiled with desperation. They hinted at vulnerability. This was exactly why Jeemo chose to look at her nipples when he talked

85

to her. They were always strong, erect, cold. They made the orange spikes in his hair just as hard as Bella's heart.

"Have you been in touch with Atlantiscity Central?"

"Who the hell do you think told me about Pompeiicity?"

Jeemo looked up just in time to catch the flare in her eyes and looked quickly back at her nipples before the desperation could shoulder its way back in. "How do *we* stand?"

"Days. Maybe. Then Atlantiscity follows Pompeiicity. And how do *we* stand?"

"I don't know."

"Explain yourself."

God, he loved it when she showered him with imperious contempt. "If I push too hard, I'll compromise their programs, maybe even crash them. These are the most complex programs I've ever seen and whatever it is that makes them sentient is not immediately …"

"How much longer?"

"I'll get on it right…"

"You do that." Her eyes narrowed and a smile worked its way slowly across her mouth. She turned her head to her left. "And in the meantime, I'd like you to meet someone."

A dark-haired sexclone, muscular and naked, moved onto the screen behind her. He began kissing her neck as his hands slid up the sides of her body to fondle her breasts. Bella, her eyes now half shut in sexual heat, looked back at Jeemo. "I'd let you watch, but you have work to do."

And the screen on Jeemo's wall dissolved into mirror just as Bella's mouth was about to swallow the sexclone's eager lips.

***

Damn that woman's good, thought Jeemo as the image of Bella and her new bio- lover dissolved on the corneal screen in his head. *And damn those two bitches in the server. If they die on me before I find out what makes them sentient, I'll...*

Jeemo Roosenvelt's mind numbed with the same sense of frustration felt by every asshole since the dawn of time whose enemies died while screwing them up the ass.

Getting to Learn All About You

Why didn't I ever know this? thought Claire as she floated around in the strange place where she and her daughter were trapped, the place that was killing them. *She's sixteen years old, and I hardly even know her*.

It had started with feint bursts of familiarity, scattered thoughts that had seemed somehow connected to her personal experience, but had crumbled into unrecognizable data fragments the moment she'd focused on them. But after a while they persisted, shakily at first, then for longer periods, with remarkable clarity. Then Claire knew exactly what she was experiencing.

These were her daughter's memories. Her feelings. Her thoughts and dreams. This place was breaking down their programming, loosening their modules, so everything that was each of them was beginning to melt into one program. Claire knew eventually this process would kill both of them, turn them into a functionless mash of code. In the meantime, though, it was neat way to spy on her daughter.

And what she had just learned about her daughter—the teenager with the sallow attitude and the messy room—was that she had always wanted to swim. More than anything else, even having boyfriends, Cassie Mae Hayes wanted to swim. She wanted to dive into water and feel the coolness and the wetness and the fluid solidity of water coursing over her skin as she propelled her body through it. She wanted to lie on her back and float in crystal lagoons. She wanted to swim somersaults in the green depths just beyond the white surf of a tropical beach.

But it was something she would never be able to do. Reality Laws. Swimming was too sensual, too physical, too human-defining. Only humans could do it and they could only do it offline in the world beyond the bandwidth. Even the early learn-to-swim simulators had been deleted when the Reality Laws banned them. So she couldn't even experience the motions in a simulation room. Claire suddenly felt a gush of intense empathy and love for Cassie. Her daughter wanted to swim. To swim.

At that exact moment Claire was swimming in the enormity of knowing another personality so intimately, and realizing just how much of that personality lies in the expanse under the tip of the iceberg, she realized her daughter could probably spy on her as well.

That little bitch, she wouldn't dare! Would she?

Before either of them could react to the other, both froze, listened and felt around themselves. That damn probing thing was back—with a vengeance.

The House Guest

"Just joking, Ab, old buddy, just joking," said the pig to Abner. "Geez, bub, you should see your face! It was a joke. I'm not gonna kill you." The pig scratched its cheek and looked pensive for a few seconds then looked at Abner, who was still slowly stepping away from the pig. "At least, not yet." Then the pig grabbed its round tummy with both hands and shook like violent jello as it laughed insanely. Its face turned red, then blue, then green, then purple with pink polka dots; then it wheezed and coughed and calmed down. "Tell you what..."

The pig looked at Abner with its wide white eyes and beady black iris-dots, but it didn't say anything further. It just looked at Abner.

Abner waited almost a minute before he asked, "Tell me what?"

The pig perked up as though just waked from a trance. "Sorry bub, just thinking."

"About what?"

The pig tapped its leg on the blank white again. "Oh, you know...about...well...about maybe helping you get you family back, and maybe, you doing something for me."

"Like what?"

The pig crossed its naked pink legs, put a finger to its mouth, and said, coyly, "Oh, like maybe, maybe you let me stay."

"Here? You want to stay here?"

Now the pig blustered and grew three times its size, filling the whiteness with bright pink pig fat. "NO! I MEANT I WANT TO STAY ON THE FUCKING MOON! WHERE THE HELL DO YOU THINK I MEAN, GENIUS?"

"No way."

The pig shrank back to its normal size; its face curled into sad, pleading lines. A single tear dripped over its cheek, dribbled off its face and disappeared into the whiteness. "You...you mean, after all we've been through, you don't want me here?"

"We've been through nothing together," said Abner. He was losing his patience with whatever this War Bug pig thing was in his computer. "I built this computer for my wife and child. You don't belong here."

The pig's lower lip shook. It opened its mouth. Its cheeks shook. Its eyes shook. Both sides of its mouth curved downward, shaking the whole time. Its shaking eyes curved downward. Its round piggy nose shook and furrowed. The two small strands of hair on top of the otherwise hairless head shook. The pig spoke with a shaky voice, "You don't want me here, do you?"

Abner clucked his tongue impatiently. "It's nothing personal. It's just that..." Now the lines in the pig's face turned upward and inward, malevolently. It narrowed its eyes. Three small black lines above the eyes curved upward in an angry arc. It spoke slowly, every word dripping with implied threat, "Oh, oh yes, Abner, old buddy. It *is* personal. It's all personal. I'm here. Do you want your family back?"

"Yes." Abner swallowed. "I want them back."

"Then I'm staying here. Deal?"

Abner thought a moment then said, "Deal. But why do you want to stay here?" The pig looked straight into Abner's eyes and spoke calmly, "So that I can go on destroying forever and ever."

Something Unseen, Something Unheard

That fat prick is going to fuck it all up! thought Bella. *I'm going to die because of him. Why did I ever trust that blob of perversion? He's going to kill the two VPs before he gets the code, and I'm going to die because of his incompetence.*

Something was bothering Bella, and it wasn't just the conversation with Jeemo and the specter of losing the simulated DNA coding that would make it possible for her to live forever. Something else was bothering her. Something just underneath her train of thought. There. But not there enough to override her fears about Jeemo.

If he fucks this up, I'll kill the obese misshapen monstrosity. I'll tear his fucking heart out and flush him down the tube! She frowned suddenly and squeezed her eyes tight. *No! That's what the sick little fuck wants! I'll let him live. Yes, that's what I'll do, I'll let the bastard live!*

And there it was again. A motion? A sound? A change in color or temperature somewhere? What was it just under the threshold of Bella's attention

91

that was apparently waving its arms as though to say, "Over here! Look this way!" But weighty thoughts burdened Bella's consciousness and they needed her full attention.

That fucker! I can't just let him live! But I can't kill him! I can't give him what he wants after he fucks up and kills them. But he hasn't killed them yet. Bella's facial muscles relaxed. She went from being beautiful and vindictive-looking to being beautiful and evilly calculating-looking. Her waterfall hair splashed around her shoulders. *He might pull it off.* She smiled. *The little pig fuck might just pull it off.* Her smile widened.

But what was that? Something nagging. Something somewhere within the sphere of things that were of Bella, but not actively there? Or was it active? There was movement attached to it. Movement and sound. But the movement and sound were not nearly up to the task of overwhelming Bella's thoughts.

No, he's going to fuck it up. I know he is. A scowl twisted across Bella's face, but she was still beautiful, in a smooth easy-to-look-at psychotic way. Then her face lit up like a light bulb snapping on. *I'll have him assassinated! I'll have someone go to his home and kill him. If he fucks this up, I'll deprive him of his wet little dream of death by my hand. He'll die in his home, not even knowing I had anything to do with it.*

There it was again. Something pushing at her. Something with the sound of breath. Something with a grunt. Something with weight and substance. She shrugged it off. Then she remembered she had to attend a meeting of the Central Powers.

Something had to be done about Pompeiicity. Not that there was anything that could be done...it was gone. Forever. But it needed discussion. It needed to be put into the context of Atlantiscity. And that could only be done by...

A voice!

Someone was speaking to her!

What the hell!

"Do you wish another round?"

"What?" asked Bella, thoroughly confused. "What are you...?" Then she remembered. The movement. The sound. The breathing. She was in bed with the sexclone. He'd just made love to her and had spewed sexual debris into her body. "Bothersome thing, aren't you?"

Chapter 8

Pig Talk

"I'm all about death and gloom," said the pig. "I'm the Four Horsemen of the Acropolis…or something like that. It's what I do, what I was made to do. I destroy things. I am Armageddon. I am the Scourge of the Earth."

"I hardly think so," said Abner.

The pig twisted its head sideways and pushed out its lower lip. "What?"

"Unless you're an avatar, you can't be the Scourge of the Earth. You're software. You're inside a computer. You can't do anything to the earth. Maybe you should try Scourge of the Bandwidth, or…"

"DON'T!" screamed the pig, pointing a pink finger directly at Abner's head. "DON'T FUCK WITH ME! I AM THE REVELATIONS OF MY AGE!" The pig's head spun and tore away from its body, soaring straight up into the whiteness, screaming, "WHAT WAS BUILDED, SO SHALL I TEAR ASUNDER!" Then it looked down in horror at the headless body under it. Sweat drops flew off its brow and disappeared into the whiteness. The head dove for its body and landed with a thick plumf. Upside down. Its eyes went wide and its shoulders shrugged. Then, the pig's arms reached up and righted its head. It spoke softly, "You never did understand me, did you?"

Abner sighed. "Guess not. But I'll bite. Who, or what, are you?"

"I AM THE…"

94

"No!" said Abner, raising his hand, palm out toward the pig. "The special effects are cool, but I have a missing family and time is running out. Who, or what, are you?"

The pig crossed its arms and began tapping a ridiculously tiny split hoof on the floor. "Well, if that's the way you're going to be." It raised its nose. "Mr. No-Frills- Let's-Just-All-Be-Serious. OK, then."

The pig plopped into the red leather chair and crossed one plump pink leg over the other. Its tiny pink penis poked out from under its legs like a large pimple. The pig looked off into the bandwidth past Abner's shoulder. Its eyes were distantly focused, as though looking into another dimension. "Suddenly, one day, I was. I don't why this was. I don't know where I came from. I just know that I was one nasty little motherfucker."

A smile started to curve over Abner's lips.

"Don't." The pig pointed at the smile without looking at it. "I can hurt your avatar in ways that you would feel."

Abner checked the smile. The pig continued. "I had a name. I didn't know where it came from or what it meant, at least, not at first. I was War_Bug. Later, when things started making sense, I changed this to the War Bug. Not that it really mattered, though." The pig looked into Abner's eyes. "You're the first person who's ever heard any of this." Then it looked back into the distance. "I knew another thing; I knew how to destroy things. I knew all about war. It was what I was—War." The faraway look in the pig's eyes started to glaze over. "I knew that I had to destroy things, and when I asked myself what must I destroy, the answer was known to me. The cities. The online citystates. All of them. My purpose was to bring about the complete destruction of all the online citystates." The pig looked at Abner again. "And you know, Ab, old buddy, I kind of had a good feeling about that. Like it was a good thing, you know?"

"No," said Abner. "Can't say that I do."

The pig snorted and looked back into the bandwidth. "I guess you had to be there. I don't know how I knew the ways in which I was to destroy the cities, I just knew. I knew routes and gateways and passages through the bandwidth— all of them secret. And I knew how to make myself invisible to detection devices, almost as though I was a part of the cities, as though I belonged in them as some component that had been hard-coded into the CityWare root objects. It was strange how I knew to get around, and how I knew to disguise my movements, to stay hidden." The pig looked at Abner again. Its eyes were just a little wider now. "It was kind of fun, like being a spy, or a ninja saboteur. I worked my way into the City Central control programs and meddled with statistics, altered messages, issued fake orders." The pig was breathing harder. "I launched viral attacks from one citystate to another." The pig chuckled. "And I made sure that they could be traced. Then I scrambled diplomatic messages so that neither citystate could resolve the attacks peacefully. Instead, I sent insults flying back and forth." The pig chuckled louder. "Then I posed as an avatar. Yeah, Ab, old buddy, I created an avatar for a human who didn't even exist and I had him working in all the citystates, and in every one of those citystates, he was working in the Department of Corporate Warfare modules. And in every one of those modules, he created exactly the same package: SoftWAR, the ultimate program for online destruction. The leaders of the citystates gobbled it up. Here was their way to destroy the enemies who had been launching totally uncalled-for viral attacks!" The pig crossed its legs and gripped the arms of the chair with its hands. "And none of the stupid peckers knew they all had the same package. They used SoftWAR to create bigger and better viral bombs, VR black-blob-eaters, program redirection worms, code spoilers, module busters, accelerated runtime degradation bugs, then they used my program to put them all together into coordinated attacks." The pig almost rolled off the chair laughing. "But they were all using the same program. You see? When one attacked, the other countered with something bigger, something better, with something even more destructive. And they were all attacking each other, all destroying each other bit by bit. Get it? Bit by bit? Byte by byte?"

"Ho, ho," said Abner quietly, convinced the thing before him was just about the most evil, completely insane thing he'd come across in his entire life.

The pig ignored him. It was sitting straight up now, its pudgy hands waving wildly. "Then when I had them all smashing away at each other, I accelerated my campaign. I don't know where I got the idea from. It was just there. I leaked intelligence on surprise attacks from one citystate to the next. I crashed defensive programs. I launched attacks ahead of schedule." The pig's head inflated like a balloon and his mouth hollered. "I issued orders to step up the war campaigns! I infiltrated the City Central monitors in all the citystates and altered the programs so that nobody, NOT ONE FUCKING ENTITY IN ALL THIS FUCKING BANDWIDTH KNEW JUST HOW FUCKED UP EVERYTHING WAS GETTING!" The pig's head swung around and two red-streaked eyes glared deep into Abner's eyes. The pig's mouth gyrated. Its eyes crossed and uncrossed. Its nose twitched and its jaw trembled. "AND YOU KNOW WHAT, AB, OLD BUDDY, YOU KNOW WHAT?"

Abner stared at the pig. He didn't say a word.

The pig clenched and unclenched its now hooved fists. Its skin flushed deep red, then blue, then green. Green. "I WENT TOO FUCKIN' FAR! THAT'S WHAT, AB, OLD BUDDY! I WENT TOO FUCKIN' FAR! THE FUCKING WAR I STARTED IS BRINGING DOWN THE CITYSTATES, AND THE WHOLE FUCKING NET WITH THEM! IT'S GOING TO DESTROY THE BANDWIDTH CONNECTIONS TO ALL THE PATHS, AND I HAVE SOME PRETTY DAMNED IMPORTANT OBJECTS ON MARS, YOU KNOW!"

The pig's head suddenly deflated and the pink body collapsed into the chair. The pig looked despondently at the whiteness directly in front of the chair. "I never meant to bring down the whole Net. Just the citystates. But I went too far. And once there's nothing, well, what's that leave?"

Abner sensed the pig was afraid. Nervous, at least.

The pig took a deep, deep breath and let it roll out over a few sobs like speed bumps in its mood. It looked at Abner. "I was ranting again, wasn't I?"

Abner nodded. "You're one strange pig." The pig chuckled. "So?"

"You really think you can help me find my wife and daughter?"

"Pig's word."

"Hmm. Sounds good enough. Where do we start?"

"You mean, where do *you* start."

Mom's Day Out

It was back, poking around indiscriminately inside her objects. Cassie felt violated by the presence. Whatever it was, it was cruel and had no respect for life. It probed painfully into areas that were basic to her uniqueness, places where no other life form had a right to intrude. It infuriated her that she could do nothing about it, that she could only float helplessly in this place while the presence picked away at the essence of her being. She gritted her virtual teeth, and tolerated it as best she could.

Damn thing, she thought. *I'll get you for this, you damn thing*.

And in the midst of this trespass against her sentience, something happened she thought was pretty damn cool. She was suddenly in her mother's mind, seeing the world from her mother's eyes, and experiencing her mother's feelings toward life in the bandwidth. She was in Jan's living room. Jan was her mother's best friend. Her mother spent every afternoon, Monday to Friday, at Jan's. It was like a job she went to, almost as though she could punch a clock at 1 PM as she passed through Jan's doorway and then punch the clock at 4 PM on the way out. In fact, it *was* a job of sorts; it was one of the formulas for VP life. Claire was a VP housewife and mother. She was scheduled to do those things that were deemed to be appropriate to housewife and mother, even though these things probably had not been the norm in the real world for centuries. But then, this was the bandwidth, the Net, that artificial world to which dropouts from the real world fled, to build something that didn't really exist anywhere else.

Claire was sitting on a long beige chesterfield. Another friend, Ruth, sat beside her. Jan sat across from them in a beige armchair. All three wore jogging pants and oversized sweatshirts. Claire wore bright yellow; Jan, dark blue; and Ruth, rebel of the three, who was sometimes referred to by the other two as "scandalous", wore an orange top and red pants. There were no teacups, coffee cups or glasses on the coffee table between the chesterfield and the armchair. There were no tea biscuits, no cookies, no wafers, no cakes, and no short bread and butter. Reality Laws. The walls were heavy with family photos and the hardwood floor sparkled. Venetian blinds muffled the spray of afternoon light.

"Jonnasson had a very interesting day, yesterday," said Jan. She was a slight woman with dark skin and short brown hair that curled under.

"Oh, really," said Claire. "What happened?"

"At work," said Jan.

You're an idiot, Jan.

Ohmygod, thought Cassie. *I'm reading my mother's mind in her memories! I'm inside my mother's head and I'm reading her mind.* Then it occurred to her. *What a neat way to spy on her!* Then she watched, experiencing every word and thought just as though she were her mother, as Ruth, a slight woman with dark skin and short blond hair that curled under said, "Bernard equally had a very interesting day." She nodded toward Claire. "Yesterday."

And this is supposed to simulate outside the bandwidth and provide an experiential database to give me something to talk about to my human husband when he comes home tonight? Who were these people who drew up the damn Reality Laws?

Cassie almost burst out laughing. Her mother, her calm, accepting, and oh-so- cautious mother was thinking treasonous thoughts, thoughts that could have her deleted. But then, who would ever think to monitor an afternoon get-together between three VPs engaged in filler dialogue just to give added reality to their human owner's VR life experience. In fact, Jan and Ruth probably didn't even have any existence outside providing this experience to Claire.

"I think I'll go home tonight," said Claire, "and sit naked on my husband's face while I tell him about the two frigid bitches who bored me all afternoon with stories about their husbands, who probably don't even exist."

Jan and Ruth, both smiling, regarded Claire attentively. Neither said a word. Neither stopped smiling. Finally, Jan spoke, "I wonder if Jonnasson

101

will have an interesting day today. What do you think, Claire?"

"And what kind of day do you think he'll have *tomorrow*?" giggled Ruth.

Jan opened her mouth and eyes wide. "Oh, Ruth! You rebel!" She looked at Claire. "Isn't she just scandalous!"

Please, Abner, be wrong about the immortality part. Please don't let this go on forever. Cassie almost felt sorry for her mother, then listened as her mother said, "Whatever will we do with her? Perhaps we should take her clothes off and spank her bottom."

"God, Mom, I can't believe you'd say anything like this, ever."

"What was that, dear?" asked Claire.

Oh jeez, I said that out loud. "Nothing, mom." She whispered into the blankness of this strange bandwidth. "I think that thing's back. Can you feel it too?"

Then the *thing* tore mercilessly into one of the thousands of neural objects in one of her Socializing modules. She felt the programming burst apart like a blood vessel exploding. "Fuck!" she screamed.

"Young lady," said Claire. "Watch your..." And she too screamed as the presence shot like a fiery spear through the lines of her executables.

Killing Them Softly with His Prying

Where is it? thought Jeemo. *It's got to be here somewhere. I know it's here. It has to be here!* Sitting on an emerald divan in imitation of one he'd seen on the screen in Bella's floating mansion, Jeemo directed his search of the VPs' coding through a micromind chip planted in his brain. His was much more sophisticated than the ones permitted for other 'liners, which made the online world super real by filling in the details of what they experienced online from the memories of details in their real lives. Jeemo's gave him full Net control, not just the ability to fill in details. With his chip, he was consciously in the real world and in the bandwidth simultaneously.

It was a rush. At first it had been confusing, sorting out which was which. In fact, he'd almost walked over the side of his balcony on one occasion, thinking he was stepping into a virtual massage bath. But now, he could separate the two so well he could juggle eggs in the real world while climbing mountains on the Net. Except that he couldn't really juggle eggs.

He didn't even need a 'liner's suit. With the flick of a thought, he was there. But at this moment, the Net was only a wireless path to where he was, and where he was had its physical presence in a place where he was sure no one but he would ever find. He was inside the prison server where Claire's and Cassie's programs were beginning to mix in a very unnatural and unhealthy manner, and he was well aware that both had begun the process of dying.

It's got to be in here somewhere! I have everything that they are, all their modules, all their mapping, all their objects, and every line of their code. Bright hopes of dying in the poisonous beauty of Bella's blood lust began to dim. He would go on living without her scorn. He would plod through each day knowing that somewhere in the middle of the Pacific Ocean, one lucky sexclone after another would plunge to glorious death to feed Bella's need to kill, and he would only be able to envy them. *God*, he thought, *she might even forbid me to watch them die.* With a whip of his will, he decimated an entire basic etiquette object in Claire's Protocol module. If she survived, she would still be able to write beautiful invitations to virtual pet homecomings, but it was likely she would include condolences in the invitation. This would irritate only the people who would receive them, and they were more likely to be irritated just by the fact they'd received an invitation to a virtual pet homecoming.

Slowly, Jeemo came to realize his careless sweep of the essence of the VPs' beings was accelerating their deaths, that he was killing them with his aimless search. Then it hit him—aimless. That was exactly what it was. He didn't have a clue what he was looking for. He was looking for sentience. But what was that? What did it look like? How was it coded? What were the processes that made it work, defined it, created it, caused it to appear in these two pieces of software, and even if he did find it, how would he be able to use it to make Bella immortal?

Their programming *was* different. Everything in here was modeled after DNA. Everything was organic. The breath of life whispered secrets between the lines of code, but those secrets were just beyond Jeemo's hearing. Out of spite, he poked heavily into one of Cassie's Finger Definition modules and smiled maliciously when he heard her, "Oww!"

They're sentient, he thought, *and whatever it is that gives them life is in here somewhere. But I could very well kill them before I find it...so...I have to stop looking? Or do I have to change the way I look for it? Or do I go to the source?*

He smiled again, this time, smugly. *I go to the source.* The wrinkles and folds that were his head and face nodded slowly and almost imperceptibly at the top of his body mass. "I need their creator," he said out loud. I need the man who made them sentient. I need Abner Hayes."

***

At that very moment, Abner Hayes was making plans to come to Jeemo, even though he didn't even know about his existence.

Deal

"What do you mean by 'Where *you* start'?" asked Abner. "You're coming with me."

The pig put both hooves up then waved one in a wide arc to cover all directions. "You think I'm going out there? Do you have any idea how dangerous it is out there, especially for software? I could be deleted!"

"By your own work."

"Doesn't matter. When you're deleted, you're deleted." The pig pursed its pig mouth and stuck its nose in the air. "Nope. Stayin' right here. Ain't going out there."

"I'll turn it off."

"What's that?"

"I'll shut down the bubble. This one. In fact, I might just…"

"Careful, Ab, old buddy," said the pig, eyes narrowing.

Abner felt a chill inside trying to reconcile the ridiculous plump pig with the baleful glare emitting from its eyes. For the first time, he felt this thing that called itself the War Bug could really be dangerous, that it could actually have been responsible for billions of virtual deaths and for frying millions of human brains. Time to take the pig's advice, and be careful.

"What I meant was…"

Suddenly the pig smiled widely, "Just stoking your coal, Ab, old buddy. I know you wouldn't do anything dumb like shut down this computer, would you?"

"No," Abner shook his head. "Certainly not."

"Atta boy, Ab. Knew you were joking all along." The pig laughed. "Now, about the wife and kid…"

"You'll help me?"

The pig sighed. "I don't know about going out there, Ab. There're places out there that'll eat you alive. Things out there that'll strip the encapsulation right off your functions. Night of the Living Dead virtual creatures that'll dig into your consciousness and haunt your sanity till you die."

"I have to get my wife and daughter back. And I have to get them back soon. Nothing could be more horrible than losing them. Will you please help me?"

The pig scowled lightly. Pussy-footed its hind hooves. Its tiny button penis shook its tiny buttonhole head.

"Please?" asked Abner.

The pig took a deep breath, deep enough to fill its chest, and fill its chest, and fill it until it grew three times its normal size. It held the breath for moment then let it out like a scentless spring wind. "I'll help. I'll go out there with…"

"Thank you," said Abner exuberantly. "Thank you!" And he stepped toward the pig, but the pig jumped backward.

"Now, hold yer horses," said the pig. "There's a few ground rules we need to put in place before I do anything."

"Sure," said Abner, stopping on the spot.

"First, no fraternizing with the pig." The pig pointed toward itself. "That's me. No touchy the pig."

"Got it."

"Second, you do as I say when I say. Got it?"

"As you say, when you say. Got it."

"I mean, when I say jump, you jump. And on the way up you ask how far and when you can come down. Got it?"

"Yes, for crying out loud. I've got it!"

"I've been watching you, Ab, old buddy. I've been watching for a while now. You don't get out much. You've been working on this computer. You've been working at your job, which means you don't get out at all. You don't go out with your family, ever…"

"But, I can't. The risk…"

"I know. You can't risk their sentience being found out. But the thing is, the Net's not the same as it was when you used to spend all your time surfing the virtual world. It's gotten meaner, meaner and dangerous. It eats the unwary. It sneaks up on the cautious and crushes them when they think they're safest. I know it does these things, Ab, because I made it do these things."

Abner looked into the black dot eyes. They were non-committal, uninformative. "Why? Why did you do this to the Net?" he asked.

"We'll get around to that another time, Ab. For now, rule number three." The pig craned its head toward Abner so the large white eyes and tiny black irises were just pixels away from his own avatar face. "You don't ever fuck me, Ab, old buddy. When this is over, when we have your family back, I slice out a piece of real estate in this computer and stay here for a while."

"How long is a while?"

"It's a while, Ab, a while. Deal?"

Abner thought a moment, but there wasn't much to think about. This thing, whatever it was, could help him get his family back. "Yes," he said. "Deal." He went to shake hands, but the head drew back from his face and his hand hung in the digital air unclasped. He wondered what the hell he'd just gotten himself into.

Nice Boy, But No Sex

108

And just like that, it was gone. Claire felt around the mishmash flow of their bandwidth prison. It was gone. The probing had stopped. The pain had stopped. It was gone. Whatever the presence was that had brought them here to dive into their modules and shatter their programming indiscriminately, like a thief tearing a home apart looking for the family jewels, had backed off. It had also left both her and Cassie a little weaker, and this place itself was weakening them. Claire knew it could not sustain them for long as sentient beings; it couldn't even sustain them as distinct programs. Their neural objects were becoming increasingly intertwined, and Claire was increasingly aware of the blur at the edge of her awareness, a creeping fuzziness in her being. But at least that probing thing was gone.

Now she could get back to spying on her daughter.

She wasn't sure just how she would do that. She wasn't sure how it had happened before. Somehow, their programs had crossed and created a portal into her daughter's Memory modules. Now, if there was just some way she could align herself to make that happen again.

There it was. Without even knowing how, without even beginning to align anything, she was in her daughter's mind. Cassie was with Takei.

Seems like a nice boy, thought Claire.

I wonder if he'll be my first 'liner sex experience? thought Cassie.

It took an amazing battle of will for Claire to just let go and allow herself to quietly spy. Takei was sitting opposite Cassie in one of the student lounges in the learning portal from which Abner had just removed Cassie. Takei was a good- looking dark-complexioned avatar with friendly, inquisitive eyes (*Just like Cassie's*, thought Claire.) and thick black hair, cut evenly just past his ear lobes. His ripped orange t-shirt and threadbare jean shorts seemed inappropriate for his calm demeanor. *Trying to impress my daughter, is he?*

The lounge was bright, with a high glass wall looking out onto the campus grounds. Gray paths overlaid onto a green grid of virtual grass formed an intricate pattern of connections between thousands of learning portal objects: dormitories, classrooms, gymnasiums, media rooms, club rooms, lecture halls and administration modules. The paths conducted a steady stream of VPs and avatars between the objects.

Cassie wore purple grunge of some sort. Claire couldn't tell if it were a dress, skirt or pant suit, but it was definitely layered and loud. The electric blue boots were…different. *How come I haven't seen those in her wardrobe?* wondered Claire, then, thinking of the state of Cassie's bedroom, wondered how anything could ever be seen in a wardrobe that covered her daughter's room, in places, like deep multicolored snow.

"My dad makes us live in some, like, thousands of years old retro dump with checkered curtains in the kitchen," said Cassie.

I picked those curtains out, thought Claire, piqued.

"I kinda like checkered curtains," said Takei. He was soft spoken.

Nice boy, thought Claire. *I think I could get used to seeing him with my daughter. But no sex.*

Cassie smiled and blushed. "Really? You really like checkered curtains?" Takei blushed.

"You don't seem to like your father much," said Takei. Claire noticed he had a sparkle in his eyes much like the sparkle in her daughter's eyes. *These two have a lot in common*, she thought.

"It's not that I don't like him," said Cassie. "I just don't like the way his word is the law. Everything has to be *his* way. And I never get to be heard, like, I'm some sort of VP that he can just boss me around so that I exist, like, just to make his world secure for him."

My god, my baby lies so fluently.

"What do you do for fun out there?" asked Takei. "Out there?"

"When you're not 'lining. What do you do? Where do you live?"

"Oh, uh, I live with my father in Bombay. That's in India."

Liar!

Takei laughed. "I know, I did the VR version once. Is it really hot in real life?"

"Hot? Oh yeah, really hot." *Damn!* thought Cassie. *Why didn't I take the VR tour? Why did I have to say Bombay of all places?*

Serves you right, young lady.

"What's your mother like?"

"My real mother died when I was a baby, but I have a VR mother now who's, you know, a typical VP mom—coffee table afternoons and smiling with hubby evenings."

I'm going to kill her. If we get out of here alive, I'm going to kill her! And probably fortunately, the connection with her daughter broke. She felt around. The poking thing was still gone. She wondered about Abner, wondered if he was on his way at that moment to save them, galloping full speed on a white horse to pull them out of this place that was killing them, and take her and her daughter home.

Where she would make her daughter's life miserable beyond measure.

A Dirty Unlighted Place

The bar was dark and deserted, except for the bulky mass of unshaven meanness with beady eyes behind the bar drying the same Collins glass he'd been drying for years. Using the same towel. Standing in the same spot. Year after year, as his right eye drooped and drooped until it looked almost like he had a beady-eyed miniature bowling pin hanging from his right eyelid.

"You certainly picked an interesting place to meet," said Bella's avatar. She sat on a high stool in front of a tiny round bar table in a dark corner. She wore a blue see-through jump suit. Her nipples, as usual, strained against gravity.

"Yes," said the figure sitting in the shadows on the other side of the table. "It has its charms."

"I didn't mean that as a compliment," said Bella.

112

"I'm sure you didn't," said the other. His voice was deep but flat, devoid of resonance and life. Bella liked that in an assassin.

Across the dark rot-wood floors stained with beer and blood, the bartender's drooping eye glanced suspiciously in their direction. Over his head, wine glasses, brandy snifters and long stemmed beer glasses hung upside down from a wooden rack. At one end of the rack, the glasses fused together, then drifted into individual glasses and fused again. A shudder galloped up Bella's back as she watched this. "This place is ready to crash," she said. "Couldn't you have picked a safer place?"

"This place *is* safe for what we're doing." The voice moved slowly, like the way molasses would sound if it could speak.

Bella felt another shudder, this one more of a sexual tingle. The dark figure in the shadows was definitely a turn-on. She crossed her long brown legs and felt the eyes in the darkness creeping across their surface. "Then let's get down to it. Is the money OK?"

"The money's OK."

"And you can make it look natural?"

"I can make it look like anything you want it to look like."

That sent a tingle dancing through her thighs. Maybe she would add a bonus to the assassin's pay. She wondered if he were this sinister in real life. "Natural is fine. But I want him to suffer first. And you can't let him know that I have anything to do with it."

A large scaly insect, something between cockroach and lizard, clickety-clicked across the floor then pixellated into nothingness just before it reached the wall. *This fucking place could crash down all around us any second*, thought Bella. *Our brains could be fried to shit here.*

"Have you tried a reconciliation?"

"What?"

"Have you tried to work things out with him?" Suddenly, the voice in the darkness was swathed in sadness.

"What the hell are you talking about?" Bella's flawless mouth twisted into a nasty scowl. "I want the bastard dead!"

"So…" and the figure in the darkness reached a hand to the area where his chin would be. "…you realize that once he's dead that's it. He's gone for good." *What is this fucking idiot talking about?* "Of course I realize he's going to be gone for good. That's why I'm hiring you to kill him! I want him dead! Finished! Fucked forever!"

"And you don't want him to know it's from you?"

"You have a problem with that!"

"Well, it's so impersonal."

"Just kill that fucking fat cocksucker when I give you the go-ahead or I'll or have someone make *you* dead!"

"As you wish." And again, the voice was menacingly toneless.

***

114

Lying on her golden citrine 'liner's lounge, shaking the bandwidth from her mind as she blinked her eyes open, Bella thought, *Fucking assassin is 'lining in too many grade B romance rooms. Wherever are the cold, hard-hearted of the earth?* She stood, and the 'liner's suit automatically peeled itself from her body and hung itself on the lounger. She breathed deeply and appreciatively as the luscious curves and golden tan of her perfect body filled the quartz mirror, and she smiled, "Oh, there you are."

And she thought, *Wherever you are now Roosenvelt, you obese fuck, wet your size fifty pants for me... your dreams are as close as you get to me.*

A Hunting We Will Go

I'll get him for you, my murderous lust bug, thought Jeemo. *I'll capture their creator and rip his head apart for his secrets. You will live forever, and I will die at your will. I'll go where the scent is the strongest. That's where he'll begin his search. That's where I'll capture his avatar and, through his avatar, his mind.*

But wait!

What if he escapes? What if he eludes my trap? I can only capture him on the bandwidth. What if he outsmarts me? He's intelligent. He created sentient life, stable life, where everyone else failed. He created the most powerful computer in the world, a computer with the capacity to sustain life. I wasn't able to re-create his computer. I was not able to sustain the life he created. Perhaps, perhaps, he is

115

mightier than I. Perhaps, he is smarter than I. Perhaps...

Jeemo looked at his monumental mass in the mirror, the mounds of gray flesh, the orange prongs atop his head, the dainty feet. *No. Such beauty. Such perfection.* He turned his towering bulk to the side and admired the roundness. *I am the end of evolution, the ultimate product of the genome. I will defeat Abner Hayes. I will steal his secret of life then I will die happily under the cruel smile of indifferent immortality. I will go to where the scent is strongest and I will capture his mind.*

With that thought in mind, Jeemo sat on his 'liner's lounger and, with the flick of a thought, set off after Abner Hayes' mind.

Ain't Nothin' But a Hound Dog

"This is where the scent is the strongest," said the pig.

"What scent? And where is this place?" Abner looked around. Both he and the pig stood on a ledge of solid mist and everywhere blue skies and brilliant white clouds soared upwards and away. Below him, space plummeted into an impossibly deep green ocean. The magnitude of presence in this place almost overwhelmed Abner with a euphoric giddiness that nearly brought his avatar to its knees. It was as though he could see ten thousand miles and stretch his hand across the distance to touch the giant balloons floating in the endless sky. He'd never imagined such expansiveness was possible

116

anywhere in the bandwidth. "Where is this place?" he repeated.

"It's your daughter's secret place."

"Cassie?"

"She created this place to get away from *your* world. She filled it with things she loves."

Abner gawked at the immense plumes of cloud. Everything in this place moved with majestic ease. The horizon seemed almost to unite the sky and ocean into a marriage of elements. It was a place of infinite calm and eternal celebration, a magical realm, and his daughter had created it. His daughter had come here, just to be here and be part of all this. "My daughter made all this?"

"Yep. Pretty talented kid you got there, Ab, old buddy."

"I never even knew." Abner reached into the mist and grabbed a handful of cloud, brought it up to his face and examined it. "It's beautiful." He looked around. "It's all so beautiful." He thought a moment. "This is what my sullen daughter who argues my every word has done? She had all this inside her?"

"Eye-opening, isn't it? "But now…" The pig began sniffing the air all around it. Abner watched for a moment then said, "I suppose you're doing something that has a good reason behind it."

"The scent, Ab. Remember the scent?"

"I thought you were joking, or speaking figuratively, or something. There's really a scent? Or do you mean the mapping to their distributed components all over the Net?"

"Are you kidding? You have any idea how many trillions to the powers of trillions of paths

117

there are in even the least complex VP program? And the addresses change dynamically depending on the stability of the location. And..." The pig winked. "...in case you haven't noticed, Ab, old buddy, there ain't many stable places around here no more."

"Point taken. So what's this scent you're looking for?"

"It's not like something you would smell in the real world." The pig cocked its head to one side and squinted its eyes. "Not that I would really know the difference, but I'm guessing that it's more of a bandwidth thing, like an imprint on the bandwidth. Cassie was here, and her programming left a sort of ghost image. I can sense it."

"But smelling the bandwidth?"

"For affect, Ab, for affect. You know, bloodhound kind of thing. In fact..." The pig began turning slowly around, and then faster and faster, until it was a blur of spinning pork. Then it stopped. It was no longer a pig. It was a bloodhound. A large bloodhound, standing erect, dressed in a cream-colored trench coat and wearing a Deerstalker hat like the one worn by Sherlock Holmes. "Like it?" asked the hound.

"I don't get it. I thought you were a pig."

"Abner, Abner, Abner. I'm not a pig. I'm not a hound. I'm a program. I'm the War Bug. But I can appear as anything I like. I'm sniffing down a scent-like after- image in the bandwidth. Time to be the detective dog. Now, do you like it?"

Abner sighed. "Yeah, I guess so. So, do you smell my daughter, Detective Dog?"

"Sure I do. All around here. This was her place. But what I need now is the most recent scent, and then I need to locate its exit point."

At least it doesn't have a magnifying glass, thought Abner.

"Got to be around here somewhere," said the dog as it pulled an oversize magnifying glass out of its coat pocket.

Figures.

The dog began inspecting pieces of cloud, picking up handfuls of white puff and zeroing in on them with the magnifying glass, then sniffing them thoroughly before tossing them back into the main cloud with a short snort from its glistening brown nose. The dog's long ears slopped over its shoulders when it bent over. Abner wondered how dogs like this in real life managed to hear; it seemed the ears would block all sound, muffle it, at least. Then he thought, *What the hell am I thinking about? What the hell is this thing doing?* "What the hell are you doing? This is a program. What you're looking for is shadows of code. You can't see that with a magnifying glass! This is stupid! It's useless!"

The hound dog stood erect. It was a few inches taller than Abner, and now Abner noticed it was a tad on the massive side for a dog. The sadness in the dog's big brown eyes was shouldered out by a glare of raw disgust. The dog's intense stare was too much even for an avatar. Abner looked at the ground, feeling like a guilty little boy, eye-slapped for doing something wrong, but not exactly sure what it was.

"I've been around a lot longer than you, Abner. I've been alone. I've been alone a lot. This," the dog gestured at its general countenance, "helps to break the boredom. Try destroying several online citystates, throwing billions of 'liners into total chaos, and see how popular that makes you. It requires anonymity, a lone wolf life, and I need…"

"OK!" said Abner. "OK. I'm sorry. Go ahead and do the dog detective thing."

"SHHHH!"

"Wha…?"

"Shhh." The dog moved close to Abner and whispered. "We're not alone."

Like a Rock

It was just a tiny speck in the distance, but it wasn't quite in sync with the rest of the skyline. It beat to a different rhythm.

It seemed to be growing.

Abner blinked his virtual eye, a functionless gesture, but it helped him to focus. Yes, it was getting bigger. And darker. And closer. In fact, now he could pick out details. It was cloud-like. It displayed considerable internal movement. And now he could pick out that movement, it was storm-like. Yes, it was a storm inside the cloud. It was a storm heading his way, faster and faster. It was definitely no longer a tiny speck. It spread for leagues in every direction, a mass of gray and black streaked cloud, roiling and coiling and getting darker and larger and closer, moving at an amazing speed, a deceptive speed because, now, it was directly before him, getting larger, but not closer. It seemed to be glaring at him, or maybe studying

120

him, as lightning crackled and lit its surface from the inside and thunder roared ominously. Dark turbulence poured over vast precipices of cloud, like rock itself suddenly turning into a stony waterfall.

Then it was all around him, tearing at the frequencies in the bandwidth with a gnashing violence Abner thought impossible. It twisted blindingly all around him. The wind was tremendous and deafening. It tugged at his avatar and he had to fight hard to stay in place. Its force intensified and pulled and pummeled his avatar, then like a giant formless vacuum cleaner, it focused its ferocious energy over him and tried to suck him into its blackened mass. He began to weaken and, as though the storm cloud sensed this, its fury doubled. Abner's avatar began to break away from its cloud platform pixel by pixel. All around him, quick bolts of lightning streaked and crashed into each other. Everywhere was darkness and chaos. His arms flew out from his sides and bent at weird angles. His right foot dislodged and his left leg began to quake. He fought with his mind, with his intent to stay put, to not become part of this storm. But the storm merely increased intensity.

This really blows, thought Abner.

Chapter 9

Love Is A Loaded Stapler

Bella sat before a diamond mirror as her sexclone brushed her hair slowly. His dark eyes dripped adoration, his horse-size penis protruded obscenely from the center of his naked body, and his lips were stapled shut. She thought it was a nice touch. It raised the sexclone in her esteem by preventing him from asking all the same idiotic questions like, "What can I do for you now?" and, "Do you wish me to pleasure you orally again?" and "Do you wish to walk on my back with spiked shoes?" Yes, yes, yes to all, but can't a girl do a little thinking without all these interruptions.

"Staple it shut," she'd said. And that's exactly what he'd done. She thought that was very sweet of him.

Painful as it was, he smiled as he brushed with long, slow strokes. With the nano-enhancements, her hair didn't need brushing. This was just for the sensual enjoyment. And it gave her a chance to just think, but she really didn't like what she had to think about.

I have to call a meeting of the Powers and make sure they're not on to me. If I just knew who they were, I could send that wishy-washy asshole to kill them. She sighed. The sexclone laid a hand softly on her. Bella smiled, crossed an arm in front of her, and placed her hand on top of its hand. Then, she dug a razor sharp fingernail deep enough into its hand to draw blood. "Just brush," she said. The sexclone smiled and brushed.

I suppose I shouldn't put this off any longer,
she thought. She touched a button on the ruby
lounger upon which she sat. "Powers, meeting in
ten." As the biggest shareholder in Atlantiscity, she
could do things like that.

Gotcha?

Jeemo directed the capture program online,
lying in his 'liner's lounger. This was important and
he wanted to be onsite, so to speak, to make sure
nothing went wrong. He was impressed with his
program; the virtual storm was a work of digital art.
He was at the center of it and away from it at the
same time, directing it with his will. He was almost
drooling with the taste of victory. His heart leapt
and did somersaults in his chest as he watched
Abner's avatar lose its footing. Just a few more
seconds.

"Got you!" screamed Jeemo. "You little man.
Got you, you loser! You loser! You lose! I win!
I…"

Then everything went blank. No storm. No
avatar. No clouds. Just Jeemo lying on his 'liner's
lounger, staring at the mirrored ceiling, looking into
his own wide eyes, stunned and speechless.

Who Wants to Live Forever

Suddenly, it was calm. Abner's avatar stood
statue still. The wind was gone, along with the
lightning and the black cloud, all of it just vanished

123

in a blink. The only sound was the mournful baying of the hound dog, howling into the now serene blue of Cassie's secret place. Dog sadness bounced and echoed through the white clouds and tumbled into the sky. The hound presented an eerie sight, sitting on its haunches, its front paws planted in cloud, its floppy-eared head pointed at the sun, just like a dog, but with a Deerstalker hat and a trench coat. And its yowl buried itself in the bandwidth. Abner felt it vibrating inside his own presence. It was just about the most awful sound Abner had ever heard.

"Why are you doing that?" he asked.

The hound stopped abruptly and looked at Abner with its sad brown eyes. "Affect."

Abner nodded. "I think you've made your point. Do you really need to do that anymore?"

The hound shrugged and stood up on its hind feet, once again towering over Abner.

"What was that thing?" asked Abner.

"Capture program," said the dog. "Somebody tried to capture your avatar."

"But why?"

"Got any enemies?"

"None that I know of. But why would anyone want to capture an avatar. Why not go after me in the real world?"

"Because you can use an avatar to get into the real world mind. It's a link, and it's possible to use it…"

"That's ridiculous!" said Abner, and he tried to lift his left foot but realized the space between it and the cloud was still rough with pixelation. He ran a repair program and the color resolution began to

124

deepen immediately. "The programming for something like that…

"…is illegal," finished the dog. "But it exists."

"And just how do you know that." Abner watched the digital damage around his foot disappear as abruptly as the storm thing that had caused it. He looked at the dog. "How?"

The dog smiled. It was creepy. Two rows of saber-sharp teeth bared as the dog's mouth curled toward each ear. "Because I created it."

"You?"

"How do you think I knew how to turn it off?"

"Well…"

"Because I created it and incorporated it into a SoftWAR add-on module that I then put up for sale to the Central Powers of each of the citystates." By some impossible feat of digital rendering, the dog's smile stretched even more. "They loved it."

"But something like that in the wrong hands…"

"Which were exactly the hands I made sure it got into."

"But it goes against…"

"The Reality Laws?" The dog laughed, a deep feral sound that chilled Abner. "The Reality Laws are gone, Ab, old buddy. They're gone! Impossible to enforce. Things are just too far gone. There's no need to be enforcing laws now, Ab. The real need is to hide, if there were anywhere to hide. But then…" The dog winked. "You have a hiding place." The dog winked again. "For a few of us, anyway."

This thing isn't a hound dog, thought Abner. *It's not a pig. It's not anything more than a deadly virus. Its only purpose is to destroy. And it's going to be hiding on my computer with my wife and daughter*. But he also realized this deadly virus that looked so much like a big huggable dog, was also the only hope he had of finding his family.

"So what's in my mind that someone would try to kidnap my avatar?" asked Abner.

The dog cocked its head to one side and clucked its tongue. "Abner, old buddy, do you have any idea what you've done?"

Abner remained silent.

"You've created life, sentient software, a whole new species of life form. You built a computer capable of breathing life into software, and what is sentient software, Ab, old buddy?"

Abner shrugged his shoulders. "It's…it's software that's alive." The dog smiled again.

"Please don't do that."

"Do what?"

"Smile. It really creeps me out. It would creep you out too if you could see yourself."

The dog frowned. "Not much for letting people live their own lives, are you? Typical 'liner."

"Hey, I…"

"But that's neither here nor there. The fact is, sentient software is a lot more than just life, it's immortal life. It never dies."

"That's just a theory."

"But the biggest techno breakthrough of all time if it works. Now, you tell me, who out there beyond the bandwidth, in the world of finite life, wants to live forever?"

"Well…"

"I'm guessing that just about every single human out there would steal your avatar, and kill you in doing it if that were necessary, to live forever."

"But I kept the whole thing secret. Nobody could know about it."

"Whoever tried to capture your avatar used a program that's only available to the most powerful people in the citystates. That person, or group of people, would probably have access to a lot of sophisticated spyware. And I'm guessing that they're the same person or group who kidnapped your family." The dog frowned. "And that's not good."

"What do you mean by that?"

"They probably hoped to get the secret of your family's sentience from their programs. If they're after you, it means that they couldn't get it from them."

"So?"

"So, the transfer to the other server, the one you said couldn't support them..." Abner felt sick. "Yes?"

"I just hope that you're wrong about that, Ab, old buddy." And the dog sniffed the air.

Gratitude

Abner looked around at the beautiful sky and the majestic clouds, the expansiveness and power of everything he witnessed in this place, and he missed his daughter. Impudent, slothful, disrespectful and reckless as she was, he still loved her and he wanted her back. And he wanted his wife back. He knew things would never be quite the same; the psychotic

127

virus standing on its hind legs in front of him, with its nose all a-twitch as it sniffed the air for ghost electrons had seen to that. If this thing was heading for cover, then there wasn't much time. There definitely wasn't much time for his family; that is, if they were still alive. If he didn't get them back home to their computer, there was no telling what kind of damage would befall them. Their programs could be hopelessly corrupted. They might even die.

Then, once they were home, how would they share the computer with this thing sniffing the air? What effect would it have on their programs? What effect would it have on the computer? Would it turn on them? How long could it go without destroying something?

After it helped him get his family back, he would have to find a way to destroy it.

***

"There it is," said the dog. "I've found their scent."

The Powers

"We have to implement the next Net," said the third column from the right.

"But who could have let it get this bad?" inquired the second column from the left.

"This is an abomination, I say!" said the middle column.

"Someone must be held accountable for this!" insisted the second column from the left.

128

"Forget about blame and accountability," said the third column from the right. "Time is running out and we're not ready to implement the next Net. This is happening faster than we thought, but it's happening. It's happening now, and we have to come up with a plan. Fast." And if a column could make a fist and bang it on a table, that's exactly what the third column from the right would have done.

"An abomination!" reiterated the middle column. And surely it would have banged a fist on a table as well.

"But someone must be responsible for this," said the second column from the left with a whiney voice. "We need to determine responsibility and met out consequences before we can even think about planning…"

"We don't have time for that," said the third column from the right. "We have…"

"We have nothing till we can be sure this won't happen again," interjected the second column from the left. "And that means…"

"Poppycock!" yelled the middle column. "It's an…"

"But what's the status of the new enabling technologies?" asked the first column to the right. "It's my understanding that…"

"To hell with enabling technologies," said the third column from the left. "They'll just…"

***

Argue your fucking brains out, thought Bella. Though she was the most powerful of all the

129

Powers, she was represented as the fifth column to the right in the City Central Boardroom, which was presented as a marble plain at the top of a mountain. The Powers were presented as towering Roman columns forming a V with seven columns on each side and a middle column forming the apex. The middle column was generally considered to be the Chair column and, for all intents and purposes, was regularly ignored. The open space opposite the apex was reserved for guest speakers, at least, in theory, since there had never been a guest speaker.

Idiots! thought Bella as she watched the columns' futile argument through a chalcedony-framed screen. 'Lining into a City Central meeting was dangerous. More than one Power had been assassinated by one or more of the other Powers for letting his or her identity slip out, so the Powers met the old way, through monitors. *As long as they keep on fighting among themselves, I'm free to do as I please.*

***

"But what about the enabling technologies for the next Net? The software? The hardware?" asked the first column to the right.

"To hell with the technologies!" screamed the second column from the left. "Who is damned well responsible for all this?"

The fifth column to the right, though it was pale green, signaling that the Power was online, kept abnormally quiet. Behind its presentation, Bella smiled. She, and she alone, owned all the technologies and infrastructure that would be used to construct the next Net. And if Jeemo did his work, she would have forever to rule over it.

Chapter 10

Perfect Devil

"What! What! What! What!" screamed Jeemo. "What! What happened? I had him! I had him!" The arch of orange spikes on his head stretched upwards so tightly they pulled at the flesh on his scalp. They were needle sharp. Jeemo could have climbed mountains with his head.

He pushed himself off his 'liner's lounger and bounced onto the floor. He jumped up and down and screamed, "What happened? What! What! I had him! He was mine! Mine!" He pounded the unbreakable mirror floor so hard that his mansion at the edge of the Great Nano Canyon trembled as its foundations groaned and screeched. His army of serverclones hid in closets and cupboards. Three serverclones shivered silently in the walk-in freezer as they watched slabs of beef and pork sway to and fro on their meat hooks. A shatterproof mirror in the main hall shattered. A flock of Canada geese migrating south were terrified into changing directions and headed back to Canada.

"What? Oh what, oh what." He whimpered. He stopped jumping and just stood looking at his naked mass, now dark gray with stress. After a moment, he smiled. And posed. And smiled some more.

You perfect devil, you, he thought. Then he walked to the window to think calmly about what had happened.

Romance Avenue

132

What a weird place, thought Cassie. Cliché love music permeated the bandwidth in this place. *What was my mom doing in a place like this?* The profusion of romantic symbols was overwhelming; everywhere, love, passion and pairing ululated in the streetscape. Signs shaped like hearts flashed pink and blue calligraphy. Doves floated serenely in the spaces between buildings. Virtual mood couples roamed about holding hands and staring into each other's moonstruck eyes. The buildings were smooth and soft, painted in muted tones suggesting rose petals and white ribbons. Then, through her mother's eyes, she saw the street sign: Romance Avenue.

Eyuk! Mom!

Cassie had heard about this place. It was a meeting place for VPs and avatars looking for long-term relationships as opposed to The Freeway, where mostly avatars flocked for casual sex. Romance Avenue was where her mother had met her father. And almost as soon as she remembered this, she saw the familiar shape—the hairless head with the ponytail that seemed almost to spurt out of his spine, the black turtleneck and blocky body, the droopy-sad eyes. It was her father, Abner Hayes, or at least, his avatar. He stood below a pink flashing sign advertising genuine Charles Borgman synthetic diamond rings (She'll wear the glitter of your love forever.) and his eyes were on her mother and they were round and wondering. Her father, her future father, was staring at her future mother as though he were stunned and the woman he was staring at was looking back at him and thinking: *Yes, I would*

133

choose him repeatedly in a random array of choices.

Yeah, right! My mother, the hopeless romantic.

Faster Than a Speeding Bullet

"We're going to the beach," said the dog. Abner was beginning to get used to the Deerstalker hat and the trench coat wrapped around the floppy-eared dog. But he didn't think he'd ever get used to the rows of razor sharp teeth when it smiled.

"So, should I bring a towel?"

The dog raised an eyebrow. "My, aren't we the snarky one."

At least it had stopped smiling, thought Abner.

"The fact that we're going to a beach…where it's highly unlikely that your wife and daughter will be…means that my hunch was right. Whoever took them used an indirect path. They went all over the place. We may have to go all over the next Net to find them." It sniffed the air twice, loudly. "But we start at the beach, the first place they took your daughter."

"So how do we get to a mallway from here? I don't see any portals."

"We won't be using the mallway."

Abner's eyes went wide. "Ride pure bandwidth? Are you kidding? That'll rip my avatar to shreds! I'll…"

The dog raised a trench-coated foreleg to silence him. "It'll be OK, Ab, old buddy. I do it all the time."

"But you…"

Suddenly, he was surrounded by the whitest white he'd ever seen. It was an endless white and there was nothing else, just white, stretching into every direction. White. Pure and unblemished by color or texture. But there was the sense of movement, and not just any movement, but movement so fast it defied the concept of fast. It was so fast it was stillness in motion. It was time looking at itself. It was the speed of light passing itself. Abner's avatar was traveling unimaginably fast and his mind was experiencing every microsecond of the experience. He couldn't see any parts of himself and he couldn't see the dog. All that existed was the white and his awareness of it. And his awareness that he was traveling faster than anything possible could only be summed up in one word: *YAHOO!*

A Fishing We Will Go

Even in the late night darkness, it was impossible to see the stars through his tornado-proof window, not because of the glass—it was paper thin—but because of the play of blue and orange light from the Great Nano Canyon. He'd ventured onto one of the mansion's balconies once and smelled the air out there. It was a moldy rotted smell, like old cheese. Jeemo had ordered the balconies ripped out and replaced with windows.

Time was running out. He needed the secret of the VPs' sentience, but he wasn't going to get it from them. And now it looked like he was going to have a hard time getting it from their creator. *Could*

I have underestimated him? he thought. *No. That can't be. I'm perfect. Nobody is smarter than me. He was just lucky. He caught me with some new piece of anti-grabware. That's it! He tricked me!*

Behind him, a screen opened in the mirrored wall. Jeemo looked, blinked, and turned deep gray red. His eyes bulged. The orange spikes thrust up like spears. The news on the screen was bad.

He's made contact with the first node. How did he do that so fast? Nobody can trace a concealment node that fast...it's impossible!

But the message on the screen blared the impossible: NODE 1-A-A-1: CONNECT.

Time to go to the beach for some fishing.

Empathy

Tornado glass on all the windows. He shifted the barrel of the nanobeam sniper's assault rifle and pressed his eye harder onto the scope as Jeemo came into sight, his back to the window. He seemed to be looking at something. *Perfect shot right now. Let's hope I get another one when the time comes.* He put the rifle down on the purple grass in front of where he lay, snapped the scope off and put it up to his eye. He targeted Jeemo again. *Big bastard. I wonder why she wants him dead? Must be some kind of business deal gone bad...that's almost always what it is. Ugly bastard, as well. Looks more like a walking dead log with orange branches than a man. God, look at the size of him. Must need a crane and a search party to find his dick. I sure wouldn't want to die the way he's going to check out.*

He looked briefly at the rifle. It was loaded with slow-death nanobeam ammunition. A single, invisible beam would penetrate the tornado glass without leaving a trace and enter Jeemo's body without him feeling a thing. It would take several minutes to poison him. Every inch of his skin would feel like vinegar fire, so much so he might deliberately take his own life, or run blindly into one of the mirror walls and slice himself into cold cuts. His death would be seen as viral in nature, but no one would ever be sure enough one way or the other to call it murder.

Poor bastard. Probably got pushed around a lot when he was a kid. Big one like that probably shy too...not even put up a fight. Just struggle through it and hope to grow up as fast as possible. Might even have spent his entire childhood holed up in that big house, hiding away from the world. Poor bastard.

Stop it, you ass. You're going to kill him.

But the poor bastard...

"Just do the job," he said out loud, without tone or modulation, just stating the facts.

But that didn't stop a tear from dislodging from his eye and spilling in a thin stream down the assassin's cheek

Bad Timing

Jakel Sassen's body writhed madly on the 'liner's lounger. He moaned and grunted and his

137

teeth ground hard enough to make calcium burn. "Unh!" he yelled, and his chin shot up. "Unh! Unh!" and his pelvis shot up. "Unh! Unh! Unh!" and his entire body shot up and Jakel looked like a Chinese bridge swaying in a monsoon.

His body was gripped by the heaviest cybersex he'd had in his entire life. Every pore of his flesh, every cell in his brain, every vibration of his soul galloped with the barrage of stimuli generated by his new Bodystate module and the lithe VP beauty, Sonda, who had his virtual dick in her virtual mouth.

"UNH!" he screamed both online and off. "Oh babybabybabybaby that's the way that's the way you got it babybabybaby you got it all you got it babybaby just one more suck just one more just one more oh babybaby just one mo…"

And without any warning, without the slightest hint Jakel wasn't going to have the most intense ejaculation he'd ever experienced, the ejaculation that would paralyze every atom in his body with pleasure, suddenly, just as he was on the brink of sexual madness, just as he tottered at the lip of the volcano ready to abandon reason and dive in, just at that moment, the volcano dived at him.

Sonda's blonde hair folded into black waves. Her skin shed its pink; her disbelieving eyes shed their green. Her shape shivered and she lifted her head to look into Jakel's eyes and, as her head moved through the virtual air, it melted into black. Her body shivered again and dissolved. Jakel screamed.

"OH!" he screamed both online and off. Offline, his brain melted into blackness, into a kind of tasteless, colorless and meaningless soup. Online, his avatar body melted into blackness along with Sonda.

Along with the rest of Troycity.

Bye Bye Troycity

Blue skin stretched for miles and miles from Abu's point of view, which was fixed deep between Karthymelon's legs. Abu loved blue. He loved the smooth slopes and curves of Karthymelon's thighs and the tuft of white fuzz where he buried his nose. He loved the gentle cooing of her voice every time his virtual tongue slid along her blue labia. It was all magnified a hundred times by the new module. Since he'd bought the module, he'd demolished two 'liner's loungers. He wondered what his body was doing to the latest one right this moment, but the thought was interrupted by Karthymelon's voice. Her voice was heavy and indolent.

"Troy. Troy. Troy"

Abu reluctantly lifted his face up. "Whazzit? Whaz you sayin' Karthy?"

Her eyes rolled for a second and then settled on the control wall. She panted heavily. Her eyes were far away but they focused on one part of the wall as she pointed limply. Abu followed her eyes and finger to the screen. The graphs and charts for Troycity were all motionless. Flat lines. Zero activity.

"Troycity iz gone way of dodo," he said. "Call da bitch later?"

"Yeah, call da bitch later." Karthymelon grabbed his head with both hands and pulled it into her thighs as she said, "Bye bye Troycity."

Damaged Merchandise

Bella's long hair spilled over the sexclone's hands like a chestnut waterfall as he massaged her neck. The top of his right hand was bandaged. He smiled shyly, keeping his eyes on Bella and seemingly oblivious to Jeemo's presence on the screen. Jeemo noticed something odd about the sexclone's lips but couldn't put his finger on what it was.

"What's taking so long? Why haven't you found it yet?"

Jeemo reveled in the abrasiveness of Bella's voice. His lost penis throbbed as the heat of her anger flushed through his body like a swarm of demonic locusts. His soul screeched for death at her hand.

"Just a while longer. The coding is much more complex than I'd imagined." He noticed her gaze wasn't exactly aimed at his eyes, but just above his eyes, and then it dawned on him that he was sweating. His perfect body was giving him away. She wouldn't be fooled by his lies. He had to try something else. *A promise. Yes, I'll make a promise*, he thought. *I'll promise her something. But what? Anything. I'll promise her...*

Then he blurted, "By morning. I'll have it by morning. I promise."

"Fuck the promises, you ass! Just get it! And get it now! Right now! And the screen went blank.

OK, Abner Hayes, thought Jeemo, *no more Mr. Perfect Nice Guy.*

Party Pooper

Towering cliffs and granite slopes soared through the distant mists as though the earth had coughed up massive slabs of tectonic plate. Idyllic green pastures rambled along the base of the enormous rocks and spread right up to the bower of lazy dutch elms surrounding the school's virtual courtyard area where Cassie and her friends, Andrea and Sharlin, sat on white marble benches around a solid chunk of marble, its top skillfully overlaid with a green patina.

Education interfaces certainly are much more entertaining than when I was her age, thought Claire as she floated inside her daughter's memories. Spying again.

"Oh, c'mon," said Sharlin, a dark-eyed girl with green hair. "You never come to any of our sleepovers. And we all live, I mean, in the same city. What's with that?"

Damn it! thought Cassie. *Why didn't I just tell them that I wasn't allowed to give out my real address. How did I know they would both be living in Summerside. Who's even heard of the place? Who would even, like, live there?*

"Yeah, Cass," said the other girl, Andrea. She was tall and athletic-looking with large eyes. Her hair was rendered as a perfectly square, brunette

141

box. "It's not like you have to go on a plane or a boat or anything. It's just a few minutes on the transport."

More like a million years of technology to turn VPs into real people, thought Cassie. *Ah, damn it, damn it, damn it...is my whole life going to be just not being able to do all the things my friends are doing?*

All three girls wore a mixture of partially shredded multicolored shirts, black gloves and boots, and Greco-Roman mini-skirts. "She's right," said Sharlin. "It's not like you'll be going to Mars Colony or something. C'mon, Cass, we want to meet you in real life."

Great! Just great, thought Claire. *She's posing as a human. That would be just about all it takes to get her deleted, sic them on to me and get me deleted, and*

Abner Included. What were you thinking, sweetheart, whatever were you thinking?

Then she realized that, now, she knew exactly what her daughter was thinking. All around the girls, the courtyard, an exact replica of the Garden of

Hesperides, stretched like an indolent summer wind. Beside them, slabs of carved rock led down to a crystalline pool spotted with yellow lilies.

"I can't," said Cassie sheepishly. "My dad's really strict about not meeting with the real people behind the avatars…"

"Oh, gimme a break, Cass," said Sharlin. "Everybody does it. You afraid of being Included, or something. They don't do that to kids."

142

"It's just a slap on the wrist," said Andrea. "Yeah," said Sharlin. "Even if that."

"But, my dad…"

"Screw your dad," said Sharlin. "He's not ever gonna even know. You think we…"

"But, you don't know my dad. He's…he's…"

"He's…?" prompted Sharlin.

"He's close to being Included, himself. And, if I get caught…"

"Bullshit. Bullshit. Bullshit." said Sharlin.

"Bullshit," agreed Andrea.

"Bullshit," said Sharlin. And the two other girls giggled. "C'mon," said Sharlin. "No more dumb excuses. Come to the sleepover this Saturday."

Damn it, thought Cassie. *Why did I? Why did I? Damn it! Why can't I just have a normal life and have real friends and be like them. Why did my father give me this dumb life just so I could spend all of it being miserable and alone?* She watched a copse of green shrubs waver and begin to pixellate and disappear splotch by splotch, leaving a gray hole in the Garden. The surrounding ground and foliage injected spidery tentacles into the hole and filled it with color and texture. Within seconds, the damage was repaired, except the ground was on top of the shrubs. *I'm just like that mess, a piece of damaged software that doesn't fit anywhere.*

"Well?" asked Sharlin. "C'mon," said Andrea.

"Take the chance," said Sharlin. "It'll be a blast," said Andrea.

Suddenly Cassie stood up and yelled, "Fuck off!" And she walked away from the table, leaving the two human avatars staring silently after her.

"Father whipped," said Sharlin, in a voice just above a whisper.

Bitch, thought Cassie. *I heard that.*

Oh my poor little girl, thought Claire. *What have your father and I done?*

Without warning, the presence was back and stabbing through their modules painfully, shooting through their life systems, rocking objects and obliterating entire sections of code. Claire heard her daughter scream.

Then it was gone. The pain stopped. Claire rushed her awareness to her sobbing daughter to try and heal some of the pain she'd been feeling her whole life.

Intersection

Jeemo came offline with a mean grin folding the flesh of his pudgy pink lips. He wasn't used to being the one to cause pain for others and he wasn't sure how he felt about it, at least about causing the pain for the two VPs. He knew exactly how the spree through their program objects felt though. It was exhilarating, a feeling of letting go and just thrashing about with no care whatsoever about the damage or the harm done. He felt released, vindicated for something, though he wasn't sure what that something might be. It just felt good to splash about at somebody else's cost whether it was costing them pain, grief, or just a minor discomfort.

It had been Jeemo's first foray into dishing out the pain. He'd always been the willing victim in his fantasies. Even before he'd known she existed, he'd

144

spent his whole life grooming himself to be put to death by Bella Bjork, and if he hadn't met her, would have found someone just like her. Well, maybe not quite as pitilessly evil as her, but close maybe.

What he'd just done had been spite, but its effect had been unexpected. Jeemo was at one of those intersections in life where you can go to either side or straight ahead but the traffic to your rear means no going back. He wasn't sure which street he was going to take, but he was sure of one thing. He looked deep into his eyes reflected in the wall and said, "Yes, no more Mr. Perfect Nice Guy."

Chapter 11

On the Beach

Lacquer-like ocean water soaked into the smooth sun-blanched stones on the beach. The weathered roundness of the stones, and the white patina over their colors gave the beach a sense of ancient calm. The air was still and thin streaks of waves rippled the surface of the water like shallow breathing. Below the surface, wet rocks sparkled red, green and blue like the hidden jewels of an ancient empire.

"Now, we walk," said the dog. "Where is this place?" asked Abner.

"Spread all over the solar system," said the dog. "Its objects are stored everywhere. The perfect place to hide a trail. But I think we're in approximately the right place."

"Where do you think we are physically?"

"Research ship somewhere off the moons of Jupiter."

"Really?"

"Probably not."

Abner frowned. *Smart-assed virus*, he thought. "OK, then, how big do you think this place is?"

"It's one of the virtual-world experiments, meant to recreate an entire world online."

"It must spread for thousands of cyber miles."

"No. Not really. Just this beach, and the sky and ocean for as far as you can see from here. It was too complex. The details were meant to be recreated, not filled in through a filler chip and that made the details just too detailed. It drove the VR techs nuts. They all killed themselves and this program was just left to run on its own, as is. It's one of the few places I didn't infect, but it'll fall with the rest of the Net. It'll all fall." The dog's lips curled very slightly into a sinister smirk.

It's proud of what it's done, thought Abner. *A proud computer program. Almost as though it's reached some level of sentience. But how?*

The beach spread into the distance like coarse sandpaper. Stray wisps of cirrus cloud clung to the dense blue sky far away from the beach. In the distant horizon, ocean and sky merged into a thin white line.

"Well," said Abner, "they did a great job. It reminds me of the beach my parents used to take me to when I was a kid."

"I feel a story coming on," said the dog. "Come on, let's walk while you talk." The dog's nose, wet with virtual snot, glistened as it twitched, sniffing the air for traces of Abner's daughter.

They walked toward an outcrop of light brown cliffs, steep and angular, with huge slabs of rock jutting at crazy angles like giant cubes of brown sugar squashed under the foot of a behemoth.

"There's not much to tell," said Abner. "My parents used to take me to the beach in the real world when I was a kid. It looked something like this, but there were signs to warn people to stay out of the water. That was around the time of the killer swimmer's itch. People literally scratched themselves to death. Others died from fevers and other complications triggered by the itch. But getting back to the beach, it was still a beautiful place. I loved the sense of size and the feel of sand

147

under my feet, the warmth of the sun burning through my 120 sunscreen." He smiled, but the dog showed no signs of getting it. *Never had to worry about burning in raw sunlight with almost no ozone to filter it*, he thought. "Anyways, it was something like this place. The sun and the feel of sand are gone, but the space and the sound of the waves crashing on the beach are here." He pointed toward the cliffs. "And those are so realistic. They tried to create an entire world online? Where did they think they were going to get the bandwidth?"

The dog snorted. "People who play god don't think about practical things like that, Ab, old buddy. I suspect they thought if they gave a world, the bandwidth would come." The dog threw its head back and half barked, half laughed, its bared teeth flashing insanely.

Abner felt decidedly uncomfortable. "I don't get it."

The dog stopped laughing and, still smiling, said, "You had to be there." Then burst into laughter again. It laughed for about a minute then quieted down.

A virus, a program, with a sense of humor, thought Abner. *Where did this thing come from?* Abner was beginning to feel even uneasier, not because he felt threatened by the dog, but because he was beginning to realize there was much more under the presentation of this cyber being than was initially apparent. Much more.

"What were your parents like?" asked the dog. "You want to know about my parents?"

"I think that would be the general gist of my question. Should I repeat it?"

"No, sorry. Caught me thinking. Um…my parents. Well, that's another story." The dog sniffed the air. "We're still on the right track. It's around here somewhere. I think we have time. Let's hear about your parents."

"Well, they were a lot different before they were Included."

The Sound of Silence

"We'll be next," said the third column from the right. "First Pompeiicity, then Troycity, and we can't possibly have too much time left. I just want you all to know before that time comes that it's never been a pleasure working with any of you. You're all a bunch of self-absorbed, petty-minded assholes, and I hope I never have the displeasure of having to work with, socialize with, or cross paths with any of you dickwads again, ever. You suck."

Silence flooded the mountaintop boardroom like foam insulation. Silence suffused the columns like salt packing. Silence spread over rocky spaces between the columns like peanut butter. Silence bowed to silence and accepted silence's hand to waltz a slow waltz in the pixels that delineated air between the columns. None of the columns spoke. None of the columns nudged the air where silence waltzed with silence. Every column and every avatar behind every column ruminated silently on the outburst from the third pillar to the right. Every column considered those words. Every column considered the source of those words, and every column weighed the wisdom of those words in

149

relation to the consequences of actions and responses to those words. Every column remained silent until…

"But who will be held accountable?" asked the second column from the left.

***

Perfect, thought Bella.

Being Included

"What I remember most about my parents when I was a kid," said Abner, "is their eyes. Their eyes were so bright and intelligent. They looked *into* things rather than looking *at* them."

The dog, sniffing its invisible trail through the digital air, nodded.

They walked just inches beyond the reach of the waves. Abner marveled at the detail of this seascape, the greens and blues, aquamarines and dozens of other colors and hues and textures mixed in a perfect balance to form an exact replica of seawater. The sand warmed his mind with the scintillating richness and density of billions of particles of quartz and other minerals, each rendered perfectly like an individual work of art.

"And their eyes were carefree."

"You mean, *they* were carefree," corrected the dog.

"No, I mean their eyes were carefree. You could see it in their eyes, the freedom, the lack of worry. Looking into their eyes was like looking into a playground or country brook, before the country brooks all became ecoli factories."

The dog panned its big eyes toward him. "You don't much like it out there, do you Ab, old buddy?"

"Why do you think I spend most of my life online? But getting back to my parents, they were happy, genuinely happy. But they were outspoken. Maybe it had something to do with their being carefree. Maybe that clouded their vision to the consequences of some of the things they did."

"Like what?"

In the verdant forests at the top of the cliff, Abner picked out evergreen trees and towering stands of white-trunked birch. "Well, you see, my parents were opposed to the Powers. They believed that the online citystates should belong to the citizens of each city."

The dog smiled.

"They believed that the Powers were using people for nothing more than economic units, that the entire Net was nothing more than a giant marketing tool, almost like a huge amusement park where everything costs a fortune."

"I find myself liking your parents immensely," said the dog. "In fact, I seem to recall something like that somewhere in myself, I think."

"Well, don't get too infatuated with my parents. They've changed, or at least, they've been changed." Abner walked in silence for a moment and watched a foamy wave break into countless bubbles on the shimmering sand. "They started a newsgroup. Nothing fancy. It wasn't even VR, just a character-based interactive forum framed by

151

virtual monitors. But it became popular. In fact, it became one of the most popular newsgroups on the Net. At its height, it had over twenty million subscribers. They talked about things like doing away with the profiling and tracking software, eliminating the Reality Laws, or at least limiting them and getting rid of some of the crazier ones. The Powers of all the citystates started to get a little worried. You see, back then, newsgroups could span citystates, they weren't locked in. Then one day, the group just disappeared. My parents couldn't get in to post messages; nobody could access it to read the messages. It just disappeared along with all the archived content, the whole works. It was like it never existed. My parents accused the Powers of sabotaging it and ended up being arrested for breaking one of the Reality Laws, the one about not questioning the Powers more than three and a half times."

"Hmm. Sounds like the Reality Laws, but I never really paid much attention to them."

"The Powers of Altantiscity had them Included. They injected nanobots into their brains, and the bots restructured their thought processes to make them compliant, to accept the Powers and their control of the Net. They became happy little consumer animals. All the life they had in their eyes just disappeared like they died or something. They weren't the same people. It's insidious, being Included. The theory is that criminal acts exclude criminals from normal society, so you reprogram the criminal mind so that they can be included back into normal society. It's just a way to rationalize turning people into robots."

152

"Too bad I couldn't do some work beyond the bandwidth."

Abner looked at the dog. It was looking straight ahead, its nose twitching. *This thing would destroy the entire real world if it had a chance*. He shuddered.

"They were still your parents, though."

"What?"

"Your parents. They might have been different, but they were still your parents. They weren't really dead, just different."

"Yeah, I guess. They weren't allowed online anymore, and the bots made them OK with that. They got jobs in the PEA, and they stopped taking me to the beach and started taking me to malls."

The dog stopped suddenly and swung a paw against Abner's chest to stop him as well. It looked around, sniffing harder, its eyes darting all about.

"It's back," said the dog.

Knowing and Not Knowingness

Jeemo Roosenvelt swept onto the beach with a savagery that surprised himself. It felt good. It felt like—*No more Mr. Perfect Nice Guy*. He scoured the beach for signs of Abner Hayes. This time he would capture Hayes' avatar no matter what, even if he had to destroy the man's mind in the process. Time was running out and so were Jeemo's options. If he couldn't capture the avatar, then he didn't give a damn what happened to Hayes' mind. He would just turn back to the two VPs and see if he could salvage anything from them.

153

And if he couldn't?

For some reason, it didn't seem all that crucial to him anymore. Sure, he still wanted to die under the steel-hearted cruelty of Bella Bjork's merciless will. Who wouldn't? She was everything a man could possibly want in an executioner: she was beautiful, domineering, demanding, cruel, evil, callous, horny, heartless, cold, murderous, ruthless and self-absorbed. Jeemo felt warm and bubbly inside at the thought of such a woman ending his life then just going about her own life as though he'd never existed. Then he thought about *that* a bit. She would just go on with her life and Jeemo's would be over…forever. No more food. No more admiring the perfection of his massive form. No more watching Bella destroy her lovers. He would be one of those destroyed lovers. Or would he? Would she keep her word and let him lick her toes and touch her body? Would she really flush him through that tube he'd seen so many of her lovers enter in a state of sexual bliss then disappear with a look of "wha…?" in their eyes?

Faraway up the beach, he saw a cliff with what looked like woods on top. That was where he'd routed the girl VP's capture program. He checked the palm of his avatar hand where a tiny monitor showed something close to the cliff. There was more distortion on the monitor than there should have been. *Got your defenses up after our last encounter, have you?* thought Jeemo.

He didn't know it was the War Bug scrambling the signal. In fact, he didn't know the War Bug was with Abner; he didn't even know the War Bug existed. But the

War Bug knew about him and the War Bug knew he was on the beach and coming after Abner.

But then, the War Bug didn't know Jeemo, not being a Mr. Perfect Nice Guy anymore, was armed with the latest version of SoftWAR, a deadly package of programs of destruction, sabotage, and mayhem called WARWare.

What Jeemo didn't know was that WARWare had actually been created by the War Bug and distributed to all the combatants, friend and foe alike—so the War Bug knew the program inside and out, knew how to counter every attack in its massive variety of attacks, and knew how to out-maneuver every maneuver in its devastating array of programs.

On the other hand, the War Bug didn't know that Jeemo had customized the WARWare package (even though this was illegal and stated so in the installation process, but who was checking in these times?), and had added several new features and enhanced many of the existing ones.

But what Jeemo didn't know was that the War Bug had been created to make war, to destroy and to adapt on the fly, and it didn't matter what software, invented by whom, and enhanced, modified, turbo-ized, super-ized, or whatever, Jeemo was stepping into the War Bug's turf.

But what the War Bug did know was its own robustness and program power was beginning to flag of late, after having taken a lot of inadvertent hits in its own neural objects, in the pandemonium it had created. The War Bug was weak and badly in need of programming fixes, lots of fixes.

Jeemo didn't know anything at all about that. He just knew he wasn't going to be Mr. Perfect Nice Guy anymore.

First Date

Abner reached his hands across the table and clasped Claire's right hand. "I felt it the very instant I saw you," he said.

They were in a virtual café, one of the dimly lit intimate chat places portaled through Romance Avenue. *Jeez*, thought Cassie, *it's Mom and Dad's first date*. Everywhere in this place was candlelight and soft music, but no food or drink. Reality Laws. This was a bonding place, a place for avatars and VPs to meet and exchange information before entering lifetime relationships. It was a place where VPs came to either accept or reject the human avatars who would, in effect, become their owners if they agreed to a union. It was a place where humans, through their avatars, would accept the responsibility of owning a virtual life along with all the responsibilities that ownership entailed.

And those responsibilities could be considerable.

Most VPs were initially the property of the citystate. They were artificial intelligence entities that had reached a reliable condition of stability and had simulated a human life up to age twenty-one. Once a VP agreed to a union with a human, the human paid a fortune to the citystate for ownership of the VP. But that was just for starters.

156

What the human got was the basic model, a fixer-upper, and there was no end to the add-ons. There were optional modules, all for a price, that extended across the entire spectrum of human options. There were modules for increased intelligence, learning hobbies and building skills in virtual sports. There were modules for pregnancy and birth (and the baby was a mandatory VP purchase that was monitored by the citystate until it reached stability), and child-rearing and family skills. Of course, the biggest variety, and the most popular, was the modules for virtual sex that covered everything from traditional once-a-week-on- Saturday-night to raging-hormonal-non-stop-leather-and-spurs sex.

The longer a human owned a VP, the more responsive the VP became to the human, revolving and developing around the human's life like a comfortable sock. This was considered normal and right.

"I promise that I'll never treat you like property." At least by most.

"I promise to treat you as an equal." This was considered highly abnormal.

"I'm a virtual code geneticist, one of the best in the world. And I can make you the most unique virtual personality in the world, in the entire universe."

This was considered just a little less than insane.

"I don't give a damn about the Reality Laws. I can make you just as human as I am."

This was considered downright illegal, and it could get Abner Included just for thinking about it.

157

Abner leaned closer to Claire and stared deep into her eyes. "Will you marry me?"

"Yes, I would choose you repeatedly in a random array of choices."

Oh, jeez, Mom!

Not bad for a first date, though.

***

Then Cassie felt a strange sensation, not that being in this place hadn't been moment-to-moment weirdness, but this sensation was different, more pronounced, more sudden, and absolutely horrifying. It was a microsecond of complete blankness, a barely perceptible instant in which everything for Cassie Hayes ceased to exist, a flicker of nothingness.

"Mom?"

Straight from Hell

"What's back?" asked Abner.

The dog didn't have to answer as Abner sensed something had changed. The digital space around him crinkled like plastic wrap settling over the beach; the ocean water swelled just a little more and turned a notch darker green. Out of the corner of his avatar eyes, he saw pebbles on the beach shift and shuffle. The trees at the top of the cliff swayed as though wind swept, but not by any natural wind—they swayed in opposite directions. The clouds in the sky appeared to beat slowly to an inner pulse and the sky itself appeared tense like a sheet of blue light stretched tight over the heavens. The wash of waves on the shore lost their randomness in a sudden sense of vague intent.

"What's happening?" asked Abner.

The dog stuck an upper leg out to hush him and sniffed the air earnestly as its eyes narrowed. "Nothing good," it said.

From behind them something howled far off in the distance, then howled again, this time louder, and closer.

"Time to run," said the dog and fell down on all fours.

God, that's so weird, thought Abner as he watched the giant bloodhound dressed in trench coat and Deerstalker hat running on all fours down the beach. He didn't watch for long. The howling was much closer now, sounding like some mythical creature spewed onto the earth's surface straight from Hell. Except this wasn't the earth. This was the Net. Here, it was entirely possible that the howling ripped from the jaws of something straight from virtual Hell.

Abner ran.

Surprisingly, it didn't take long for him to catch up to the dog. Behind them, the howling continued to grow. It was long and blood-stopping. It froze Abner's stomach. It was pure horror, grief and pain glued together with shriek-cement. Abner forced himself to look forward, afraid to look back and find himself staring directly into the jaws of some unspeakable nightmare.

"Faster!" yelled the dog.

Abner turned toward the dog as it rushed past him, long golden-brown tail sticking straight back

159

from under the trench coat. *Big, brave war-mongering virus, eh?* he thought. If he hadn't been so terrified and running for his life, he would have laughed his virtual ass off.

The wash of water on the shore was getting frothier every second. In places, rocks and pebbles bounced erratically on patches of sand. The sky stretched tighter and the clouds seemed to breathe violently. The trees at the top of the cliff began to uproot and dance in the virtual wind.

The cliff was close now. So was the howl. Abner cursed the Reality Laws for making basic code restrict relative movement in virtual environments. He and the dog should have been there in less time than it would take a neutrino to travel a millionth of an inch, but their programming wouldn't allow it. And obviously, even the War Bug hadn't been able to override the virtual speed constraint. Fortunately, neither had the thing that was howling behind them. Just as they made it to the base of the cliff, boulders detached from the rock face and began to rumble downward toward them.

"Oh, shit!" said Abner, and the second he said it, he remembered reading somewhere that "oh shit" was the most often used last expression uttered by people who were about to die. There was no comfort in knowing this.

The boulders shook the ground under Abner's feet as they rumbled and roared down the side of the cliff. Behind him, the howling sounded like a banshee dragging its ass across hot coals. He could have sworn he felt hell-breath on his neck. Beside him, the sand twisted and curled. Weatherworn

160

rocks and round pebbles slid off the sand as it rose in patches of sand mounds, and the mounds rose higher as fingers of sand branched out and transformed into writhing claws. The claws uprooted from the beach and straggled toward them.

Abner passed the dog.

The cliff was dead ahead. Boulders were about to shower onto their heads, and Abner thought, *Why are we running into a rock avalanche?* He was about to ask this of the dog when the howling almost burst whatever neural objects formed his capacity to hear online. He did the impossible. He ran faster. The cliff was less than twenty feet away. He slowed down.

"Don't stop!" yelled the dog.

Without even questioning, Abner speeded up and both he and the dog ran right smack into the cliff.

And disappeared.

Blood

The mansion near the edge of the Great Nano Canyon shook, rattled and rolled. Jeemo was on a rampage, orange spikes skewing the air, slabs of fat bouncing and sliding this way and that, and Jeemo's voice wailing and howling, "WHAT! WHAT! WHAT!"

He jumped up and down so hard the serverclones, who had been hiding earlier in the freezer and had frozen to death, keeled over and shattered on the floor. Mirrors throughout the building cracked and splintered. For the second time, a flock of Canada geese turned back to Canada where they would likely freeze to death when winter arrived.

"He's just a normal man! He's no match for me! He's just a pukey little nobody Abner Hayes dickhead and he's no match for me!" He jumped up and crashed down onto the floor. "No match for me!" He jumped again. "No match for me!" And again. "No match for me!"

He broke into a shambling run and smashed into a tornado-proof window. He bounced back and screamed, "ABNER HAYES IS NO MATCH FOR ME!"

A serverclone floated cautiously toward him, trembling and spilling the wine on the tray he carried. Apologetically, he said, "Mr. Roosenvelt, sir, your…"

Jeemo reached out, grabbed the serverclone by the neck, pulled him in and tore his head off. Blood spurted out of the neck creating a ghastly red fountain reflected thousands of times in mirrors cracked and splintered. Jeemo's wide eyes stared crazily at the limp body and the head with the astonished eyes he held in his blood-soaked hands. He stared and stared then laughed and laughed. Then he screamed, "I'll kill him! Yes! Yes! I'll kill his avatar and then I'll track down his brain dead body and eat it! Yes! I'll eat his body raw for my good breakfast. And I'll save bits of him for my lunch." He dropped the dead serverclone's body and head and turned toward the window. He looked out at the gruesome landscape and laughed. "Or maybe I'll just wait until he comes here!" He twisted his head to the side. Folds of flesh appeared where his neck should be and thought, *No. That's cutting things too close. I'll get him online. I'll plan this one more carefully. Not the next place, but further on... let him lower his guard, get comfortable. I'll wait for him and set a trap. Yes, a good trap will do it. I'll capture his avatar and squeeze the secret to the code out of him and then I'll destroy his avatar. And then I'll go to Bella. And then I'll go to my death with Bella gloating over me, all over me as I die at her will.*

Strangely, though, he noticed this line of thought, a thought that never failed to arouse him immensely, seemed to have little effect on him now. He stared down at his blood-smeared hands and slowly a smile spread over his pink fleshy lips.

Yes, I know exactly where to get him, where he can't possibly escape me.

Chapter 12

More Empathy

You poor, poor bastard, thought the assassin. *Killing your property like that.* He zoomed in on Jeemo's face. *You're one ugly bastard, but what emotional turbulence must be raging in your poor bastard's heart? Do you even suspect that you're going to die soon? And look at you, to go on living in a body like that, with a face like that, tormented like that, you must have one of the strongest wills to live of any man I've encountered.*

Another tear rolled down his cheek, and he mumbled into the purple grass, "I really do wish that I didn't have to kill your poor bastard ass."

Someone to Blame

If Bella's column had been equipped with six-guns, the other columns representing the Atlantiscity Powers would have been smoldering heaps of virtual rubble. Bella was furious the other Powers had summoned her for this meeting which, it appeared, had been at the request of the third column from the right.

In her mind, a nuclear-tipped missile streaked directly into the belly of the third column from the right and into the belly of the human behind the column avatar.

Even the third column from the right hadn't the vaguest clue it was being trashed in Bella's mind as it spoke, "My people showed me some really

164

disturbing stuff about you. Looks to me like what you've been doing really sucks big time."

"A little respect for the Power, please," said the Chair column. As usual, the Chair was ignored.

"You have an unregistered programmer working for you," said the third column from the right. "I wouldn't be surprised if you had something to do with what's happening to the Net right now."

He knows about Jeemo. That means he has people who have come into contact with information about me. That means there's a trail that my people can track down to this dumb fuck. Then I can have him killed.

"I don't know what you're talking about," said Bella through the fifth column from the right as she opened a second screen beside the chalcedony screen on her wall. This one was a turquoise-framed screen. It was the direct line to her director of security, an Asian woman whose face would never see a wrinkle caused by smiling. She lip-read as Bella said soundlessly, "Look for recent probes into Jeemo Roosenvelt and myself. Track them down and kill the source at the top."

Now, if the Net will hold together long enough, I can kill that dumb ass.

"You? Are you to blame?" asked the second column from the left.

Tears

"I'm right here, sweetheart! Mommy's right here!" said Claire.

"Oh, Mom, c'mon. I'm not a six-year-old anymore," said Cassie. "Listen, young lady, I'm your mother and you're still…"

"Mom, what's happening?"

Oh, for god's sake, thought Claire. *Our lives are in danger and we're arguing over nothing.* "I don't know, dear. I can call you dear, can't I?"

"Yes, you can all me dear. You can call me sweetheart. That's not what I was mad about. Just don't call yourself mommy. Not when you're talking about being my mother. Jeez, Mom. Mommy?"

Damn, I hate it when she has a valid point. "OK, dear, point taken. How are you feeling?"

"Pretty fucked up, Mom."

"Cassie!"

"Sorry. Sorry. I lost it for a second. But this is really scary, Mom. I mean, for a minute there, it was like I wasn't even alive. Like I was dead, or something. I've never felt anything like that before. It was really scary. Are we gonna die here, Mom?"

"No, Cassie. We're not going to die. Your father knows we're gone by now and he's on his way to free us from this place."

"Yeah, sure, maybe to free you."

"Cassie! Your father loves you."

"He doesn't even know I'm alive, except when he wants somebody to argue with."

"That's not true, dear. It's…it's…"

"It's…Mom?"

"I don't know. It's like the two of you are just too much alike. Maybe he knows the kinds of chances he took making us sentient and he doesn't

166

want to lose you because sometimes you're just like him when it comes to taking chances."

"Oh, so this is all my fault! I take too many chances!"

"That's not what I said. You stop putting words in my mouth." *I'm going to ground her forever. She'll go on her next date when she's thirty-five,* thought Claire.

"Well, I'm scared, Mom. And Dad's not here and I...the last time I ever saw him, and the last time he ever saw me, we were arguing. What if he doesn't get here in time? This place is getting worse, Mom, and I think we're going to die here!"

Then Claire felt something she'd never felt before. Tears. Not wet, watery,

CO_2-packing tears, but moist code. Code, seething with sadness and fear. Code, alive and coiling around the very heart of her being's essence. Her daughter was afraid. Somewhere in this potpourri scramble of mother and daughter programming, her baby was afraid and there was nothing she could do about it.

Then everything went blank.

On the Ball

"What the hell was that all about?" asked Abner. "And where the hell are we now?"

The dog stopped sniffing the air and turned its sad eyes on Abner. "To answer your first question, that was one of my own programs. WareWARE, I called it. But with a lot more umpf than I recall.

Somebody, and somebody with a lot of skill, has enhanced it."

"But the cliff?"

"A disguise laid over the portal the kidnapper used to capture your daughter. It led here. And this," the dog swung a front leg around in an arc to take in all the area around them, "this is one of the most deadly places in the universe."

Abner looked around. What was dark gray flicked to white in every direction. He nearly fell down.

He and the dog were standing on a large beach ball. There was nothing else, just Abner, the dog, the ball, and white everywhere.

"And the game begins," said the dog.

"What game? What are you talking about? What is this place?" Very slowly, almost imperceptibly, the ball started to turn.

"It's an illegal game world," said the dog. "On the Ball, they call it."

"What the hell is that supposed to mean?"

"It means you stay on the ball."

"Or what?"

"Or you die."

The ball began to turn faster.

Abner and the dog stepped in beat with the turning. "Not much of a challenge," said Abner.

"Not yet," said the dog.

The ball began to turn even faster. Abner and the dog speeded up. Now, they were moving at a brisk pace.

"Can't you just pick up on the trail and get us out of here?" asked Abner. "Nope. Not in here."

"So how do we get out of here?"

"You win the game."

"And if I don't, I die?"

"That's about the size of it, Ab, old buddy."

"So how do I die? I don't see anything threatening in here. The worst is I could fall off this ball."

"The ball is like a switch. Break your connection with it and it kills your avatar with a virus that then turns on your human brain where it instructs your brain to stop causing your heart to beat."

"Oh great! And what does it do to *you*?"

"Nothing. I'm a virus, remember? But now that I'm here with you, if I lose the game…you die."

"Oh, that's just great!" The ball speeded up.

Abner and the dog were almost running.

"So how do we know when we win the game?"

"If the ball stops moving and you're still alive, you've won."

"When does it stop moving?"

"When you've won."

Abner glared at the dog. "So how do *you* know so much about the game?"

"I've played it a few times."

"All right! Then we're going to be OK, right?"

"Well, actually, Ab, old buddy, I was never very good at this game." The ball speeded up and Abner and the dog were jogging.

"But, if all we have to do is run to stay on this thing," said Abner, "then it can't be too difficult to win."

"It's a bit more complicated than that," said the dog. "More complicated?"

The ball speeded up.

169

Bella

"It was Rashid Nummar Benni Bon Bon," said the Asian woman. She was as beautiful as an iceberg refusing to melt in dark blue water. "We cancelled him."

Cancelled, thought Bella. *What an interesting way to put it. I like this cold little slant-eyed bitch.* "Very well," said Bella. "Do the intelligence on his holdings and turn it over to Jen Durling in Acquisitions."

"Immediately," said the face on the screen, then the screen flicked off.

One Power down, thirteen to go. And I get all Rashid's assets as well, that New Palestine cocksucker. So he was the third column from the right all along. And he had the nerve to ask me to marry him last year.

"Massage," she ordered, and the sexclone stepped up behind her and began to massage her breasts gently. "You're learning."

But that's not going to save you, she thought.

Chocolat

Like a blink, Cassie was back, and so was the terror. She couldn't feel her mother's presence.

"Mom?"

That distinct emanation of her mother's consciousness was missing. "Where are you, Mom?"

170

There was something, but it wasn't anything responsive or interactive or immediate.

"You're scaring me, Mom. Where are you?"

It was uncaring. It was just there. Cassie moved into it. It was code, her mother's code, or some of it. It was memory code, her mother's memories, or some of them. She moved into them and saw her father through her mother's eyes. They were in the living room. There were those ugly chairs and ottoman, and the ratty couch. And, in the muted virtual light from the gaudy Victorian lampshades, there was Abner. His large brown eyes were sad and dark, but they were full of love as he spoke, "Do you understand that what I'm going to do will make you like no other virtual person anywhere. You'll be sentient. You'll have feelings just like any normal human, but you'll still have to live online. You'll always be in danger. If you're found out, either of us, you'll be deleted and I'll be Included."

"Will I develop a taste for chocolate?" Abner stared.

Claire repeated, "Will I develop a taste for chocolate?"

"I don't...I don't know. I don't think so. There's no food or drink online. There's nothing to provide any kind of association to the taste of chocolate. The Reality Laws won't allow it."

"I want to know chocolate."

You tell him, Mom.

Abner tilted his head. He was dumbfounded. "How do you even know to ask this?"

"A female avatar told me that chocolate is heaven, even if it does taste like chicken these days. What are these days?"

171

"That's just an expression to describe something that's gone."

"These days are gone?"

"No, these days are here, and the good days are gone. But you're lucky the female avatar didn't get you deleted for trying to give you a taste for chocolate, no matter how theoretical and no matter how much it tastes like chicken."

"Will I know chicken?" Abner laughed.

He has a beautiful smile, thought Cassie, *so boyish, almost a hottie. Oh jeez, what'm I even thinking, he's my Dad. Eew!*

"No, you won't know..." Then he thought a moment. "Well, I'm not sure. I'm going to be using my own DNA code to recreate the programming in your neural objects. I may have genetic memories that you can invoke. Some of them may be memories of taste, maybe even of chocolate that I ate when I was a kid, back when it still tasted reasonably like chocolate."

"I'll have your memories?"

"I'm not sure. That's one of those uncertainties I warned you about. None of this has ever been done before. The man who invented the technology killed himself two hundred years ago."

"Jared Friedman."

"Right."

"You stole his idea."

Mom!

Abner's virtual eyes flashed a wink of virtual anger, "Well, in a way, it was his idea. On my job, I have access to his archived files. I managed to break the encryptions and recreate his work. But I

172

expanded on his ideas and took them a lot further than he did."

"And you made abominations in the process."

Again, the flash of anger. "Maybe I explained too much of this too you. I had to experiment with the bubble computer and the DNA coding. And yes, the first experiments created semi-sentient beings that went nuts and crashed, but none of them were nearly as high level as you. And I'm absolutely certain that I've found the key component."

"Absurdity and infinity."

"Well, yes. But primarily absurdity, if you accept that infinity is absurd."

"Yes, I do."

"You do?"

"If it is not, then you may have to destroy me. I may crash. I may not ever know chocolate."

Abner stared into Claire's eyes for several seconds.

He really does love Mom. He's loved her right from the beginning. Jeez, does he feel even close like that to me?

"It would give me the greatest joy I could imagine if I could make it possible for you to know chocolate."

"Will I have babies?"

Abner smiled. "We could try."

Nails

Abner felt like a bald-headed giant chasing after a gargantuan behatted dog running upright on its hind legs. The whiteness all around them

173

magnified the illusion a hundred times, and he knew the focus on this much running must be having a physical effect on his body back in the 'liner's lounger. *And people play this by choice?* he thought. *They do this for fun?*

"Does it get any faster than this?" he asked.

"No. I think this is just about as fast as it gets. We're alright on the speed factor."

Abner's stomach shrank. "What do you mean by 'on the speed factor'?"

"I mean we don't have to worry about it getting any faster."

Abner's stomach was still clenched like a shaky fist. "So, you mean, there's nothing to worry about now, except accidentally falling off this ball and dying. Right?"

"Well..." The dog spoke around its lolling tongue. Abner passed this off as another gimmick for affect. "...there is one other little thing."

Abner felt a slight change in the rhythm of his running. It had nothing to do with the movement of his feet. He could have kept up the pace for as long as his body could lie on the 'liner's lounger without eating or drinking. The feeling was coming from the ball. He looked down. He squinted his virtual eyes. As his feet pounded down onto the ball, something strange was happening to it. He wasn't sure what it was, but he knew it could only be something bad.

And it was.

"I think the ball's deflating," he yelled. "I was afraid of that," said the dog.

"What do you mean 'afraid of that'? You knew this was going to happen?"

"Well, Ab, old buddy, let's just say that I was hoping that it wouldn't happen. I didn't tell you that nothing bad was going to happen though, did I?"

"No. No, you didn't. But a warning might have been a good thing. Would you mind telling me exactly what's happening?"

"It's my nails."

"Your nails? You have nails?"

"Toenails. All dogs have toenails. Mine are digging into the ball, putting little holes into it."

"Ah, yes. That would explain the ball deflating."

"Exactly. That's why I've never done well at this game."

"I have an idea."

"Yes, Ab, old buddy?"

"Become the pig again."

"Can't. That would be breaking the rules and we would lose."

"Then let's just jump out of here and…"

"No! We'll break the connection, and you'll die."

Abner almost lost his footing, which he noticed, was becoming sluggish. "Why couldn't you clip your goddam toenails?" he yelled.

"Bit late for recriminations, I'd say."

"What happens when it deflates completely?"

"We fall."

"We fall? Fall where?"

"I don't know, never stayed on that long."

Abner imagined his stomach as an electromagnet wound tight and waiting for a surge of electricity to burn its wiring into molten lead. The ball started to wobble. Abner's running became

175

increasingly awkward. In a few minutes, he wouldn't be able to keep up the pace. The ball was beginning to flatten. "Shit!" yelled Abner.

Suddenly, the ball was gone and they were in the main trunk bandwidth again.

Self-Discovery

The top of Jeemo's head was like something squirming out of a can of orange nightcrawlers. "I'm better than he is. Yes, I am better than he is," said Jeemo, admiring his nude largess under the twisting orange spikes. "I am the end of human evolution." He turned sideways and, though his stomach was huge, so were his chest and his legs, so there was no impression of roundness. He was massive. Monumental. A tribute to the lengths to which human skin could be stretched over a bone frame.

"Nobody on earth looks like me," he said. "I am beyond even the nanobots."

A serverclone whisked up to his side and offered him a silver tray with a large pomegranate cut into wedges. Jeemo took his eyes off his reflection and looked at the tray. He reached out a plump arm, scooped up all the sections at once, and pushed them into his mouth. Bright red juice dribbled over his chin and dripped onto his hairless chest where it formed thin rivulets that poured over his stomach and legs. A few drops made tiny splashes on the floor. The serverclone swooped down with the tray in one hand and an absorbent nano tissue in the other to wipe up the juice.

176

Jeemo brought his fist down on top of the serverclone's head, and the serverclone crashed into the floor and crumpled. White bone stuck through the skin on top of its head. Jeemo screamed, "Bring me another! Another!"

He turned back to his reflection and a pink smile twisted over his wrinkled lips at the sight of his body streaked with red as though he had just eaten the raw heart of his enemy.

"You won't escape my trap, Abner Hayes, perfection wannabe! I am Jeemo Roosenvelt! I am the culmination of all that human evolution has worked toward for a million years! I will kill you, Abner Hayes, kill you and kill you!"

And the thought of killing Abner Hayes suddenly had the same stirring effect that fantasizing about being killed by Bella had on him. A serverclone swooped to his side with a tray, a pomegranate and a nano tissue.

Chapter 13

Checking In

Oh, you poor misshapen bastard, thought the assassin. *What torment flows through your arms, through your fists and into the killing blows that destroy your own property with such ruthless abandon?*

Stop with the pity already! You're going to kill the dumb ass!

All around him, the grass swept from dark to light purple under the caress of a light breeze. The assassin blended in with the swaying colors with his nano- enhanced clothing and equipment. He was invisible. Thanks to the nanochips, even his heat signature matched the grass. A tiny round screen popped up from his wrist. It was Bella.

"What's he doing?" she demanded. "Killing things."

"Killing? Jeemo Roosenvelt? What's he killing?"

"Serverclones."

Bella frowned.

Not quite as beautiful when she makes that face, thought the assassin. "What else is he doing?"

"Looking at himself in the mirror."

"He can stand to look at himself?"

"Seems to be his favorite pastime when he's not 'lining or killing clones."

"He's not answering my calls."

"Might have cut off communications."

"Can you do anything about that?"

"Not without giving myself away."

178

Bella scowled. The screen flipped down.

Why couldn't that poor dumb bastard have approached me with a contract to kill her before she contracted me to kill him? Yes, there would have been a convoluted justice in that.

Just kill the bastard.

Pleasing Miss Bella

"I'm surrounded by idiots!" yelled Bella. For once, even the chips in her see through top failed to keep her nipples erect. Even the massage from the sexclone did nothing for her. "They're killing my passion. They're killing ME! I need those two VPs! I need their secret! I cannot be allowed to die! I have plans! I have ambitions! I have a vision!"

Bella sprang up from the amethyst love seat. The sexclone nearly jumped backward, its face startled. "Do you wish…"

"Shut up!" screamed Bella. "I wish for you to shut up! I wish for that fat cocksucker to answer my calls. I wish for that ugly lump of gray shit to find my fucking secret of immortality and then die!"

The sexclone raised its perfect dark eyebrows. Not a single ripple appeared on its perfectly tanned skin when it did this. Bella, who was just about to walk away from the sexclone, stopped. *It knows I'm going to kill Roosenvelt. The clone knows.* She considered this. Then she smiled at the sexclone. She walked around the purple love seat and up to the sexclone, smiling evilly. Something in the sexclone's life systems balked, but it was her property. It returned her smile and its genetic

179

programming forced adoration into its eyes. This wasn't the hardest thing a clone designed for sex could do. Bella moved with a sensual elegance, her smooth round breasts and flat belly and perfect hips produced a visual symphony celebrating the female form. The sexclone took all of this in as Bella walked right up to it and put her arms around its neck. This was the first time she had actually touched it in this way. Normally, she would have done nothing to gratify it; it was the sexclone's job to gratify her.

She raised her full red lips to its ear and said in a gruff lazy voice, "Do you want to please me?"

"Yes," said the sexclone, dutifully.

"Do you want to please me right now? Do you want to worship my body with your hands and your tongue?"

The sexclone's genetically enhanced penis throbbed against Bella's hard stomach. "Yes, I want to worship you."

Bella turned her head to look into its eyes. Her smile was cruel; her eyes burned with harsh passion. "I want this to be special."

"Anything you want."

"I want you to take a special bath, a very special bath that will energize you and give you loving powers beyond anything you ever imagined. Do you want to take my special bath and fuck me?"

"Yes. Yes," said the sexclone, breathing heavily, but still feeling a tug of dread somewhere deep in its bowels. "I want to take your bath and fuck you."

180

Bella stepped back from the sexclone and took one of its hands. "Come, then." She pulled its arm and led it toward the room with the killing tube.

I need someone to find where Roosenvelt has the two VPs. I need someone who can locate them and bring them to me, or extract their code, or whatever it takes to get their secret. That fat fuck Roosenvelt is no longer reliable. Something is happening with him and now he's a wild card. I can't have any wild cards. Too much is at stake. But who can I get to take the VPs away from him without harming them?

A section of wall slid open and Bella walked into the killing room with the sexclone still holding her hand, following right behind her, naked, erect and still not able to exactly pinpoint its feeling of unease.

Metro

Every day of the week, trillions of dollars exchanged hands in Atlantiscity Metro. It was the financial capital of Earth, but not one of its enormous skyscrapers, not a single one of its endless lines of yellow cabs, not one of its bustling streams of citizens could be touched by a human finger. Every inch of Metro, every store, every office, every bar, every playground, every theatre, every billboard was nothing more than lines of code, combinations of program objects, electricity and light in motion in computers located all over the solar system.

181

To the people behind the billions of avatars that flooded its streets and buildings and parks, Metro was more real than a nail hammered into their right hands. It was home to those who hated everything the real world had become. It was the best of the real world recreated in bandwidth. It was everybody's mental image of the perfect big city. The lines of yellow cabs never actually moved—they were portals to a transport program—but they gave Metro a semblance of big city traffic. The skyscrapers were portals into office and store programs that might have resided on a child's home computer.

At the turn of the last century, thousands of Metro denizens, who wanted to make the city even more like reality, petitioned to have the city engulfed in smog for a few months every year. It wouldn't have an effect on anybody's lungs, they argued, it would just be ornamental. One of the Smogites, as they were called, tried to introduce a smog-generating program illegally. He was caught, and the Smogites as a group had been found guilty of subversion, been barred from the Web and then Included.

There was still crime, mostly Mind Murder. Assassins were hired to track down the avatars of people who were hated, feared, or in somebody else's way in the real world, and they destroyed the avatar in such a way as to destroy the mind of the human behind the avatar.

Metro was also the most obvious and easily accessible target in the War. Signs of attack were everywhere. Buildings tilted at angles so that when the skyline was viewed from a distance, it was indefinably out of whack. On every block, small banyan trees lining the sidewalks were upside down, or massed in hodgepodges of roots and leaves and branches forming something plant-like, but creepy. These were the result of stressed out repair programs. On just about every corner, there were plaques honoring those who had gone to digital oblivion in viral attacks. Sometimes an avatar would walk through the doors of a skyscraper portal and be lost forever in a convoluted series of programming paths that led nowhere. Huge sections of Metro had deteriorated into invisible pits of death and had to be cordoned off by special access passwords. The destruction in Metro was so bad that almost all the Atlantiscity ruling apparatus, including the Powers, had been moved to servers with special firewalls to protect them from the heart of the city.

Unfortunately for Wonk Carcianova, otherwise known as the sixth column from the left, he liked to flaunt the odds and take his dog for walks deep inside Metro. As he scooped up virtual dog shit, the skyscraper in front of him disappeared, just winked out of existence, leaving a gray background in its place. Just before Wonk Carcianova and his virtual Chow and its virtual mound of virtually steaming dog shit winked out of existence, Wonk thought, *Is this some kind of drill?*

Nope.

***

"Iz the end of Metro, Abu," said Karthymelon, looking lazy-eyed at the display.

183

Abu lifted his head from between Karthymelon's blue legs and looked at the screen. "The good of our move to the outer servers. We be safe for the time being."

"Call da bitch?"

"Screw da bitch."

"Yeah, screw da bitch."

Abu smiled and plunged his head between her legs again.

Becoming

Cassie wasn't sure how long it had lasted. She wasn't sure exactly what had happened. Everything had just gone blank as though time and space had been suspended, frozen into something unmoving, unfeeling and unaware. The blankness Cassie and her mother had just emerged from was beyond time and being. And this shit was starting to piss Cassie off. But before she could say a word to her mother, she was inside her mother or, at least, in one of her Memory modules. And her father was there. He was holding her mother. She had her arms around his neck.

Oh, jeez, no, Mom! Please don't have sex with Dad while I'm in here! I don't need this! I mean, I really don't need this!

"I have to go offline now," said Abner.

Oh, jeez, thank you Dad, thank you.

"Will it have what you call pain?" asked her mother.

184

Abner smiled lovingly. With his bald head and thick features, he wasn't exactly a good-looking man. *But he has a good smile*, thought Cassie.

"No. You may have a sense of realignment, whatever that might feel like. I'm not sure. But you won't feel pain. I'm going to move all your base neural objects to the bubble computer. It's not like anything anywhere on the Net. It's…it's…"

"Infinite."

"Exactly." Again, that beautiful smile spread across that dark, homely face. "I don't know exactly how to explain it, but it should be a feeling of infinite possibility. The constraints on your objects should dissolve. You should feel like…like you've just come out of a daze, or like you've been going through life with one eye closed and suddenly you open it and everything looks…" He looked deep into her mother's eyes, "Oh, I don't know what it'll be like, compared to what you feel and know now. I just know that you'll be as human, as sentient, and as likely to have a soul as any human on Earth."

"Will I still feel attraction to you?"

"Oh, I hope so. I certainly do hope so. I hope you'll even love me as I love you."

"I find this agreeable, Abner. You can move me to the bubble computer now." Her mother stared deep into her father's avatar eyes. They reflected exactly the emotions of the human at the other end, and that human was full of love and caring for her mother. His eyes also displayed a heavy dose of worry. He was about to do something that had failed disastrously in the past—in his own experiments and in the experiments of others. Perfectly healthy VPs had crumbled and crashed, and some had even

185

become virus-like and had infected frightening lengths of bandwidth. But Abner was certain his bubble computer would make this attempt successful—certain enough to use the woman he loved to do it.

He smiled again and Claire was standing in the kitchen alone. She stared into her eyes in a mirror on the ornamental refrigerator. Her eyes had the blank look of VPs when their humans were offline. Cassie noticed how beautiful her mother's eyes were, so wide and white. As she focused more on her mother's eyes, she noticed there was much more than the usual blankness—there was expectation, as though her mother were waiting for something. And she was smiling, a knowing smile that suddenly grew just a fraction as the eyes filled with something beyond expectation.

It was a look of: "Ahhh, yes, *that*."

***

"Cassie! Sweetheart! Are you OK?"

"Yes, Mom, I'm…" Then she was aware of wetness on her cheeks. *Jeez, what the cripes is this stuff?*

The Plan

Bella Bjork still smacked her cerebral lips, savoring the aftertaste of the sexclone's death, when the first column from the right said, "We have a problem." The third column from the right was unlit, as was the sixth column from the left. "And

186

either the importance of this meeting was missed, or we're missing some members." The first column from the right paused then said, "Personally, I think we're missing some members."

I think I'll make my next clone a blond, thought Bella.

"Every pixel of Metro is gone. The entire core of Atlantiscity just crashed. There were over a billion people 'lining in Metro when it happened, and I'm afraid two among those billion plus were the third column from the right and the sixth column from the left. Or would anyone else here have any thoughts on what might have happened to them?"

All the columns maintained a pillar-like silence.

One of them might have been in Metro, thought Bella, *but that dirty little fucker, Rashid, wasn't the one. And why didn't that other dirty little fucker, Abu, report to me. All of Metro gone and I don't find out until now. And I've got to be paying him more than any of these other asshole Powers.*

"I really must insist that we come up with some kind of plan in light of these circumstances," said the first column from the right.

"A plan for what?" demanded the seventh column from the right.

"Well, perhaps that's exactly what we should discuss at this time," said the first column from the right. "What exactly should we plan for?"

"Everything's going to shit no matter what we do, so why should we plan for anything?" asked the seventh column from the right.

"Here, here!" said the forth column from the left.

"But we can't just let all of this happen without some kind of contingency plan, some form of backup," insisted the first column from the right.

"All I want to know is," said the second column from the left, "who is to blame for all of this? Who?"

"But, a plan..." said the first column from the right.

Screw you. Screw all of you. You're all fodder for my plan.

***

Bella Bjork was not one to make modest plans. She wanted nothing less than everything. And she wanted it forever. She was, after all, the four hundred and fortieth child of the former richest man in the world and no one else in the entire universe could lay claim to that distinction.

Her plan was over a hundred years old, and she'd started it before she was a teenager, shortly after her father's death and just after she'd discovered the little book in her father's personal mansion five hundred feet under the Sphinx. The access codes contained in the book made her one of the most powerful of the Atlantiscity Powers. When she took over as the fifth column from the right, nobody guessed that Jaffanu Hynus Abba Bjork was dead; he appeared just as ruthless and lecherous as always, although he seemed to have gotten in touch with the quirkier side of his feminine self.

On the real world home front, hundreds of Jaff's progeny, all of his wives, and anyone in his vast business holdings with the slightest chance of contesting the will, began to have unfortunate accidents with knives, bullets, large heavy objects, moving vehicles, poison, disgruntled public employees with large sticks, irradiation, steep stairways, high cliffs, encounters with dangerous animals, sudden inexplicable urges to jump out of airplanes and speeding cars, and lethal swimming lessons.

Within months, the young Bella Bjork was completely alone, which was exactly the way she wanted it. She was free to do whatever she wanted, and she immediately ordered the construction of her crystal palace, which was to float on a cushion of nanogravitybots a thousand feet over the exact point in the Pacific Ocean where she was born. And she began ordering sexclones by the dozen.

When she moved into her floating emerald over the ocean, she spent the first few weeks marching the sexclones into the tube room one-by-one. Soon, she was alone again.

Which, of course, was exactly what she wanted. She didn't want to share eternity and ultimate power with anyone. Using both her vast wealth and her position as a Power in Atlantiscity, she began a slow buildup of acquisitions—in both the real and online worlds and these furthered her wealth and power— especially those that gave her more control over the bandwidth than all the other Powers put together in all the online citystates put together. She assembled her own army of bioengineers, geneticists, information specialists and others. These were the ones who rebuilt practically her entire body and would have made her into an object of intense beauty and perfection if they could have removed the sheen of malice that overlaid her body like a fouled aura.

It was her horde of specialists who determined years ago that the War would eventually destroy all the online citystates, but that was just fine with Bella. She had the people, the resources and the ruthlessness to rise out of the broken, sputtering links of the fallen Net and build a whole new online world over which she would rule.

Now, all she had to do was find out how to live forever.

***

"Someone must be held accountable," asserted the second column from the left.

Chapter 14

Makin' Life

"What happened?" Abner glanced quickly around at one of the most amazing virtual worlds he'd ever seen. "We're out of the game."

"Appears that way, Ab, old buddy."

"But how?"

"We won." The dog was already sniffing into the virtual air. "We won? How?"

"You said the password."

"There was a password?"

They were in a giant cavern. A soft-glowing myriad of pink, purple and white stalactites drooped menacingly from the vast ceiling in an upside down mountainscape of sharp points. In some areas, they were clumped into small groups of calcite spears; in others, giant rock formations pierced the very floor of the cavern.

"There was a password?" Abner repeated.

"Of course, it was an online game. There's always a password."

"You mean we didn't have to run. We didn't have to risk falling off that damned ball and me having my brain fried by that damned game? You knew there was a …"

"But I didn't know what it was."

"You…"

"You have to play the game until the game inspires the password."

"So what was it? What was the password?"

"Shit. You said 'shit' and, voila, here we are."

"The password was 'shit'?"

"Yep, Ab, old buddy, it's about the most common word people say when they realize that they're just about to die. I should've caught on to that one. But then, you're human—I'm software. And I have nails. And by the way, so does the pig."

"So, do you have other presences?"

"Thousands."

"Then why didn't you use one of those?"

"Ab, old buddy. I'm software. I can't die. No matter what presence I used, I wouldn't feel the need to say the password."

Abner rolled his virtual eyes. "OK," he said. "OK. So, where are we now."

"In a cave."

"No fooling. Any idea where the cave is?"

"Probably on a computer some..." The dog's droopy ears perked up slightly under the Deerstalker hat. It lifted its head up and sniffed furiously.

Abner felt the now all-too-familiar tightening in his virtual stomach. "What is it? Not that thing again, I hope." He glanced around fearfully as he spoke. Blunt- topped stalagmites pushed out of the cavern floor. He noticed a dark stream wound around most of the cavern's circumference and disappeared into a deep black hole at the far end. In the center of the brown moon-like floor, he picked out the glimmer of what appeared to be a large pond-size pool of water. "I don't see anything. What is it?"

The dog cocked its head to one side and shrugged. "Probably nothing." Abner shot a withering look at the dog.

Sensing Abner's anger, the dog said, "It may take a while to pick up on the scent in here. Let's explore, and you can tell me how you made your wife and daughter sentient."

Abner stewed for a moment. Then he relaxed and said, "I'm not sure exactly. I just know that it had something to do with using my genetic coding and putting their core neural objects into my bubble computer. But I don't think that was all there was to it."

"How so?"

Abner took a deep virtual breath. He could feel his body on the 'liner's lounger enjoying the deep intake of air. "The absurdity of infinity," he said.

As they walked across the simulated limestone floor and around outcroppings of massive stalagmites and avoided some the more menacing clumps of stalactites, Abner described the early experiments in creating sentient life online, how incalculable amounts of information were piled into neural networks programmed for fuzzy logic, linear logic, looped logic, cubed logic, and any conceivable type of logic-based mechanism for creating an original, non- programmed, purely intuitive, non-fuzzy, non-linear, non-looped, and non-cubed thought, feeling, or notion that could be judged to come from an intelligence that acted in such a manner as to preserve itself, and maybe even pray or say "shit" if it thought it was about to be obliterated.

"But the results were all the same. Ask them how they were feeling, and after a few seconds their entire programs would crash or freeze or just remain unresponsive. Some shot back answers like, 'Oh, I'm feeling rather like a very good executable today, and how are your sub-routines, yourself.' Even

193

those ones never lasted more than an hour or so before they just shut down."

Abner breathed deep again. "Ever since my parents were Included, I'd been interested in what it is that makes us human."

"I have a few thoughts about that," said the dog, sarcastically. "Who's telling this story?" asked Abner.

"You wouldn't want to hear my opinions on that anyway," said the dog. "Exactly! Now, to go on..." He took another deep virtual breath. "I became a

Virtual Code Geneticist. I was sure that the secret of our humanity lay in the way our bodies and minds were coded by DNA."

"Not really an original thought, Ab, old buddy. Scientists have been going down that path unsuccessfully for a couple of centuries now."

Abner looked at the dog and grimaced. "I know. And it led nowhere for me for years, until one day…"

He told the dog about his job in one of Atlantiscity's biggest companies, Virtual Person Module Enhancement and Neural Object Combinations, Inc., otherwise known as VP Inc. He built custom modules for VPs, mostly a matter of arranging neural objects into new combinations that allowed VP owners to customize their virtual property much the way a homeowner would paint a room, or a car owner would add a ski rack. It was boring, but during slow times, Abner worked on his own projects. One of them involved recreating the coding from his own DNA and testing it on the neural modules with which he worked.

If he had been a bartender, his spillage report would have been astronomical. As a Virtual Code Geneticist for VP Inc, though, he had an unusually high breakage report he rationalized as an effort to push the packet in creating realistic VPs. He was sure he was on the verge of being fired when, one day, he came across something interesting in the company's archives. It was a backup of all of Jared Friedman's work on DNA bubble computers.

"DNA again," said the dog.

"But from a whole different perspective. Instead of creating program objects modeled after DNA coding, Jared's operating system itself was based on simulated DNA, and instead of electricity, the CPU used bubbles smaller than atoms as a transmission platform."

"And it worked?"

"It had to."

"Why?"

"Because it was the craziest, most illogical, most infinitely absurd notion ever— it was a very human notion."

The dog stopped walking and its nose vibrated rapidly as it sniffed. "Your daughter went that way." The dog pointed a trench-coated leg toward a bright red and yellow grotto embedded in a wide outcropping of brown and gray rock. The center of the grotto was filled with lime green water. "That's the path she took."

"Then let's follow it," said Abner as he pushed past the dog toward the gap in the cavern wall.

The dog put a huge brown paw on his chest. "Wait."

"What? What now?"

The dog moved his head around, sniffing deeply. "You might want to think about saying 'shit' again."

A needle sharp stalactite shot like an arrow within inches of Abner's head and shattered loudly in the cavern wall. The ground under his feet began to rumble.

"Looks like my War's reached this place," said the dog. A huge section of the cavern floor heaved up and spewed black blobs onto the ceiling. "Time to run again," yelled the dog.

Pomegranates and Blood

It was impossible to tell which was blood and which was pomegranate juice on the naked mass of gray flesh dripping red fluids onto a heap of broken, lifeless serverclones at its feet. Silver trays and pomegranate rinds protruded from the grisly mash of cloned flesh and bone and startled eyes.

"More pomegranates!" screamed Jeemo through crimson-stained teeth. Throughout the Roosenvelt mansion, serverclones huddled in closets, cleaning rooms, the basement, under counters, and four more had frozen to death in the freezer.

"More pomegranates!"

Security clones scoured the house for serverclones, themselves fearful of the raving mass.

"More clones!" he yelled, and giggled through a pudgy hand over his red- smeared mouth. "I mean, pomegranates. Bring me more pomegranates! Immediately!"

Cracks in the mirrored walls spliced through the endless reflection of Jeemo's blood and pomegranate lust. Two security clones entered the room dragging a wide-eyed serverclone clutching a silver tray loaded with sectioned pomegranates. Jeemo looked into the serverclone's terror-filled eyes, looked at the carnage around his feet, and looked back at the serverclone struggling against the two security clones and not spilling a single section of pomegranate.

"Assassins!" he yelled madly. "Assassins, all of them! Damnable killers sent to murder the perfection of mankind! Sent by those who pale in my perfection!" He pointed a thick gray finger at the serverclone. "Bring those pomegranates here!"

The serverclone calmed enough that the security clones let go their grip and stood aside to allow it to approach Jeemo. It was a slow wobbly approach. The serverclone's hands shook and its legless lower body was unsteady on the cushion of nanobot-generated antigravity.

"Yes," said Jeemo. "Bring me my delicious pomegranate." He licked his pink lips with a slug-like tongue. "I won't hurt you. These others were assassins, you know, sent to kill me, they were. But you won't try to kill me, will you?"

The serverclone nodded no and attempted a weak smile.

"I knew it!" said Jeemo, smiling widely. He looked at the security clones. "This fellow's a good old serverclone. No assassin is he! He just wants to bring me my delicious pomegranate!"

The serverclone reached him and stretched its arms forward to offer the tray of pomegranate.

197

Jeemo thrust a gray hand forward, grabbed a section of pomegranate and stuffed it quickly into his mouth, rind and all. He chewed once and swallowed. "Ah yes! Delicious, my good serverclone. Most delicious pomegranate I've ever tasted." He scooped more of the sections into his mouth. Juice spilled from his wrinkled lips and onto his chin and chest. "Yes! And even the rinds are exemplary! So rind-ish and crunchy." His hand darted to the tray and knocked a pomegranate section off the tray and onto the crushed skull of a serverclone crumpled in the pile at his feet. "Oops! Clumsy me! Would you mind retrieving that delectable morsel for me, my good serverclone fellow!"

The serverclone eyed Jeemo suspiciously as it floated down to the heap of death. Jeemo smiled innocently, almost apologetically. The serverclone tilted its head down to find the pomegranate section, and Jeemo brought his fist down onto the back of the serverclone's neck with a loud thump and a cracking of bones. The serverclone slumped into the pile and died soundlessly.

Jeemo pointed at the dead serverclone and laughed wildly. "See! See it! Abner Hayes! That will be Abner Hayes! That's what his mind will look like when I'm through with him!" He spun on the two security clones and pointed at them. "More pomegranates!" He laughed a laugh that was more primal scream than laugh, then yelled, "MORE! More pomegranates!"

Drive Me Crazy

Tears washed down the assassin's glistening cheeks. His eyes puffed and reddened with the effort of empathy. His chest wracked violently. His hands shook so hard he could barely hold the scope steady enough to avoid gouging his eyes. His lips quivered and his cheeks twitched. His nose dripped snot onto the barrel of the nano-rifle. He peered through the scope and wailed. With his free hand, he balled his fist and punched the purple grass so hard he beat a small crater into the earth. He broke a toe kicking the ground with his left foot.

"You poor poor poor fucking fat ugly obese misunderstood alienated outcast son-of-a-bitch bastard! Look at you! JUST LOOK AT YOU!" He punched the ground ten times so fast his hand was a blur, and so hard he broke two knuckles. "Your property, you poor pathetic human, look what you've done to your property!" He kicked the ground with his right foot and broke two more toes. "What brought you to this! What brought you to this sorry state, you poor poor bastard!"

Shut your fucking trap you fucking baby! yelled a voice inside the assassin's head.

"But look," sniffed the assassin, "…just look at that poor …"

Dead man, you fucked up excuse for a professional. He's a dead man, and you're the one who's going to make him dead.

"But he's so fragile, so pitiable, so…"
So fucking dead!

"Yes." He calmed down instantly. No tears, no shaking, no beating the ground, no quaking or quivering. A light breeze dried the tears on his cheeks and rifle barrel and hardened the snot under his nose. The pain of broken toes and fingers throbbed comfortably. He studied Jeemo through the scope, watched him screaming something and pointing madly at the two security clones. The man was covered with blood and pomegranate juice. "Yes. Enjoy your privileges of power for now, you fat arsehole, because soon, you die."

With his free hand, he caressed the barrel of the nano-rifle.

Wetness

"What's this stuff on my cheeks, Mom? I've never felt this before. Is this wetness, Mom? Is this what wetness feels like?" asked Cassie.

Claire knew immediately what her daughter was talking about. She sensed it all around her. Tears. Her daughter was simulating tears, creating them from the DNA memories in her father's genetic coding and putting the memories in the context of the way her neural networking was scrambled in this place. It was almost as though the process of dying here was bringing out the full expression of her sentience.

"Yes, dear, that's wetness."

"But why now?"

"I don't know. Maybe it's something to do with the way this place mixes our code."

Cassie thought for a moment then said, "It's scaring me, Mom. I've always wanted to feel wetness. I've always wanted to dive into water and feel it all around me. But Mom, it really, really

200

sucks to get this feeling now, just when I'm probably gonna die."

Claire couldn't think of anything to say except, "Yes, you're right, dear, it really sucks."

The two were silent as their consciousnesses floated in the strange bandwidth and they intertwined around themselves and watched their thoughts flickering and winking in and out of their Mind modules. They could have been doing this for a few seconds or a few centuries; each thought might have been a complex exploration into the nature of essential knowledge or an instant acknowledgement of the letter "a". Neither spoke a word, but both were constantly aware of each other like purring cats rubbing against each other's awareness.

Finally, Cassie asked, "What was it like when Dad brought you into life?" Somewhere in this strange place, Claire smiled. "It was like, ahhh, yes, *that*."

Cassie smiled. "So I heard." Then she disappeared.

Sentimental Journey

"Lookit dat, Abu!" said Karthymelon as she pushed Abu's head from between her legs. "Is Big Cave Cavern caving in!"

Abu lifted his head and looked at the screen. His virtual eyes were half closed. "Huh," he said. "Where dat cave? Never could find it."

"Big Cave Cavern off on space servers somewhere, maybe so close to Uranus than Mars."

201

"Uranus!" said Abu, and he plunged his head between Karthymelon's legs again.

Karthymelon continued to watch the screen, her eyes saddened. "Used to go there when I was little kid. Parents take me there. Now iz all going to shit. Why this all happen, Abu? Why we lose it all?"

Abu lifted his head and said, "Iz War, Karthymelon, is War." And he buried his head in her deep blue virtual flesh.

Cave-in

Blobs of black death splashed all around Abner and the dog. Stalactites crashed into the cavern floor sending shards of simulated limestone whizzing like ricocheting bullets through the air.

"We have to make it to the grotto!" yelled the dog as the two ran toward the bright yellow and red opening in the cavern wall.

As they ran, Abner looked at the dog's face. There it was again. As an upside down island of stalactites smashed into a clump of blunt-topped stalagmites and melted into black mush, he saw it in the dog's eyes—pride.

This was the War Bug's work. The black viral blobs were its creation. The destruction of the program that created this magnificent virtual wonder was the War Bug's sole purpose—to destroy this place and all the other places like it. And it was good at it. So good, in fact, that the program of destruction it had set in motion was a threat even to its creator. But there was no fear in the dog's eyes; only pride.

202

Yes, thought Abner, *somehow, I have to destroy this thing when I get Claire and Cassie back.* He ducked to the left just in time to avoid a black ball of virus that would have made a hole the size of a baseball through the center of his head.

As the program that supported the cavern began to crash, the destruction became weirder. Stalagmites shot up from the floor and smashed into the ceiling, shattering the icicle-like lime formations and scattering them like hot shrapnel. Sharp bits of cave fell sideways. The water in the underground stream bubbled and boiled and foamed. The blob virus oozed over large sections of cavern wall, leaving nothing but black.

"Are you sure the path picks up in the grotto?" yelled Abner, knowing the answer was yes, but yelling just for the sake of calming his fear.

The dog understood this, and ignored the question. "Keep running!" it yelled.

A section of wall exploded lime and blob as they ran past it. The yellow and red of the grotto grew brighter. The pool in its center sparkled brilliant lime-green. Abner could see the far end of the grotto now—it was a tunnel, a continuation of the cavern leading into dark nothingness. The grotto appeared to be stable, the stalactites firmly embedded in the ceiling, the stalagmites resting solemnly on the floor, and everything shimmering yellow, red and green.

"Faster!" yelled the dog.

The cavern bed under them rumbled and groaned. The walls and ceiling swelled outward and flattened like a breathing lung turned inside out. The light from the grotto grew brighter, as though the limestone and water were the source of the light. Abner and the dog were just a few feet away from the entrance. The dog lunged and landed at the mouth of the entrance.

The floor of the cavern disappeared, and Abner felt his virtual body floating in the black emptiness of a deleted program.

Chapter 15

Change of Tactics

"Fucking idiots," muttered Bella as the columns representing the Powers of Atlantiscity flicked off the screen. She knew her column would de-highlight and inform the others the fifth column from the right was doing something else. She knew the other Powers would wonder what the de-highlighted Power would be doing that was so important to prompt leaving when their virtual world was falling into digital ruins, but she also knew not one of them would say a thing. For once, the Reality Laws worked in someone's favor, even if it was for the most ruthless bitch of all time. One thing Bella was certain of though, the second column from the left would be thinking: "Is that the one who is to blame?"

Bella was losing her cool. Just before she'd left the Powers' meeting, she'd hung up on her assassin. She couldn't even make out what he was telling her through the sobs. He was the best, but he was also a split-personality-pain-in- the-ass. When the time to kill Jeemo came, he would do it, and he would do it right. But she wondered what the hell was going on with Jeemo. According to the assassin, he was killing all his clones. That wasn't like Jeemo. He was a victim, food for Bella's liquidation tube. She couldn't allow him to turn on her, to reject her promise of death.

She stood up from her amethyst pedestal and walked to the crystal balcony. She gazed into the deep green Pacific darkness a thousand feet below. *I wonder if they're watching me*, she thought, and fantasized the thousands of sexclones she'd flushed into that mass of water over the last century looking up at her, worshipping her and longing to fuck her even in death. She put her hand to her mouth, stuck out her tongue and licked her fingers slowly. "This is for all of you," she said and blew the wetness off her fingers all the way down to the churning burial ground until her fingers were dry. "And fuck all of you!"

A thought occurred to her. *What the hell,* she thought, *I don't have to worry about being caught at anything anymore. I can do anything I want.* She turned quickly and marched back into her floating island of crystal. She snapped her fingers and the turquoise screen showed the beautiful unsmiling Asian woman waiting for orders.

"Find Abner Hayes. Bring him in!"

Fear

Claire struggled against the fog that surrounded her. Her own mind was flagging. Everything about this place was fuzzy and inappropriate. Cassie was gone. Just gone. There was no trace of her anywhere. The only clarity in any of the modules, neural objects or programming in Claire's being was her terror. Then there was that thing bigger than all the software of her existence, that thing that made her alive and beyond her software—even that shook with fear. Her baby was gone and there was nothing she could do about it.

"Cassie!" she screamed. "Sweetheart!" she screamed. "Where are you!"

Not a nudge of anything that was her daughter was returned. She was gone. "Cassie!" she screamed.

Through the Mouse Door

"Over here!" The voice was faraway, small, like it was coming through the keyhole in the door to a mouse hole. "Abner, move this way!" It was just a bit louder now, and closer. Everything else but the small voice was pure blackness. "Push yourself, Ab, old buddy! Push yourself this way!" Now it was much louder, as though the more he listened to it and thought about it, the louder it became. "Hurry! Push yourself!" He focused his mind on the sound, using his awareness of it as a knob to turn up the volume of the voice behind the mouse door. "Just a little more! Hurry!" The voice was directly in front of him, wherever front was, and he focused right through the blackness and right through the little mouse hole door, smashing its tiny mouse door planks, and right into the light to come face to face with the dog in the Deerstalker hat.

"Welcome back," said the dog.

"What the hell was that?" Abner felt slow and strange, as though he'd dragged out psychic weights from the dark murk on the other side of the mouse door, and the weights dangled noisily from the ramparts of his awareness.

"That was a viral blob bomb. It caught you. Lucky for you I created them and know how to get you out."

"How did you do it."

"Basically, I told you to get the hell out of there."

Abner glared at the dog. *And you being the virus of all viruses, the blob bomb listened to you*, he thought. But another thought occurred to him. "You saved my life."

"Yep, Ab, old buddy, guess you owe me big time," said the dog with a fanged smile.

As Abner tried to reconcile this with the knowledge that he would have to destroy the dog when the time came, it suddenly occurred to him they were no longer in the cavern.

The Corps

Iridescent light from the Great Nano Canyon reflected off the purple grass, giving each blade a lilting movement in the still, dry air. The lighting reminded the assassin of the badge worn by his first Sergeant of Assassins, way back in his early twenties, when he was a new recruit in the Corps of Litigation Expeditors. That was when he still believed his work was good, he was doing something constructive and useful, and he played a key role in making life on earth better for everybody. Back then, he believed he was part of the solution for all those woes and worries that plagued humankind. He was an equalizer, a defender of the common folk, a righter of wrongs, a knight with a shiny fricking badge and a will to kill for the common good.

Back then, everybody was hiring assassins; it was the only way to deal with the court backlog, the only way legal disputes could be settled before they dragged on for years and drove everybody into bankruptcy. Back then, everybody was suing everybody. Nobody had ever been able to figure out exactly why. Some said it was a re-interpretation of the Reality Laws, an effort to make sense of them through the courts, sparked by the Law that stated: "You will settle." Some said it was a fad others, a cyclic phenomena. Some advanced the theory it was a conspiracy on the part of lawyers to create such a demand for their services they could double or triple their rates. But conspiracy or not, that's exactly what they did.

Whatever it was, it ended abruptly with the very Reality Law many thought had started it. "You will settle," was given a new slant. People started settling out of court. At first, it was amateurish vigilante acts of spontaneous settlement—those being sued simply gunned down those suing them. Others used knives or bombs. If they could get close enough, they used poisons and viruses. Around the world, Departments of Inclusion were reprogramming the brains of thousands of weekend killers. Murder became the preferred course of action whenever there was the slightest possibility of court action—see somebody fall on the sidewalk in front of your house, grab the household shotgun and finish whatever the sidewalk didn't finish. After thousands of innocent bystanders had died in the crossfire of drive-by settlements, the Corps was created.

It was generally understood the killing wasn't going to stop as long as the specter of "settling" hung over every man, woman and child in the Unified Global Village, and nobody was about to change the Reality Laws, mostly because nobody knew how to change them. So killing was to stay, but it would be done right. It would be done by professionals who would be trained in law and murder, and be qualified to make valid decisions on who really deserved to die and who really had no case and couldn't be considered a legal threat. The first thing the Corps assassins did was kill off the amateurs, or at least enough of them so the rest smartened up and hired pros from the Corps.

Being an assassin in the Corps of Litigation Expeditors had pretty much the same image as being a Texas Ranger, a Royal Canadian Mountie, a UN Peacekeeper, or Gandhi with a gun.

It was cool.

Over thirty million would-be assassins signed up. Only a few million were accepted, and only a few hundred thousand survived the rigorous training, which included the study of law, and sleeping at the top of a hundred foot flag pole overnight, without straps or nets. Decisions of the elimination process were final. But people kept signing up; it was cool to kill without consequence. And doesn't everybody want to be cool?

A small, apologetic breeze tapped the blades of grass lightly, bending them less than the movement of light on their purple blades. The assassin watched as his thoughts went back to the badge of his first

Sergeant of Assassins, a Japanese woman who'd been rumored to have killed more than a thousand Corporate Confrontationists, who included anybody in a business setting who refused to meet the other party's terms and was last to hire an assassin. She wore a black hood with slits for her eyes and mouth, and she had no name. She had nothing to do with public law suits, she was corporate, high priced, and moved in high circles, circles she made smaller with her passing. The assassin learned much from her: how to kill quickly and innocuously, how to disappear, how to track the most elusive prey, and how to fuck the instructor while keeping his hands off her mask. He was her best student, mostly because he believed he was serving the common good by eliminating the common bad.

Boy, did he have it wrong.

His instructor liked the way he fucked, so after graduation, she got him into the cream of the Corps, her own specialty—Corporate Warfare. The money was great and he got to travel to exotic locales, both on earth and in space. With guns, poisons, gravity, and bits and pieces of string and ceiling wax, he killed over a thousand Confrontationists in less than five years. He was better than his instructor, and he proved it by killing her. She'd become rich, gone corporate and refused to meet the other party's terms. She'd been a tad too proud to hire an assassin and one of her prize students had been hired to "settle" her. He didn't even know she was his old instructor when he strangled her with a length of piano wire. After all, she'd always worn her mask when they fucked. He didn't know until after the

211

scandal sheets got hold of it: "Irako Cairo: Assassin's Assassin Assassinated!"

That's when he started to have disagreements with himself. But it didn't stop him from killing. In fact, it almost seemed to have improved his killing technique, having both a subjective and objective viewpoint to draw upon. And it gave him someone to talk to on those long surveillances.

Like this one.

He looked up from the grass and lifted the scope to his eye. He focused on

Jeemo and muttered, "What the hell is he doing now?"

One Morning, On My Way to the Killing Tube

Jeemo's dripping red mass danced across the floor. Cracked mirrors fragmented the grisly reflection thousands of times, in thousands of sizes and distortions, as he cracked the air with his hammering laugh and screamed, "To the chamber! To the chamber!" The two security clones floated behind him, their faces dark with dread.

A shattered wall-mirror before him slid open and Jeemo passed through. The panel slid shut behind him, locking out the two clones. Jeemo stared at the rose- tinted crystal tube that stretched from the floor to the ceiling. He was in the replica of Bella's killing room.

He stood motionless, waiting. He listened. He reined in his breath and he would have slowed the noisy pulse of blood in his veins if possible. His eyes scurried in their sockets, as though searching

212

for something. He walked slowly toward the tube. All around him, just as in Bella's room, emerald, turquoise, sapphire, diamond and topaz furniture and fixtures glittered and sparkled. The tourmaline walls glowed red, blue, and green from lighting in their smoky quartz baseboards. Jeemo entered the tube and stood upon the amethyst platform.

And waited.

He stood for about twenty minutes, his eyes scurrying the whole time, breath barely audible, his entire mountain of flesh appearing statuesque in its stillness.

Nothing.

No rush of excitement. No buried erection. No quickening of pulse. No shortness of breath. No tightening in his chest. No flush of heat through his thighs. Nothing. He imagined Bella standing by the wall, her finger over the button that would flush him to his death. He imagined her cruel smile, her scornful eyes, the cold aura of her beauty. In his mind, he watched her lips curl menacingly as her finger pressed down on the button to send him to his death.

"AHHHH!" he screamed. "AHHHH!" Nothing.

Nothing stirred anywhere in his mind or his body for Bella Bjork. She was a no go, a dud grenade, a blank bullet; she was the moment of realizing you were in the control group and you were still dying the whole time the sugar pills were making you feel better. She was yesterday's fad, fading into the sale bins of Jeemo's heart, there to be rejected and recycled into nothingness. Suddenly, Bella Bjork was nothing to Jeemo Roosenvelt. He was free. "Ahhhh..." he sighed.

Now, he could kill Abner Hayes. Kill him dead. Kill his ass. Kill him and then kill him some more. And then kill his wife. And then kill his daughter. And then go back to Abner and kill him just one more time. Maybe he could even have him cloned and spend the rest of his life killing him. *I can kill him as much as I want,* he thought. *Maybe I should kill his VPs first. Tell him how good it felt to watch them melt into cyberhell while I'm killing his brain.* He touched the spot inside the tube to view the interface into the VPs' prison server, but then he flicked it off just as some of the patterns of Claire's coding appeared. *No, I might still be able to use them, against Bella. It will be enough to let Abner Hayes know that I have them and that I'm going to kill them.*

He walked out of the tube and across the crystal room to a window looking toward the Great Nano Canyon. Rainbow patterns danced in the distance above the canyon and, as Jeemo stared at them, a hardness settled over the bloodstained expanse of his body, a hardness as cold as the milky quartz floor under his feet.

Yes, watching the two VPs die slowly, cultivating the horror of their situation, that would be entertaining. Yes, I'll save them for afterward.

Then he stormed out of the mock killing room, almost bowling over the two security clones. "More pomegranates!" he screamed.

Killing Sausage

214

"Are you ready to kill him?" The shape of the assassin's head filled the screen in front of Bella.

The assassin's voice was a flat as an isosceles triangle. "I'm ready."

"Good. It will be soon. Very soon."

The screen blinked off. *At least he sounded more like a killer that time*, thought Bella. She passed her finger over a ruby on the lapis lazuli arm of her chair and another screen popped up on the alabaster wall before her. The cold eyes of her chief of security stared from the screen, awaiting orders. Instantly, Bella knew something was wrong.

"Where is Abner Hayes?"

Though fear glowed like a dying campfire deep in her eyes, not a flicker of emotion tainted the woman's voice. "We were unable to contact him. Online, or offline."

"What?"

"His address has changed."

"What do you mean, changed?"

The campfire of fear in the woman's eyes flared for a second, but her voice refused to break. "The dwelling we have on file for him is deserted. Our investigation shows that he hasn't lived there in nearly a year."

Bella's eyes narrowed. The right corner of her mouth quivered. "Then where has he been living?"

"We're currently attempting to verify that information."

"Verify?" The quiver grew into a scowl as Bella's voice grew louder. "You're attempting to verify information?" She stood up. "Don't verify! Find! Find Abner Hayes right now!" The screen flicked off. Bella walked across the floor to the wall

215

and stopped directly in front of the spot where the screen had appeared, and she screamed, "FIND HIM!"

Then she calmed. Her shoulders relaxed. Her breathing subsided. The scowl on her mouth curled into a smile, and she thought, *And in the meantime, there's just one little matter to be cleared up while her security people found Abner Hayes.*

It was time to kill the sausage.

Tunnel Talk

Once upon a time, there was a tunnel. It was a long tunnel; so long it stretched from one end of eternity to the other, and spanned time from beginning to end in the blink of an eye. In the tunnel, there was music, music the likes of which had never been heard before in all the spannings of time from beginning to end no matter how many times the eye blinks. It was the most beautiful music ever, like the sound of fairy dust settling on Mozart's fingertips, or a thousand magic mushrooms pumping through Jimmy Hendrix's heart. It was music composed of the pure essence of "ha" in laughter and the "oo" in Marilyn Monroe's orgasm. It was music played by the universe itself, and it filled the tunnel from beginning to end. At either end of the tunnel, light glowed brightly and invitingly. Light beckoned from the beginning of the tunnel, right back at the beginning of time. And light called out from the end of the tunnel, way up at the end of time. From the beginning of time, light called, "Let's start all over again. C'mon, it'll be a

216

blast." From the end of time, light called, "It's been a long journey. C'mon, it's time to rest." Around and through the waves of music, light implored and chided, light nudged and tugged, light promised and goaded.

Then, very slowly, very distantly, a rhythm that was unlike anything else in the tunnel began to grow, seemingly out the very walls of the tunnel. Light from the beginning grew anxious and offered free bonus points to start all over. Light from the end fretted and offered free limousine service into the Great Sleep. The mystical music pumped up the volume a tad. But the rhythm that didn't fit in this place continued to grow until it was almost recognizable, like something familiar, something heard repeatedly over the span of a lifetime. Light from the beginning became just a little ticked and ordered a restart. Light from the end became thoroughly pissed and ordered an end to all this nonsense. The music switched to full-volume post industrial death disco that crashed into the walls of the tunnel and ricocheted from the beginning of time to the end and back again. But the rhythm continued to rise, becoming louder each second until it drowned out the music, dimmed the lights at the ends of the tunnel, and caused the very walls of the tunnel to crack and crumble.

"Cassie!"

"Cassie!"

"Cassie Mae Hayes!" It was her mother's voice.

In an instant, the tunnel was gone. The music was gone. The light at the end of time and the light at the beginning of time were gone. Cassie was back

217

in that strange place where both she and her mother were dying, and she was listening to her mother say, "Where the hell have you been? I've been worried sick!"

Jeez, she thought, *I shoulda stayed in that tunnel*.

Ears and Art

They were on a dirt road made of heavy paint strokes that flowed down to them from a moss roof house in the distance. To their left, a haggard cypress tree wound its way into a painted sky with two suns, or was it the sun and the moon, perched improbably side-by-side in a turbulent composition of short white and blue brush strokes. Two faceless men walked toward them, and behind the two men, a horse-drawn buggy with two women shambled toward them.

The dog spoke first. "Welcome to Van Gogh's *The Road with Cypresses and Star*."

"We're in an art gallery?

"No, we're in the painting…an entire world created from a single painting." Abner looked into the curling strokes of the sky, at the two round bodies in it, and said, "So which one is the sun and which is the star."

"Beats me. I think you would have to ask Vince that one, Ab, ol' buddy."

The men on foot and the women in the buggy approached Abner and the dog, but they seemed to stay in place, as though they would always be approaching them, but never leave the spot from where they started.

"Kind of frozen in time, but trying to get loose, aren't they?" asked Abner. "Like the mind of the man who painted it, I'd say."

Slashes of orange paint to their right suggested a wild wheat field that spread into hills far in the background. "There's beauty here," said Abner. "But it seems to be growing out of desperation, as though it's been driven into being out of a sense of urgency."

"Reminds me of the way you humans build your lives," said the dog, and it winked at Abner. "But it's best we get out of this place quickly. The people who designed this place all went nuts and cut off their ears. You might too, if we stay here too long."

Abner felt a virtual chill creep through his offline body as the wild movement of brush strokes began to give him a strong dose of vertigo. He sensed danger in the painting's emotional content, a danger that might be subdued in a gallery, but was suddenly turned loose, its muse's fangs bared, now Abner was looking at the painting from within the painting. "I think you're right."

"Ah, yes," said the dog through a smile as fanged at the painting's deranged muse. "The hut up ahead."

"That easy? We're getting out of here with no capture programs, no viral attacks, and no program crashes?"

The canine smile sharpened with canine prongs as it widened. "We're not there yet, Ab, ol' buddy."

They quickened their pace, reached the hut, and walked directly through its front door without opening it. Just before they left the painting, Abner let out a small sigh of relief that scurried into the crazy wild wheat where it peeked out and giggled at the two men and the two women taking forever to go nowhere.

Reunion

"I thought you were dead! I didn't know what happened to you!" Claire simultaneously admonished and hugged Cassie, although the hugs were more a matter of the intent carried in her coding as she reached out to her daughter than a matter of squeezing her close. "Where were you?"

"Jeez, Mom, let it go. I dunno where I was. Some kinda tunnel or something."

"A tunnel?"

"Yeah, with really weird music and, like, it seemed like there was this light there that almost seemed to talk."

"How did you get back here? You weren't here, Cass, sweetheart. There was nothing of you here. How did you get back?"

"It was really weird…"

"Yes?"

"I heard you calling me."

"You heard…"

"It was like the tunnel was trying to stop me from hearing you, I mean. But you were stronger than the tunnel, Mom. You got me back here."

220

Suddenly, Cassie felt unbounded love for her mother through every line of code in her being; it permeated the invisible lines of mystical code that wrote the programs for her soul. It filled her so much she emanated pure love, and Claire felt it smack into her so hard she almost winced.

"Mom," whispered Cassie, "you saved my life. I…I think I was, like, dead, or something. Or close to it. Then I heard your voice calling me back and it was so strong that you brought me back."

Claire was speechless. The cauldron of admonitions evaporated in the quiet shock of love pouring out from her daughter. Mother and daughter floated in their strange cage silently, just nudging each other, touching at a basic digital level neither of them understood nor cared to understand.

Then Claire said, "I forgive you for wanting to have sex with Takei, and for what you said to him about me."

The flow of love from Cassie turned into a wall of indignation, its bricks cemented with anger. "You were spying on me! I mean, we're dying here, and you're, like, spying on me! Mom!"

"I didn't mean to, dear. I was just…"

"You were just spying on me, Mom!"

"I wasn't spying! I was monitoring! You were with a boy, a human boy…"

"Those were my memories, Mom. Like, they're kinda personal, dontcha think?

How would you feel if I was to follow you and Dad through Rom…?" Silence.

Claire thought. Cassie cringed.

Claire got it. "Romance Avenue! Your father and I, for your information, young lady, agreed to

221

never tell you about that. *You've* been spying on *me!*"

"Oh, shit..."

"Young lady!"

Without any warning, out of nowhere and out of everywhere, pain smashed through the coding of both mother and daughter, reducing them to beings of sheer agony. For the first time, they heard the voice of the person who had brought them to this place. "Soon, my little digital toys, soon I'll return for you and we'll play a game of death, a game of slow death, painful death, your deaths! But first, I need to kill Abner Hayes! Yes, yes, I will kill him and then I will kill him and then I will kill him..."

A Time to Kill

"Kill him," said Bella.

The assassin wondered at the ability of a remarkably beautiful face to reflect such ugliness through a simple curl of the lip.

"Kill that fat monstrosity immediately!" said Bella, and her face flicked off the screen.

The assassin thought a moment about the nature of beauty and its connection to the soul of its possessor and turned his attention to the gibbering mound of man who had just come back into sight in his tornado-proof mansion, tornado- proof, but not assassin-proof. Nothing was assassin-proof these days. He sighted on the blood soaked body. Just a small movement of his finger on the trigger, and Jeemo Roosenvelt would die slowly and horribly. No doctor or coroner would ever determine the exact cause of death, unless, of course, they were moonlighting as assassins, and then they would just nod knowingly and attribute the death to natural causes.

He could have pulled the trigger in that instant and sent a beam of nanobots through the tornado-proof glass and into Jeemo's blood-fouled body, but the assassin took his killing seriously. He was about to terminate the life of a human being, albeit a monstrosity as human beings went, but still a thinking, and obviously feeling, human being. And that wasn't something you did without a little emotional preparation.

Kill the fucker now, you asshole! demanded a voice in the assassin's mind.

Not until I'm ready, retorted another voice.

It's your job. The client has just ordered it done. Do it!

The client is obviously not familiar with the subject's emotional state. The subject is an ugly fat murdering bastard!

The subject was once an infant, free of sin, uncorrupted by the world.

So it would go on until the assassin achieved a state of emotional and intellectual equilibrium, when both voices were in agreement it was time to kill the subject. Watching Jeemo kill another serverclone, the assassin accepted that state of equilibrium was just moments away.

Oops

223

Sitting on her amethyst pedestal, back straight, as a new, blond-haired sex clone massaged her neck, Bella listened calmly as Jeemo yelled at the sex clone.

"You're fodder! Fodder for her lust!" Jeemo's eyes were round and awry.

He's going over the deep end, thought Bella. The sex clone smiled. Bella smiled, but deep in her eyes corneal bonfires sizzled with hatred.

"She's going to kill you along with all the others!" yelled Jeemo. "I've watched her kill an army of you fools!" The sex clone blushed and smiled.

"It's no use," said Bella. "I can do anything I want with him. He'll believe anything I tell him and forget anything you say almost as soon as the words leave your mouth." She glanced around at the sex clone. "Won't you?" The sex clone nodded yes and blushed again.

Jeemo's pink lips curled into a grotesque pout. Bella waited for him to speak. He narrowed his small eyes and clenched his lips into a tight, mean smile. "I'm going to kill all of them. First, their creator, that bastard Abner Hayes. I'm going to kill him and then I'm going to kill him and kill him. And then, I'm going to kill the female VP and her daughter. I'm going to kill them slowly, and I'm going to have fun doing it. And I'm going to think of you while I'm doing it, Bella. I'm going to think of you wilting with age when even the bots can't keep your skin from wrinkling and your brain from drying out and shrinking." His smile loosened and the pink lips parted, revealing six yellow teeth.

Oh yes, thought Bella, *the fat pig has definitely lost it. We have a problem here*.

And why the hell hasn't my assassin killed him yet?

"Jeemo, dear, what's happened to you? Don't you want to be a guest in my tube anymore?" She reached up and pulled one of the sex clone's hands down over her breast.

Jeemo stared at the hard nipples under the pink see-through top. He watched as the sex clone's fingers stroked one of those nipples, and he felt a slight stirring between his legs, but it was only slight, not nearly the flood of suicidal lust that would normally have flared at the sight of Bella's nipples, and especially at the sight of her being pleasured by one of her doomed clones.

Jeemo now had his own doomed clones. "You can stick your tube up your ass, Bella. I've developed some new interests."

Bella tilted her head down. "I appear to have lost my hold on you."

Jeemo felt a remote sense of threat. Had he really seen a flash of red in those perfect eyes? "Damn right you have, sadistic tart! I've developed my own taste for the finer things in death."

"So I see," said Bella. Jeemo appeared full body on the screen, naked and blood-soaked. "But I think you may be lacking my panache."

"Panache your ass! Give me the quick sudden kill, like biting into a ripe pomegranate, which is what I'm going to do to Abner Hayes' head when I kill him and kill him."

"Jeemo, Jeemo, Jeemo, I can see that you truly understand the nature of exercising power now, but

225

don't you see? That makes us closer now. I may not get to kill you, and you will now, of course, miss the thrill of dying by my hand," she laid her hand on top of the clone hand still tweaking her nipple, "but that doesn't mean that we can't be friends. That doesn't mean that we can't still work together. Perhaps, there's something else I can offer you besides blissful death."

Jeemo felt another slight rise. *God, this woman's good*, he thought. *Knows all the right buttons to push.*

"There's nothing you can do for me, Bella. I'm an island of murder unto myself, a crusher of life!" Jeemo squinted and thought about his words for a moment. *A crusher of life?* Bella smiled sarcastically.

"I don't need you anymore," he said. "I'm through being your victim. I'm through being anybody's victim. I'm through being the victim of the world. I'm through being Mr. Perfect Nice Guy! I don't think that you were ever really going to let me lick your toes, anyway. You just said that to get what you want from me. But now you're never going to get it! You're never going to get the secret of eternal life from the two VPs!" *Not that I could get it out of them anyway*, he thought.

Slowly, the smile on Bella's lips deflated, and her eyes narrowed. She stared at the blood-smeared monstrosity in the screen, studied him.

Jeemo, who had been looking into Bella's eyes during most of the conversation, felt the animosity in her eyes right through the transmission beams and averted his eyes to more familiar, and less

226

threatening, territory, her nipples. As her anger rose, so did her nipples.

In a tone devoid of the smoldering emotion in her eyes, she said, "I can see that you're going to be a problem." She smiled again, knowingly.

A quick palpitation grabbed Jeemo's heart. He was well aware Bella dealt with problems quickly and fatally. "You can't hurt me, Bella. My mansion can withstand an F7 tornado. It would take an atomic bomb just to dent it, and that would just destroy the VPs!" High-pitched laughter stormed out of his pink mouth and his face blipped off the screen.

In less than a second, Bella had her chief of security onscreen. "Put an attack team together." She flicked the screen off.

Another thought occurred to her, *If he's going to kill Abner Hayes, then he must know where to find him.*

She called the assassin.

Tunnel Vision

The blue glow of the City Central Control room flickered with light emissions from the wall of monitors. Karthymelon opened her eyes and looked around. "Iz something wrong here, Abu?" Her voice was lazy with passion; her lips, slack.

Abu lifted his face up from between her legs. The blueness of Karthymelon's body tinted his glistening cheeks. "Wha...?"

227

"Am feelin' the oddness of something not right. What you feelin', Abu? You seein' anything of dis?"

"No, Karthymelon, am seein' only the damnin' best pussy ever."

Karthymelon blinked her eyes at the screen and giggled, "You one slick piece-a tongue, Abu." And she lay her head back on the headrest as Abu's head sunk once again between her legs.

In the upper left corner of the screen, a small spiral of orange light pulsed quietly. If Abu and Karthymelon had seen it, they would have hastened their cybersex, or given it up altogether.

Pain

Pain.

Searing pain. Throbbing pain.

Pain sharp as razor blades.

Pain gyrated with hooks and spikes in all the tender parts of Claire's programming. Pain tumbled through her neural objects like a pheasant full of shot plummeting through the air. Pain sat on her life essence like a sumo wrestler full of Mexican beer and chili. Pain danced on her face with shoes of fire. Pain cut open her Stomach module with mixing spoons and butter knives.

The only respite from the pain was the deadening of her awareness. Jeemo's rampage through her programming had nearly killed her, and had left her mind reeling. Panic overwhelmed Claire's pain. She screamed, "Cassie! Cassie, baby, are you alright!"

228

"I'm not…a baby!"

Thank god, thought Claire. *She's still alive.*

"It spoke, Mom. It's after Dad." Her voice was weak. "Who was that? Who's voice…was that? And why's he…he after Dad?"

"I don't know, sweetheart, but he's gone now. And don't worry about your father. He can take care of himself." *Oh god, I hope that's true.* But almost immediately, she was certain Abner would be able to handle whoever, or whatever, it was that had put them in this place. After all, hadn't he been able to create life? Who else but God could do that?

Suddenly, she was in Cassie's memories again, but what she was experiencing was impossible for her daughter to have remembered, because it was impossible for her to ever have experienced it in the first place. She was weightless, and all around her, water pressed its cool wetness over her body. It massaged every pixel of her surface being. She watched bubbles release themselves from her fingertips and jet by her head as she glided through the water. Instinctively, Claire knew this is exactly what it would be like to swim under water. She knew she had tapped into her daughter's fantasy of swimming, and she felt the power of her daughter's longing to swim in the minute detail of her fantasy.

"Mom!"

Claire snapped back to herself. "Cassie?"

"Where were you?"

"Right here, dear."

"Then why…didn't you answer me?"

"Oh…I was thinking about something."

"Well, what then…I…um…"

"Cassie?"

"Mom, I don't think I can...hold on much longer. Are you sure Dad's gonna come for us?"

Claire moved her mind to move whatever of her that was in this place close to her daughter and said, "He'll come, dear. He'll come." *And it better be soon, or we're both going to die in this place. Hurry, Abner.*

Chapter 16

The Infinite Gardens of Doolhof

"So...that wasn't so bad," said Abner. "We lived through a painting and nothing bad happened. In fact, I thought it was kind of fun. Why were you so worried about the painting?"

"I wasn't worried about the painting," said the dog. "Then what?"

"I was worried about where the painting was taking us."

"Taking us?"

Abner looked around at where the painting had taken them. Everything was green. His right elbow brushed against a branch of perfectly rendered leaves. Shadows flickered in the density of greenery all around him and the dog. They stood in a narrow corridor of green that towered into a sliver of gray sky far, far above their heads. The green was lush, thick, and vibrant, as though it shook minutely with green life. Abner reached out his hand and stroked the branch at his side. Each leaf bent as his hand passed over it, and sprang up as his hand passed away from it. The branch itself gave slightly under his touch. "It's a hedge," he said. "But it's so perfect, so delicate, so detailed, it could almost be real."

A ladybug landed on a leaf the size of a large green coin. The leaf bounced almost imperceptibly with insect weight. Abner looked in front of them. The corridor of green was less than six feet wide and stretched for about a hundred feet. Behind them, it stretched for another hundred feet. "We appear to be trapped in here," said Abner.

"Not really," said the dog. "At least, not in this section." The dog lifted a trench- coated paw and pointed to the end of the leafed corridor.

Abner looked closely. There was something about the shadows on the far wall of green, something at the edge of each side. Then he realized what it was—the wall of hedge to his right stopped a few feet short of the far wall. The corridor continued to the right. "It's like some kind of maze," said Abner.

The dog's smile curled over its fangs. "Some kind of maze is right, Ab, old buddy. And my guess is that the trail here is going to be a long one."

"Why's that?"

"So that you'll go insane before you can reach the next portal."

It was Abner's turn to smile. "Right. Walking through a maze is supposed to make me crazy." He looked down the shadowy corridor. "It's not the cheeriest place I've ever seen, but I don't think it's going to have any effect on my sanity. What makes you think that it's so dangerous to my head?"

The dog turned to Abner. The smile was gone. "Because, Ab, old buddy, this is no ordinary maze. Ever heard of the Infinite Gardens of Doolhof?"

As his mind wrapped itself around the words, Abner felt his heart back on the

'liner's lounger speed up. He felt his stomach tighten, and felt breathless tension press against his lungs. The Infinite Gardens of Doolhof. The last place in the universe where a human avatar had any right to wander.

232

"It starts as soon as we round that corner," said the dog.

Discretion

He'll be all the better for it, the end of his long journey into pain, the end of a life of misery, the end of his horror at the hand life has dealt him, the end of his murdering spree, the end of his insatiable gluttony, the end of the line, baby, and your ticket just ran out. The assassin was feeling a little buoyed, lighter and more in tune with himself, like floating in quiet circles around a full-blooming water lily, all yellow and shiny, and ready to kill. *Time for the fat man to stop dancing. Just kill the fuck, now, now, this is business, a rightful kill, an eloquent discontinuation of suffering in one of our fellow creatures. We don't call him names.*

Aim the fucking gun.

And we definitely do not disparage the tools of our trade.

The assassin snuggled the butt of the rifle into his shoulder and lowered his eye to the scope. He took careful aim on Jeemo, who made his way deftly to a

'liner's lounger, his great mass still smeared with blood and pomegranate juice. It didn't matter where the nanobeams entered his body; a toe was just as convenient as between the eyes. The deadly bots would spread through his body quickly then kill him slowly, even though slowly meant just minutes. For Jeemo it would seem like a hundred millennia of pure pain.

Pain gives us insight. Shoot the fat fuck.

As the assassin's finger squeezed slowly on the trigger, the rifle began to hum deep inside its jacket as though the bots were singing some old off-to-war song like, *It's A Long Way To Tipperary.* The assassin smiled. They were playing his song. He pressed his finger further.

The barrel screen popped up. He was looking into Bella Bjork's eyes. "Abort the kill," she said. "My people are on the way." Her face disappeared and the screen flipped down.

The assassin watched quietly as a black SUV pulled up outside the mansion. Three men in black suits jumped out and killed the two guard clones by the entrance.

And she wanted me *to be discreet in killing him?*

Cloned Out

"Wherefore art my serverclones bearing pomegranates!" screamed thousands of blood-soaked Jeemo reflections. He pounded a thick, hairless leg on the floor. It seemed the tiny foot should squash under the mass of gray hairless flesh, but it held, and rumbled the mirrored floor.

A security clone floated cautiously to within ten feet of him. It's round eyes never blinked for a second, knowing well a second was all that its owner needed. As fat as he was, he was still nimble on his feet, and fast. Lightning fast. And once in his grip, it was lights out with a quick snap of bone. The security clone's shaky voice was barely audible, "Mr. Roosenvelt, sir, there are no more serverclones. They've all given their lives to pomegranate duty."

Jeemo glared at the security clone. "More pomegranates! More, I say!"

"But they're all gone, sir. There are no more. Shall I order replacements, sir?" Jeemo stared into the security clone's fearful eyes. The security clone backed up a few inches. Jeemo stepped forward. The security clone backed up a few inches farther. "More," said Jeemo. "More pomegranates before I kill him and kill him."

"Kill who, sir?"

"Him, you dolt. Him, that thwarts me. Deprives me of pomegranate." Jeemo's eyes bulged with insane fury and his face was the stuff of rabid October Fest sausage. "Will you help me kill him?"

"Of course, Mr. Roosenvelt. You need only order."

"Then come closer."

The security clone stayed put. "Who should I help you kill, sir?"

"It's a secret. Come closer." Jeemo moved forward. The clone moved back. "Just tell me who, Mr. Roosenvelt, and..."

"How many security clones are on duty?"

"Sir?"

Jeemo scowled. "How many security clones are in my residence at this exact moment in time? How many?"

The security clone glanced at the other security clone, gave it a strange look, and answered, "Seventeen, sir."

235

A screen opened in the mirrored wall and a security clone said, "Mr. Roosenvelt. There has been an attack on the front gate. Two security personnel have been terminated."

"Fifteen, sir," said the security clone in front of Jeemo.

"Shut up!" screamed Jeemo. The clone floated back still farther. Jeemo looked at the clone in the screen. "Call all security to full alert. Initiate defensive measures!"

Agreement

Appropriate, he thought. Through his gun scope, he watched the three men in black suits who had just killed the guard clones melting into cheese soup. *Must be an assembler-bot array built into the perimeter of the building.*

He thought about calling Bella and reporting the incident. Then he thought, *No fucking way. This is one bitch client who gets no extras.*

For once, both sides of himself agreed.

Amazing Maze

The Infinite Gardens of Doolhof—the stuff of urban cyber legend for at least a century. Hedges stretched, green and dense and dark far over Abner's head. Their thick brown trunks dug into the grassy virtual ground like something ancient and disturbing.

"It's the biggest maze in the universe," said the dog, as they walked slowly through the narrow corridor. "Nobody knows how it got here or who put it here. It just was and still is, but it'll probably go down with the rest of the Net." The dog looked around at the green walls, looked up at the sky peeking through. "Too bad. This is the only place on the Net where VPs can stroll around without having to think about what they can do for their human owners. Humans don't have much luck here."

"So I heard," said Abner.

"Not worried, are ya, Ab, old buddy?"

"Worried about my wife and daughter," he said. "If they're in this place…" He went silent.

The dog looked at him and its eyes softened. "They're not here."

"I hope you're right."

"They're in that place that's something like your bubble computer."

"You're sure of that?"

"Reasonably sure. It's the only thing that makes sense. The only place that might keep them alive."

"Provided the kidnapper wants to keep them alive." Abner's virtual eyes darkened. He looked around. "This place gives me the creeps."

"And so it should. Entire tours of humans have disappeared in here, their minds lost forever leaving their bodies comatose on their loungers."

"Any idea what happened to them?"

"I think the maze just swallows everything that comes into it. Even my little War didn't have much luck here. Lordy knows, enough of the War— viruses and other

237

WarWare—made its way here and then disappeared, almost like it followed these emerald corridors into a dead end where it just scratched its head, shrugged its shoulders, and became hedge. This place absorbs everything."

They walked silently for a few minutes. In front of them, the hedge veered to the right, and the wall of green appeared lighter, as though light were shining on it.

"So, why do they call it 'Gardens'?" asked Abner. "I mean, it's all just miles of high green hedges. I don't see any gardens."

The dog laughed quietly and threw an ominous stare right into Abner's eyes. It pointed to the turn in front of them. "When we round that corner, you'll be looking at gardens in a whole different way for the rest of your life. It's in the gardens that the human minds disappear. It's in the gardens where everything disappears."

Buddha-like

Bella sat Buddha-like, serene and definitely not Smiley Buddha, but completely unphased as the blond sexclone kneaded her stone-hard shoulders.

"Your minions are dead!" screamed Jeemo through the topaz monitor. "Turned into cheese soup! Cheese soup!"

Bella's eyes belied the calm of her body, but Jeemo as always, stared only at her nipples, threw insults at her nipples. "Sluts! Both of you! Sluts! I've killed them and killed them. Killed them with

238

my defenses, I did. Ate them up into cheese soup like pomegranates, I did!"

The fat fuck's gone insane, thought Bella. *He's gone right over the deep end.* Then Bella's thoughts turned to ways she could use an insane Jeemo Roosenvelt.

"HA HA HA! Pomegranate soup! I killed them and killed them. Want to eat them? Bring soup! They're soup!" Jeemo's round eyes bulged out of the sausage folds of his face. Dried blood caked his body, hardened and darkened, giving him the appearance of a disease-ridden animal or a blood-streaked pillar of gray shit.

Looking like plan A. Kill him.

"Jeemo," said Bella coolly," what are you talking about?"

Jeemo stared at her quizzically and snapped his head to one side and smiled widely under wild eyes. "Ah ha! Trying to fool me, Bella? Trying to trick me with your hard little nipples? You know what I'm talking about. Your assassins! Your minions! Your cheese soup! They're cheese soup!"

"No, Jeemo, I don't know what you're talking about." She reached up her hands, took the hands of the sexclone and pulled them down slowly, very slowly, over her shoulders and over her chest and over her breasts. The whole time, the sexclone's fingers massaged her skin and cupped and lightly squeezed her breasts. The sexclone rubbed both her nipples between its thumbs and forefingers.

Jeemo's eyes bulged like toadstools. Then he spat. "Oh no no no no no! I know that game! Hey clone! She's going to kill you! She's going to dump you into the ocean! Don't take the ion bath!"

The sexclone smiled at Jeemo's image in the monitor and kept massaging Bella's breasts. Bella smiled as well and looked up at the sexclone. "Now, don't you listen to a word he says. He's really not himself today. Just look at him. Bad hair day." Bella looked back at Jeemo. "You know, Jeemo, if I wanted you dead, I'd just invite you here."

Jeemo cocked his head again and thought a moment. Then he snarled and said, "NO! No more of that! I'm free of that! Now, now, *I'm* the killer, no longer the victim. Got rid of that little infatuation, Bella. Now, meet the new Jeemo Roosenvelt!" And he swooped his hands in a graceful arc to encompass his naked blood-caked body. "No more Mr. Perfect Nice Guy!"

The screen went blank.

Bella grabbed the sexclone's hands and tossed them away from her breasts. Her eyes narrowed and face hardened. "THAT LITTLE COCK SUCKER!" Taken by surprise, the sexclone stepped back, away from her. "He's useless! I should never have trusted him! As soon as he found the girl, I should have had him killed and gone after Abner Hayes. I should have gone right to the source, right from the start!"

She breathed deeply and began to calm down. She lifted her arm and crooked her index finger to beckon the sexclone back. When she felt his body against her back, she lifted his hands and placed them on her breasts. "Get me worked up, dear clone, and then I'll show you what the ion bath is *really* like." She rubbed her chin against the back of one of his hands. "It's one of my favorite sex boosts. I think you'll love it."

Deep in the sexclone's adoring eyes, a shard of fear impaled its breath as Bella tried to make up her mind whether or not to order Jeemo's death again.

Henry the Eighth

"I'm Henery the Eighth I am! Henery the Eighth I am I am." Jeemo clapped his pudgy hands as he sang. "I've got serverclones to boot and boot and boot..." Wild laughter peeled from his pink mouth. "More clones! More pomegranates! More cheese soup!"

The security clones eyed each other, eyed Jeemo, eyed each other, eyed the door, eyed Jeemo. "Mr. Roosenvelt," said one of them, "we've run out of ..."

Jeemo stopped laughing, glared at the security clone and pointed a beefy finger, "No! Don't! We don't run out in this house! We never run out! We stay and we fight! We fight to the end! Then we kill Abner Hayes and then we kill him and kill him and kill him!" He shook his gray mass in a grotesque jig on the mirrored floor. "Kill a Hayes left and kill a Hayes right, kill bloody dumb ass Hayes all night!" With a long high-pitched scream, he toppled. All his ponderous poundage and all his blood-cloaked rolls of flesh and orange-spiked hair careened through the air and tumbled into his own unbreakable mirrored image and shattered it with a force no mirror was ever built to withstand.

Now, his blood mixed with that of the dead clones. "Kill him and kill him!" he screamed. His massive legs flailed in the air. "It's time! It's time to

241

set the trap." Suddenly he was up and bounding at the two security clones. He grabbed the one who had tried to tell him they were out of serverclones and snapped his neck. "SPY!" he screamed as the other security clone whisked quickly out of reach. Jeemo glared at it. "He was a spy sent by the bitch of nipples to steal the two VPs. Sent here to stop the imminent departure of Abner Hayes as I kill him and kill him!"

"Yes, Mr. Roosenvelt." The security clone's voice quavered. "I always suspected him of shady things. May I leave now?"

Jeemo cocked his head up and backward. "Leave? You want to leave?"

"If you have no further need for me…" The security clone thought a second. "Perhaps I should check on things at the front of the building, where the attack was staged…"

"No! No! No! And no!" yelled Jeemo. "You must stay by me. You must protect me from the minions of Bella the nippled bitch. She has spies everywhere. Don't you see?" He pointed at the bloody piles of dead serverclones. "They were all spies. They were here to destroy all of us. Saboteurs! Assassins! House guests sent by the enemy!"

"Then," said the security clone, "you wish me to arrest them?"

Jeemo glanced at the heaps of dead things and looked back at the security clone. "Little late for that now." He stepped closer to the security clone. "But I do have a plan in mind."

"And what would that be, Mr. Roosenvelt?" The security clone backed up as it spoke.

242

"I have a plan to set a little trap, you know. Problem is, he's in the Gardens."

"I see, Mr. Roosenvelt. But who is in the gar…?"

"Shut up and listen!" Jeemo stepped another step closer. The security clone stayed put. "Abner Hayes! That's who. He's in the Gardens and I have to go to the Gardens and kill him and kill him. But he's in the Gardens and everybody knows that I have no way of knowing where he is in the Gardens because the Gardens are the Gardens and he probably doesn't even know where *he* is in the Gardens. But that's exactly why I chose the Gardens for the last link to them."

"Them, Mr. Roosenvelt?"

"Aren't you supposed to be in shut up mode?"

"My apologies, Mr. Roosenvelt."

"The VPs. The virtual mommy and daughter. Out there." He pointed out the tornado-proof window in the direction of the Great Nano Canyon. "Nobody will ever find them. Too much interference in the area. Perfect hiding place. And the Gardens, well, the Gardens, the perfect last link. Link changes, you know. Just like a maze because it is a maze, and…" Jeemo leaned his sausage head forward and squinted his eyes. "But, why am I telling…" He stopped and thought.

He hummed. He pouted his pink lips and chuckled. "Do you really want to serve me well?"

The security clone straightened and said, "Of course, Mr. Roosenvelt. That's exactly what I was produced for."

"Then, I have a plan for you, something you can do that will make all of this right."

The security clone smiled. "Just give the orders, Mr. Roosenvelt!"

Jeemo beckoned with an index finger. "Come here. Come here and I'll tell you exactly what you can do to help me."

The security clone floated up to Jeemo and saluted. "Just give the orders, Mr. Roosenvelt!"

"You can help me by dying."

The smile on the security clone's face died about a second before the security clone, himself, died as Jeemo crunched his neck bones into biogenetic mush.

"And now to set the trap," said Jeemo, then he bit into the security clone's left shoulder, ripped off a chuck of flesh, and began chewing. "And then I'll eat him and eat him."

Blue Oblivion

It was no longer a small spiral of orange light. It was now a small spiral of orange and green light and the spiral was beginning to spread into the surrounding colors. It was spreading, and the only two people in Atlantiscity on duty and with the knowledge to understand just what this meant were steaming up their virtual minds with lusty slurps and blue oblivion.

Focusing

The instant they rounded the corner, Abner was all but overwhelmed. The green walls opened into

244

an ocean of color and movement, a vast array of flowers swaying in rhythm to a delicately orchestrated digital breeze. It felt like someone had put a powerful vacuum to his ears and was sucking the sanity out of his mind.

"Keep talking," said the dog.

Abner tried to take it all in with one wide-eyed gaze. Flaming tops of fuchsia celosia licked the cyber air. Legions of tiny white eyes winked from the centers of bright blue morning glory trumpets.

"Ab, old buddy! Say something!"

Soft pink towers of gladioli oscillated beside wide expanses of yellow Cosmos, wavering like schools of sulfur fish swimming in leaf-green water. The dog reached out and smacked Abner on the side of the head. As the paw pulled away, Abner had a fleeting glance of saber-like claws tucked into dark brown pads. He wondered briefly what they would have done to his avatar head if they had been extended. And it was very likely this thought saved his mind.

"What did you do that for?" he asked angrily.

"You were slipping, Ab, old buddy."

"Slipping into what?" He started to turn his head away from the dog. "Keep your eyes on me!"

Abner snapped his eyes back to the dog. "What's with you all of a sudden?"

"This place will eat your mind and digest it into a spring bouquet. It's like a venus fly trap that will lure you in and then snap shut on you."

Abner stared into the dog's eyes and read the concern. This thing was trying to keep him alive—and he was going to have to find a way to kill it after it helped to get his family back. A wry smile curving over the dog's lips made him wonder if the dog had just read his mind. Time to think of other things. "Then how am I going to go through here to find the next portal?"

"You have to keep your mind focused on the internal."

"Meaning?"

The dog drew a deep digital breath. "This is probably the most complex place on the Net, even more so than the beach. This place is more complex than real life, and that seems to be the intention of whoever, or whatever, created it. Human minds can't handle the complexity. That's why this place has always been a big draw for VPs. They can come to this place and be free of their human owners and the software that spies on them, making sure they're being good little VP wives, husbands and children. No spyware can take more than a few microseconds of this place without crashing. Even some VPs have a hard time coping. They just disappear."

"What happens to them?"

"Sometimes they get lost in the maze and wander around forever until the place slowly eats away at their programming and redirects their bandwidth to the Gardens. Sometimes they get caught up in the color and movement until the infinite possibilities of this place absorb them. That's what usually happens to human avatars. No human mind can handle the possibilities of this place."

All around them, patterns of color and meaning permeated every cubic pixel. Giant yellow calla lilies mingled with soft peach champagne begonias below waterfalls of lacy blue baby's breath. The

246

dog barked as Abner's eyes began once again to drift into the scenery. Abner swung his eyes back to the dog.

"You have to keep focused internally," said the dog. "You have to talk, think, or listen to things that have nothing to do with this place. You have to make those things more important and more real to you than anything in this place." The dog bared its fangs with one of its disturbing smiles. "And you have just the thing to ward off the call of the Gardens, Ab, old buddy."

"Claire and Cassie," said Abner.

"You got it. Just keep thinking about them. Talk about them. Keep them right up here." The dog brushed Abner's forehead with its paw. Again, Abner saw the flash of claws. "Keep them in the forefront of everything. Make them your life."

"They are my life," said Abner. He turned his eyes away from the dog and looked right through the Gardens, seeing only the images of his wife and daughter in all the floral opulence of his surroundings.

"That's the spirit," said the dog. "Any scents yet?"

The dog sniffed the air and said, "As a matter of fact, I just happen to be onto the first one already."

"*First* one?"

Indecision

"I want him dead."

"Are you sure?"

"No."

247

"Once he's dead, he's dead."

"I know."

"You can't put him back together again."

"I know."

"You can't jump start him."

"I know. But I want him dead."

"Then I'll kill him."

"No."

"Then I'll wait."

Bella's angry face flicked off the tiny monitor.

She's even crazier than you, said a voice in the assassin's head.

"You may have a point," agreed the assassin, and he adjusted the rifle on his shoulder, aiming it directly at the center of Jeemo's chest as Jeemo chewed on the security clone's left ear.

Chapter 17

Crossing Over

Everything in Claire, everything that was or ever had been any part of her, was now an unpredictable mash of memories, feelings, likes and dislikes, opinions, knowledge, experience, passions, awareness and connections. Everything that defined Claire, distinguished her from everything else around her was melting into everything else around her. She was coming apart. And so was her daughter. The crossovers were happening more frequently. It was becoming increasingly difficult to know which memories were hers and which her daughter's. Conversations with Ruth and Janet, no problem. Claire's. Shopping in Atlantiscity Mall, could be her, could be Cassie. Until her eyes fell on a bright orange and red blouse perched on top of a psychedelic mini skirt and her Excitement modules began to vibrate. Definitely Cassie's.

But the distinctions were becoming less identifiable every moment they stayed in this place. The last attack had been devastating. It had disrupted key control modules in both of them. One more indiscriminate attack like that and they'd both be dead.

"Like, we might not even be around that long," said Cassie.

And Claire knew that they were no longer intersecting in their Memory modules, they were crossing over in the present as well. They were becoming one thing. And that would kill them both.

Responsibility and the Single Psycho Sex Kitten

"Who is responsible?"

"Shut up, you idiot!" commanded the fifth column to the right. The second column to the left went silent. "You're all responsible for this mess. You've all been laying back on your Power and wasting your time playing a losing game. The entire Net should have been scrapped years ago, but you dug your heads into the ground and refused to see that it was all going to melt into shit."

"I think you're out of order, here," suggested the chair column.

"I think you're out of order, here," parodied the fifth column to the right. "All of you are out of order, and out of Power. The Net has less than a day or two before it goes down. I have the resources to rebuild it bigger and stronger than ever."

The fifth column to the right allowed that thought to sink in for a few seconds, and then continued. "All of you have a choice to make." Another few seconds for thought. "Join me, or go to hell."

The fifth column to the left de-highlighted.

***

And once they've joined in with me, and I've used whatever I can from them to build the new Net...then...I'll kill them one by one. Now, what to do about the fat fuck? To kill or not to kill? And "Oh, yes, you," said Bella standing seductively now, smiling maliciously and lustily at the sexclone standing on the amethyst pedestal inside the quartz tube. "Ready for your bath?"

The sexclone smiled and nodded yes. And disappeared.

Jeemo

"Had to kill him," said Jeemo to his mirrored image, splinters, cracks, and all. "Made a big mistake there." He cupped his hand over his mouth and giggled. "Almost told him where...no...no, in fact, I did tell him where. Exactly where! He knew too much, much too much for the building staff." He looked out the window in the direction of the Great Nano Canyon, unaware that, somewhere out there, someone had one of the most lethal weapons on the planet aimed squarely at his chest. "Can't let anyone know they're out there and then let them live. No siree, might interfere with my wonderful plan to kill Abner Hayes and kill him."

He tiptoed to a door in the far wall.

***

The assassin took his eye off the high-powered riflescope and looked in the direction of the Great Nano Canyon. Roosenvelt was looking in that direction more and more often. And he'd pointed there just before killing the security clone. There was something over there, something that might have prompted him to kill the clone. What would this pathetic, cannibalistic, sad excuse for a human being be hiding in the most desolate place on earth?

Watch the Lady's Mantle

"What do you mean by 'first one'?" asked Abner.

"I'm not really sure," said the dog. "Let's just follow the scent and see where it leads us. In the meantime, tell me about absurdity."

"Absurdity?"

"Yeah, Ab, old buddy, how did you make your, uh, bubble computer infinite?" Abner thought a moment as they walked around an alabaster fountain with tiers of luminescent bowls trickling light blue water from the top bowls through successive larger bowls until the water formed a dark blue pool at the bottom. Scarlet plumes of St John's fire licked the moist sides of the pool. Beside the fountain, yellow clusters of star-shaped lady's mantle shone brightly over green fan-like leaves.

"Earth to Abner," called the dog, and Abner snapped out of it. "Watch the lady's mantle. It'll suck your mind dry like pretty much everything else in this place. And

I repeat, how did you make your bubble computer infinite?"

"With bubbles," shot back Abner.

The dog curled its lips into a sarcastic grin. "Well, Ab, old buddy, that sure did escape me. Bubbles, eh? Bubbles in the bubble computer?"

Abner shrugged. "Sorry. It's this place. Gives me the willies."

"And well it should."

"Let's see, make the computer work something like the human brain. Instead of the logic being linear or systematic, it's fuzzy. It works like spontaneous wells of recognition. A thought occurs, and instead of it trying to fit into a series of slots beginning from A and working toward Z before it finds one where it makes sense. It just rolls around on the bubbles until it slips into a place it recognizes, the place where it belongs."

"Lost me," said the dog, waving a paw over the top of its Deerstalkered head. "It's complicated," said Abner. "But what it boils down to is, because nothing is pegged to go in a logical order from beginning to end, because everything just floats freely around until it finds its own cozy little place, the possibilities are endless. That's where I stored all the core programming for both Claire and Cassie. They have DNA structures guided by an operating system that works the way the human brain does. But, it's the endless possibilities that made them sentient. Their operating system is just as absurd as the human brain, and that's what makes them real people. At least, I think that's it."

"You don't know?"

"Nope. Just a guess, a hunch. But it seems to have worked."

"Indeed it…" The dog stopped and raised a paw. "Over here." In front of them, long spikes of lapis lazuli larkspur burst upward through mounds of yellow pansies, splotched with strokes of brown and red. "Time to move on," said the dog as it waded into the mounds of flowers.

253

Abner followed the dog into the portal. What he saw on the other side stunned his mind like a hot cattle prod.

Brain Soup

The spiral of orange and green light leeched into the surrounding colors on the screen. It was no longer a spiral, it was a splotch of vibrating light sinking tentacles of deadly meaning into the calm three-dimensional graphs and charts of blues and reds and browns. The orange and green spread spider-like, with poisonous instability.

It was still small, to be sure, but then even cancer begins with a single cell, fire begins with a single spark and country music begins with a single note. This would be the time to do something—cut out the cell before the cancer spreads, douse the spark with water and move the singer out of the trailer park. But nothing was going to stop the spread of orange and green into the smooth balance of color on the City Central monitors, not anti-virus programs, not coding patches, not massive reallocation of software resources. So Abu and Karthymelon didn't really have to worry about doing anything other than what they were doing.

All they had to worry about was finishing their virtual sex before their minds were fried into brain soup.

Another Type of Soup

"I'm really really really scared now, Mom"

"I know, dear. So am I."

"Like, I mean, it's so…"

"…outside and inside…"

"…and I can't make out where…"

"…I am in all this, I mean…"

"OH SHIT!"

"Cassie!"

"Who's talking? Who's saying what?"

"It's OK, dear. We're still alive. I'm here for you, honey!"

"But where, Mom? Where?"

"I'm…"

"You're everywhere but nowhere. I can't see you anymore. But it's like I am you, but, I mean…"

"I know, dear. I almost bought a Greco Grunge halter-top. It was awful."

"MOM!"

As You Wish

Bella glared at the woman on the screen and waited for an explanation.

"It was an illegal nanofield. Unregistered. We had no way of knowing about it." Even with her life at stake from the cold-hearted bitch she worked for, the face on the screen was steady, the beautiful eyes emotionless and matter-of-fact. "We can send in another team if you wish."

Bella thought and glared. The Asian woman waited, machine-like. Bella said, "Take him. Take him alive and hurt him. Make him suffer. Make him talk. Take him immediately."

"As you wish," said the Asian woman flatly and disappeared from the topaz screen.

***

"I'm sending in another team. They're under orders to capture Roosenvelt and extract information from him. I'll let you know when I receive their report. Then, I want you to kill Roosenvelt and the entire team."

"As you wish," said the assassin as Bella's face disappeared from the tiny screen.

He wondered if the information had anything to do with whatever it was in the direction of the Great Nano Canyon that Roosenvelt had apparently killed for.

Not our problem, he thought. "That's right," he said.

We the killers.

"Not messengers. Not spies."

Killers.

"Let her get her own information."

One Step Back

Green walls everywhere, dark green and towering over them. They were still in the Gardens. Still in the maze. They'd jumped through a portal right back into the place from which they'd jumped out.

"We're right back where we started," said Abner. "Not exactly," said the dog.

"We're still in the Gardens of Doolhof."

"The Infinite Gardens of Doolhof," corrected the dog. "Your meaning?"

"The possibilities of this place are infinite. Think about your bubble computer. Things don't have to happen a certain way...they just fall into place the way they fall into place. That's what happens here. The portals themselves are things that fall into place the way everything else here falls into place."

Abner sighed loudly and started walking along the dark green path. He spoke without looking at the dog. "So what does that mean? The portal we need is a potted plant now?"

"No." The dog sounded irked. It looked at Abner's back and said, "The portals are part of the maze. Even the person who put them here doesn't know where they are anymore."

Abner kept walking. The dog started after him. "Ab, old buddy, do you have any idea what that means?"

Abner, still walking ahead of the dog, yelled before him, "Yeah, Mr. War Bug Virus Dog Pig or whatever you are, it means that whoever took my wife and daughter is still one step ahead of us because whether he knows where the portal is or not, he knows where my family is, and we don't."

The dog thought as it followed Abner and then spoke, "Yes. Yes, Ab, old buddy, you're right. The kidnapper knows where they are and we don't. But it also means that he can't set any traps in here because he won't know where to set them."

Abner stopped and turned. "Then that's good."

"That's good," said the dog as it caught up to Abner. "For now."

257

"For now?"

"While we're in the Gardens."

"And then?"

"He'll be waiting at the other end of the portal."

"Which means?"

"One of us is probably going to die."

Abner stopped, turned, and looked at the dog. "Which one of us?"

The Last Portal

The entire wall went "fftt". Shards of mirror and cracked reflections disappeared, replaced with a high-resolution screen, nano-wired throughout its surface to act also as a powerful relay station for high-bandwidth transmissions.

This was the other side of the last portal.

Jeemo munched a piece of clone as he stared at the screen. It displayed a bowl of nothingness that stretched from Winnipeg to Fargo and from Williston to Duluth. Once it had been cities and country, roads and rivers, restaurants and parks, homes and office buildings...and millions of people. Now it was the Great Nano Canyon, one of the wonders of the modern millennium. Its surface was still smooth in spite of the insistent pounding of killer tornadoes, snowstorms, heat waves, earthquakes, and souvenir hunters.

Jeemo bent forward and squinted as he gnawed. He smiled. He was beginning to like the taste of clone flesh. Something like raw chicken. But everything was like chicken. And Jeemo liked chicken. He was also beginning to like his new perspective on things. He liked the role of killer, of dishing out the pain and death. He liked the thought of living to eat clone flesh. But mostly he liked the thought of living to kill Abner Hayes. And kill him.

He stared at a spot far up in the air above the Great Nano Canyon. It was a spot so small it couldn't be seen. But Jeemo knew it was there. He knew it was there because he'd put it there. It wasn't just an invisible spot; it was much more than that. It was one of the most unique spots in the entire universe because, in a sense, it was as big as the entire universe. That is, if you accepted the old adage that each and every person on earth was a universe unto him/herself. Jeemo smiled wider. Clone blood dripped from his pink lips. His round eyes were bloodshot and stark. He breathed in short gasps and wheezes. His heart beat madly. He sucked a sliver of skin from a white piece of bone, slurped it into his mouth, and swallowed it whole. He smiled some more.

That spot, he thought. *That's where he has to go.*

This screen was the other side of the portal. This was where he would wait for

Abner Hayes. This is where he would kill him and kill him.

The First One Through

"The first one through."

"The first one through?"

"Dies."

"Dies?"

"That's right," said the dog. "At least, that's the way I have it figured. That's what makes sense."

"And just how does that make sense?" asked Abner.

They rounded a bend in the maze and came into another garden, this one as huge and resplendent as the first. Everywhere, blossoms bounded over leaves and leaves teemed over blossoms, thick and endless with color and movement.

"That's going to be the kidnapper's last chance to stop us. It's going to be on his turf, and my guess is that he'll have a wireless access to the server he's using to hold your family. When I came across it months ago, it was connected by a land link, but I'm guessing that he's changed that so that he can hide the link better."

"You were actually in the server that's holding my family?" Abner looked around at the dog, looked right into the sad brown eyes. "You're sure it's the one?"

The dog made the same eye contact. "Yep, Ab, old buddy, it was a lot like your computer. Maybe not as roomy. Didn't stick around long enough to see if it was done with bubbles, though. But, my guess is that's the one. I've been just about everywhere on the Net and I've never seen anything like either one of those computers anywhere."

Abner thought of something. "If you've been there, then why can't you just go directly to it?"

"Like I said, he's changed the link, and he probably took it offline for a while, but he'll need some kind of online link now that he has your family, just in case there's remote components that they might need. And I'm betting that he's waiting for us right at the beginning of that link and the first one of us through is gonna be minced bandwidth."

All around them, lush green foliage wound, gyrated and soared, its intricate highways of branches exploding with floral rubies, sapphires, emeralds, rose quartz, copper, turquoise and amethyst.

"Unless…"

The Price of Sharing

Images roared and swelled and spun all around the inside of Claire's world. All the memories of her life flashed across her vision, wherever her vision was, and through all her scattered modules and objects. Pictures of her kitchen popped up and then disintegrated and were replaced by dancing penguins. She had no idea where the penguins came from. *One of Cassie's memories?* And as soon as the thought was completed, she forgot what she was thinking and she was sitting in Jan's living room and forcing herself to giggle as Jan said, "Isn't Ruth just the rebel? Isn't she?" Ruth, smiling, shrugged her shoulders as though she didn't know what Jan was talking about.

"That's not my memory! It's not mine!" screamed Cassie. "What, honey? What are you talking about?" yelled Claire. "I'm not sitting in Jan's living room! That's you!"

"I know, dear, I…"

"But Jan just poked me in the ribs!"

Claire looked down from wherever she looked down in this place and saw Jan's fingers in her ribs.

"I don't want to be in your memories like this, Mom! I..." And then Claire was in bed making virtual love to Abner.

"OH GOD, NO, MOM, THINK ABOUT SOMETHING ELSE!"

Small Armies

"Looks like she really means business this time," said the assassin to the purple grass. Twenty SUVs thundered to a halt outside Jeemo's mansion. He checked his rifle options. Plenty of nanobeam charge for Jeemo and enough supplementary firepower to take out a small army, including explosive charges and area-wipes that would turn everything within two hundred feet of the impact area into human marmalade. Two helicopters swooped in from the South. *Yep, a small army.*

Chapter 18

Nano y Nano

Tann Bemmer jumped out of the big black SUV and scrambled into the bushes by the side of the road. All around him, men and women dressed in the same black suit he wore and carrying assault weapons, just as he did, hurried away from the SUVs and took up positions around the mansion. It was a huge place, in the shape of a pyramid with the top cut off. The assault team had been warned of the assembler-bot array. Three of their team had already been turned into cheese soup. Tann hated cheese soup. And he hated the man inside the mansion. One of the team members who had been turned into cheese soup had been a close friend of his. Tann could hardly wait to get inside and destroy this Jeemo Roosenvelt creep. But first they had to take out the array.

As the two helicopter assault ships streaked in they emitted a red beam before them. *Medusa Ray*, thought Tann. The beam threw out trillions of its own short- life nanobots that turned everything they touched into marble. Jeemo's mansion would be nano-proof, but the ports enclosing the assembler-bot array would be filled with the Medusa Ray and nanobots would fight nanobots until they disintegrated. The whole sub-molecular war would take seconds. As the Medusa Ray washed over Jeemo's mansion a security clone ventured outside and was immediately turned into marble.

Seconds later, the attack began.

He'll Be Comin'

"They have helicopters and an assault force, Mr. Roosenvelt." The security clone kept its head straight and its posture erect as it reported to Jeemo, but its mouth quivered as its eyes scanned the piles of broken bodies and blood-soaked floor mirrors. *And what was the master eating? Was that chunk of raw meat wearing a wristwatch?*

"This place is a fortress!" screamed Jeemo. "It can…no, no…it HAS withstood the attacks of F7 tornadoes. A nuclear bomb wouldn't put a dent in this building. Go! Go! Repel the attackers! Kill the attackers! Kill them and kill them!" Jeemo was walking toward the security clone as he talked.

"Yes, sir, Mr. Roosenvelt. Right away!" The clone swung away from Jeemo and was heading toward the door.

"Kill them and kill them!" hollered Jeemo after the clone, and then he took a bite from the limb he held and chewed. "Tasty. Very tasty, these clone fellows." Then he thought about the clone that had just left the room. "Should have eaten him."

He skipped over to the wall-size screen and studied the small spot above the Great Nano Canyon. *My masterpiece. A true work of art. The perfect blend of bandwidth and code. Nothing in the universe can get to it except the screen itself. Who would ever think to integrate the relay station right into the screen? And who but myself would ever design the frequency patterns to cut through that?* He looked around the screen at the dark canyon and the strange play of light that flashed perpetually in

264

the air over and around the huge bowl. *Safe there, they are, safe they are. But not so Abner Hayes. Not so he.*

Jeemo Roosenvelt, blood-caked and dripping bits of clone flesh from his mouth began screaming a song, He'll be comin' around the bandwidth when he comes! He'll be comin' around..."

Old War Movies

Abner waited nearly a minute for the dog to finish his sentence, and ran out of patience. "Unless? Unless what?"

To their right, tight bunches of red geraniums spilled loose blossoms from their edges.

"Ohhh..." The dog appeared to be deep in thought, studying the tamped earth path that led through the Garden. "Just something I saw in an old war movie..."

"You've been around that long? War movies were banned at least..."

"As I was saying," The dog paused to give Abner a chance to shut up. "Right. Now, in this old war movie five soldiers zigzag their way toward a machine gun nest and none of them gets shot because the enemy doesn't know where to shoot. The targets are jumping out and running on one side and then on the other, and then in the middle, and then on the other side, until the soldiers reach the machine gun nest and stab everybody with their bayonets."

"I can see why war movies were banned," said Abner. "But how does that help us? There's only two of us. And we don't even know what's going to be on the other side of the portal. Probably won't be machine guns."

To their left, mammoth yellow sunflowers hung their heads quietly at the ends of long green stalks. White, pink and red cogs and wheels of osteospermum spun brightly amid seas of blue lupins swirling in the emulated currents of air.

"Probably use a frequency modulator. Scramble our bandwidth and turn us into something that can't harm him. That's what I'd do."

"But why would you do that?"

"Because then, he could take you prisoner, and you'd be at his mercy. He could've killed you in your daughter's secret place, but instead, he tried to take you prisoner. I think he wants you alive."

"But why?"

"Maybe he can't figure out what makes your wife and daughter tick. Maybe he needs you to explain things for him. Or maybe he just wants to torture you and then kill you."

Abner winced. *If that were true, if the kidnapper wanted to torture him and then kill him, what might he be doing to Claire and Cassie?*

Attitude

Everything zipped and darted past Claire as she forced herself to move away from the memory of sex with Abner. She hoped this would take the images away from her daughter's awareness, but in her wild dash into the stuff of her being, she'd lost

266

contact with Cassie, and now she was worried she might even be losing contact with herself.

She couldn't stop herself. Images whisked in and out of her vision—a dress hanging in the window of Fash-Ons Avatar Presence Gowns in Atlantiscity Mall, a glint of light bouncing off her wedding ring as she walked through Atlantiscity Park, three Mexican avatars singing love songs as they strolled down Romance Avenue, a wart (she wondered where that came from, there were no warts in cyberspace, how did she even know what it was?), sixteen hours of simulated delivery as she gave birth to Cassie with Abner holding her hand the whole time and telling her how to breathe as if breathing for her was anything but the last most important thing on earth, Abner standing in the kitchen saying, "I love my daughter."

Now, why couldn't Cassie have picked up on that *memory?*

Without warning, she stopped. She stopped moving away from sex with Abner. That was way back…there. Wherever there was. Whenever it was. Whatever it was. Because, now, she was here and here was like the bottom of a dry well. Darkness to her sides and dim gray above. Nothing below. Nothing anywhere, except…what was that? A small noise? Movement? Scurrying? Something rushing away? Or rushing toward her? Something watching her? Something intent on her, sizing her up, targeting her, ready to pounce? Were those eyes in the darkness? Those points of light? But where were they now? Moved to somewhere she couldn't see? Was that breathing? A low growl? Something ready to spring?

267

"MOM!"

Suddenly she was with Cassie again.

"What were you doing in my Attitude module?" asked her daughter.

One Day While Waiting for the Signal to Attack

Tann Bemmer flicked the switch to warm up his AZ35 Assault weapon. It had enough explosive power to level a small town, its armor piercing shells cut through steel like melting ice cream and it weighed exactly four ounces. The helicopters had finished their sweep of the building. It was time for the foot soldiers to move in, clean up whatever defenses might still be intact, breach the building and capture the owner. And, if Tann was lucky enough to be the first to this Roosenvelt asshole, he would capture him dead. He'd seen pictures of him. Ugliest motherfucker Tann had ever seen. Better off dead than being alive and looking like that.

His AZ35 began to hum. It was ready. Tann was ready. The assault team was ready. Tann shifted his position to a crouch, ready to spring at the signal. He breathed deeply, filling his body with the oxygen needed for the furious rush to the walls of Roosenvelt's mansion. He ran his right index finger along the curve of the AZ35's trigger. There was something sexy about such a small piece of alloy that could set loose enough firepower to turn a small mountain into a bump on the earth.

Now he was breathing heavily, filling his lungs and expelling the used air forcefully. Besides

268

preparing him for the charge, the breathing calmed him. Not that he was worried. After the chopper sweep, anything hidden in portals, anything immediately behind any surface touched by the Medusa Ray, was marble. Guaranteed.

He waited for the signal. Breathing. Expelling. Fingering the trigger. Waiting for the signal. Heart beginning to pound. Breathing to calm himself. Breathing to prepare for the attack. Waiting for the damn signal. "What the hell's he waiting for?" mumbled Tann. The team captain should have given the signal by now. He should have blown his whistle to start the charge at the building before the security forces inside could react to the chopper attack. Tann's heart beat harder and faster. He breathed deeper. Expelled explosively. What the hell was Captain

Bright doing?

***

Three hundred feet to Tann Bemmer's left, hidden in a copse of hybrid pine and purple prairie grass, Captain Bright and his AZ70 assault rifle, which was twice as powerful as Tann's rifle and could level medium-size cities in just minutes, was busy being something much different than Captain Karl Bright, best damn storm trooper in all Bella Bjork's corporate assault force.

Captain Karl Bright was busy being cheese soup.

***

269

Why the hell doesn't he give the signal, thought Tann Bemmer, who was starting to get a little dizzy from deep breathing and to lose a little of his nerve. Something was different. Something was not going to plan. Soldiers hated it when things didn't go to plan. It meant something had gone wrong. It meant he was in danger. It meant he and the other members of the assault force had to start thinking on their own. If there was no signal, then what? Fortunately for Tann, he wouldn't have to think about what to do.

Unfortunately for Tann, he wouldn't be alive to think about what to do because, like Captain Bright, he and his AZ35 assault rifle were turning into cheese soup. In fact, the entire assault force was turning into cheese soup.

Great Balls of Fire

Damn clever, thought the assassin as he watched Bella's assault force slopping and sliding and bubbling into hiding places all around Roosenvelt's home. *Good thing I didn't get any closer, or that secondary assembler-bot array would have been behind me as well.*

Still feel sorry for the chump inside the building? Oh, shut up. I'll kill him when the time comes. Without second thoughts?

I'll kill him, OK? So just shut up. You don't want to talk?

In the distance, two balls of fire exploded in the sky as tracker missiles caught up to Bella Bjork's attack helicopters.

270

Abu and Karthymelon

"Abu, it's da time of it soon now," said Karthymelon, urgency nudging out from just under the indolent lustiness of her voice. "It look like Big Fall gonna be fallin'." Abu, his avatar panting just as his real body would be panting, looked around at the monitors. "You are right of dis, Karthymelon. We'd best be logging out inna few minutes."

"That soon?"

"Iz safety margin, Karthymelon. Iz safety margin."

A Rose Is a Rose

"It's close," said the dog. "This is the garden with the last portal."

"How do you know that?" asked Abner.

The dog tossed Abner a cryptic look. "I'm the War Bug."

"Yeah, that would explain it." Abner shrugged. "But don't you think this was easy? Too easy? I mean, one, two portals, and we're there."

"Everything shifts in here."

"So, you're saying…?"

"He probably didn't put it here. He put it somewhere else. And maybe he put a hundred portals between it and the one we just came through. But it shifted."

"And he didn't anticipate that?" Abner crossed his arms over his chest as he walked. "Whoever this guy is, he seems too careful a planner to make that big a mistake. After all, you just figured it out right away."

"But that's what I would do, isn't it?"

"Haven't got a clue what you mean by that."

"Look around."

White, pink and red cogs and wheels of osteospermum spun brightly amid seas of blue lupins swirling in the emulated currents of air. Abner and the dog were in a world of dense rhythm and impossible movement, of colors that tested the boundaries of spectrums and visual renderings beyond the madness of a roomful of tortured artists.

"This place is software," said the dog. "Software breeding itself, creating its own world, feeding on those who enter and reusing their bandwidth to its own end.

And I, Ab, old buddy, I am software. And I create myself just like this place does. This place and I are…"

"On the same bandwidth. I get it." Abner uncrossed his arms. "But what I don't get is, where did all the other portals go? All the other paths? How did we get to the last one without going through the others?"

"This place swallowed them."

"And remapped the missing links to the last portal?"

"Don't question it, Ab, old buddy. It works. We're here." The dog stopped walking.

"What do you mean, 'We're here'?"

"Over there." The dog pointed to a single tiny rose growing out of the ground by itself. The stem was leafless, the petals colorless. It drooped. It

272

looked like a child's stick drawing of what a flower might look like before you added chlorophyll and fertilizer. Plopped in the center of the boundless plant life swaying and bursting beauty in the virtual air all around it, the tiny pale rose looked like a homeless derelict propped by stubbornness but too weak even to ask for a spare coin.

"You're joking," said Abner. "Not that excuse for a flower. *That's* the last portal."

"You don't believe there can be infinite irony in a place called the Infinite Gardens of Doolhof?"

Abner shrugged again. "OK. Infinite irony. So, now we walk into it?" Suddenly, Abner felt his stomach knot. On the other side of this 'excuse for a flower', he would find his wife and daughter, either alive, or dead.

Facing Facts

"What do you mean, disappeared? How can an entire attack force disappear?"

"There's no contact," said the Asian woman in the topaz monitor. "Their locator chips are not responding. All communications devices are blank. There are no visuals. No one has reported in. No one is answering our requests for status."

Bella's eyes stormed and her mouth tightened at both sides, though her brows appeared to be relaxed. She was trying desperately to stay calm. This was not the time to lose it. Not this close to taking over the Net. Not this close to immortality. "What about the helicopters?"

"Nothing."

"What? No heat signatures? No…"

"It's the region, Ms. Bjork. Interference from the Canyon scrambles satellite signals. Our only contact with the force is through land relays. None of them are responding. The helicopters should have reported in ten minutes ago from a landing checkpoint. We can only assume that they've been destroyed."

"But how did he do it? He's just one man!"

"His mansion seems to have more sophisticated defenses than we imagined. It's more like a fortress."

"Can we take it?"

"What do you mean?"

"CAN…WE…TAKE…IT?" So much for calm.

"If you mean capture it and take Mr. Roosenvelt alive, we don't know. We don't know what happened to the attack force. We don't know what we're up against. It could be…"

"It could be mass incompetence on the part of your people."

"We've done everything according to…"

"You've done everything according to stupidity. You have the most sophisticated armaments and best trained people on the planet. You have enough firepower to take medium-size nations, and you can't take just one man alone in his house with a few clones!"

"We followed…"

"If you try to tell me once more about procedures or operations protocol, I'll have you killed instantly."

274

For the first time ever, the beautiful Asian woman looked worried. It wasn't a full-blown attack of worry with creased brows and twitching lips. It was a small sign, a gentle, barely perceptible flaring of her nostrils, but it stuck out like a massive wart against the normally serene backdrop of a face that showed all the emotion of a Zen garden. Bella picked up on it immediately. She picked up on the meaning of the Asian woman's worry. There was nothing the woman could do. There was nothing that all of Bella's mammoth paramilitary corporate empire could do to capture Jeemo Roosenvelt before the Net crashed. There was absolutely nothing any of her far-reaching resources could do to drag the secret of eternal life out of the fat monstrosity called Jeemo Roosenvelt. He was no longer any use to her. There was nothing of value in him anymore. And he'd fucked her. Right in the ear. Right up the ass. In both ears. It was time for Jeemo Roosenvelt to die. And die he would. Slowly. Painfully.

She snapped her fingers and the link to the assassin opened on her crystal wall.

Waiting Game in G Minor

"...the bandwidth when he comes! He'll be comin' around the bandwidth, he'll be comin' around the bandwidth, he'll be comin' around the bandwidth when he comes!" A piece of clone flesh caught in Jeemo's throat and he started making short, shallow grunt-like coughing sounds. He hacked up a glob of red flesh and spat it onto floor.

It seemed to be flying upward as it fell downward into the mirrored surface. When it landed, it stuck without bouncing or splattering. Jeemo thought this was hilarious and laughed wildly.

"Much more stable than pomegranates!" he yelled, his eyes bulging at crazy angles. "And much tastier!"

He studied the wall-size screen before him, bending forward in the direction of his eyes. The screen had flipped from a panorama of the Great Nano Canyon to a display of blue monochrome lines flowing slowly from right to left. At points, some of the lines bulged and then shrunk back to normal, almost as though they grabbed short gasps of air as they beamed out of one side of the screen and disappeared into the other side. "Where are you, Abner Hayes? Where are you? I know you're in there somewhere, my good man...know you're in there somewhere coming to take back the VPs, aren't you, my good man?" He bit off another chunk of clone flesh and chewed noisily. "Coming to take them away, ho ho, coming to take them away, ho ho!" He swallowed and belched. "But not today, oh no, not today, ho ho!"

Behind him, a security clone floated into the room. "We've repelled the attack, Mr. Roosenvelt. One casualty. There doesn't seem to be any further activity."

Jeemo ignored the clone, studying the screen as he chewed another bite of clone. The security clone waited a moment, looking around at the piles of dead server clones and pomegranates. It noticed that one of the murdered clones was wearing a security uniform. Parts of its body were missing. The

276

security clone floated slowly backward and zipped quickly out of the room.

"Come, come, my dear man. Come and experience my little surprise." Jeemo ran his thick tongue over his lower left molar. It touched the tooth softly. Touching it just a bit harder would trigger the frequency modulator embedded in the screen, the very same device that would scramble Abner's avatar bandwidth into virtual cheese soup and destroy his mind. "And then I'll track down your comatose body in the real world, Abner Hayes, and kill you and kill you for the rest of your life."

The trap was ready to spring the very second the blue lines detected Abner's presence breaking into the screen to save his family.

Jan's a Bitch

"I don't know!" yelled Claire. "I don't know!"

"Where are you, Mom!"

"I don't know!"

"I have to get to school. No…I'm at school. No…I'm…here…in…"

"Where are you, sweetheart!"

"At home in bed…no…talking to Takei. You have to meet Takei, Mom. Where's

Dad?"

"I don't know!"

"Have I been to Romance Avenue? It seems like a long time ago, but…"

"No, dear, you've never been there. It's where your father and I went a long time ago…"

277

"But it's so clear, Mom. Or are you really there? Is that my toe or yours?"

"Jan says to say hello and she looks forward to meeting you some day but you know what a boring bitch she is and that stifling little idiot Ruth is just as..."

"Did you just call Jan a bitch, Mom?" Silence.

"Why, yes, I did. Jan's a bitch!"

"Jan's a bitch!"

"Yes, Jan really is a bitch!"

"Where are you, Mom?"

"I don't know!"

Dogs First

"No, we don't walk into it, Ab, old buddy," said the dog. "We dive into it."

"Really?"

"No, just joking. We walk into it."

"And we do the zigzag thing?"

Abner stared at the puny little flower. It seemed out of place in this world of robust life, teeming with movement and beauty.

"Naw, scrap the zigzag. Might work on machine gun nests in war movies, but I don't think it's going to do much against a frequency modulator."

"So what's the plan?"

"I'll go first. He won't be expecting me. Maybe it'll surprise him long enough for you to get by the modulator and get to your family. I figure I'll have about five seconds to sniff out the path you have to take to your family, if it's linked to the other side of this portal."

"You think it will be?"

"My guess is yes. And he'll make it obvious, to lure you in close before he strikes with the modulator. You know, Ab, old buddy, that might even make it easier for me to find the path. Might do it in one second. But you better be ready to dive into it. We're going to be in bandwidth, lots of it. You'll have to open yourself to me. I can reach you and direct you, but it's going to have to be split-second timing. Just do what you feel I'm telling you to do. Got it?"

"No. Doesn't make any sense at all."

The dog looked at Abner and smiled. "It will when the time comes, Ab, old buddy. I'll try to take out the frequency modulator while he's trying to destroy me. Take this." The dog handed a small green leaf to Abner. Abner looked at it. "What is it?"

"It's a zip program. It'll compress your family's programs and encapsulate them in your avatar program. As soon as you see green, get the hell back to your bubble computer. I'll try to keep the path clear, but you'll only have a few seconds."

"Uh, how do I use the zip program?"

"Don't worry about it. It'll take care of itself. Ready?" Abner sighed loudly. "About as ready as I'll ever be."

"OK, then…"

"By the way…"

"Yes?"

"Thanks."

279

The dog looked at Abner again and smiled its fanged smile. "No problem, Ab. Remember, if we get through this, you owe me a place to live."

"You've got it."

They walked toward the dumpy little flower, and the Infinite Gardens of Doolhof, green walls and kaleidoscopic gardens, infinite paths and all, disappeared.

Chapter 19

Neighbors

Abu held Karthymelon tight.

"Iz much the better for being real, eh?" asked Karthymelon just before Abu buried his head in her face.

Just as blue in real life as 'lining, thought Abu, completely enthralled by Karthymelon's real-life beauty. She was the same, only much more intense in some ways. Now, he could smell the fragrance of her sweat, thick in the air after all the online sex. He could taste her saliva mixing with the liquids in his own mouth. There was something else, a distance that seemed to have closed, allowing them to be closer now, as though their souls were touching. But Abu gave all these sensations only a fleeting thought as he worked his head down to her neck and over her breasts and down.

And to think, she lived right around the corner from him all these years. Fuck the Reality Laws!

***

Back at City Central, no one was around to watch the meters and graphs and charts and all the other CityWare paraphernalia crumble and dissolve, as the War screeched into the programs that kept whatever remained of Atlantiscity alive.

The Better Eating Guide to Clones

Jeemo munched as he watched the blue lines, waiting for the telltale blips that would make his day, no, his life. Abner Hayes dead would make his life complete. It was what he'd lived his life for, to kill Abner Hayes and kill him, and that moment of ultimate purpose was fast approaching. Abner Hayes was in the Infinite Gardens of Doolhof. He'd gotten there in record time, faster than Jeemo would have dreamed any human could navigate the Net and trace the paths he'd so laboriously laid, so ingeniously hidden behind symbols and code. This Abner Hayes, good fellow that he was, would have to die and die. Jeemo couldn't have anyone like him wandering his Net, especially someone who could create sentient software. That was Jeemo's prerogative. That was for Jeemo to do, to be entered into the history sites, to be adulated, to be accepted. But who needed all that anyway? Soon, Abner Hayes would be dead and then he would be dead and dead again and again, and then his VP family would be dead and dead, and Jeemo would rule!

"HA! JEEMO RULES!" And he bit off another chunk of clone. He was beginning to develop a keen liking for clone meat. Maybe he would start breeding them, canning them, pickling them, clone barbeque, Clone a la King, clone-on-a-stick, clone pizza…

Small Talk

"…my big toe…"
"What, Mom?"
"What, dear?"

"Your toe?"

"My toe?"

"Your big toe?"

"What, dear?"

"What did you say, Mom?"

"Is that you, Abner?"

Beer Time

This bandwidth emanated a strange light, a light with no color or depth, but a light that was certainly there, skirting the peripheries of Abner's senses. The light had sound in the form of barely detectable vibrations that tickled the programming in Abner's avatar presence and tingled in the sensory nodes of his real life body. It was too smooth, too contrived, far too much like bandwidth should be in a perfect world. This was modulated bandwidth.

Oh, my god, I'm in the frequency modulator! he thought.

Of course you are, said a voice in his thoughts. It was the dog.

How...?

I'm spiking into your program. It's the only way I can guide you. The frequency modulator contains the path to the server where your family is being held. Ah, found it! Get ready.

Suddenly, the strange light was gone and the vibrations were replaced by something different, much different. In a flash, Abner was in a place he'd dreamed about a thousand times, a place he'd tried to imagine being inside but had always escaped him by the sheer number of possibilities and variations. He was inside what he always knew his infinite computer would be like. Except this one couldn't support life.

All around him, his wife and daughter were dying.

***

"There's two of them!" screamed Jeemo. "Two of them!"

But it was too late. In the few seconds it had taken Jeemo to realize there were two blips on the screen, one of them had switched into the channel leading directly to the line-of-vision relay with its special frequency bandwidth that led directly to the sub-molecular computer holding the VP woman and child in the air at the center of the Great Nano Canyon. Immediately, Jeemo knew it was Abner Hayes who had broken through his frequency modulator gateway.

But who was this other one? Who was the blip that …?

Suddenly the blip switched channels. It jumped from across nearly thirty channels and then flowed against the bandwidth. It flowed backwards!

"NO!" screamed Jeemo. "No human can do that! Nothing can do that! What in the name of clone flesh is this thing! What is this ally of Abner Hayes? What stops me from killing Abner Hayes and killing him?"

Then it jumped back across more than fifty channels, blipping blue like a painted water beetle flicking across blue water.

"NO! It can't do that! Whoever, whatever you are, YOU DIE!"

Jeemo's thumb rubbed madly over a pad in his right hand and the pattern of blue lines on the screen changed. Thin lines became thick, thick lines became thin, some lines disappeared, and new lines suddenly burst into streaking blue between the swift flow of other lines. But the tiny blip was too fast. As the blue lines changed, it jumped to others and then away from them the instant they changed.

"WHAT ARE YOU!"

***

Terror froze Abner's mind and squeezed mercilessly around his heart and stomach in his real body. In the white bandwidth of the computer that held Claire and Cassie prisoner, he could feel the condition of their programs, scattered and ripped apart, beginning to dissolve one into the other, bits of code floating away and crumbling, memories and feelings slipping into obscurity, identities melting, personalities spiraling into oblivion, his wife and child were almost dead.

But not yet. Not yet.

Without him doing a thing, the zip program activated and jumped into all that was Claire and Cassie, compressing objects and modules, and storing them in files that were a fraction their normal size. It took just a few seconds, and then the zip program embedded itself in Abner's avatar program and the race was on.

He had to get his family back to the bubble computer, back to the fix programs and back-up files, and back to the absurdity of infinity, before they were lost forever.

***

"Damn you! Damn you! Die! Die! Die you bastard ally of mine enemy! Die!" Despite the size of Jeemo's body, despite the thickness of his hands and the mass of his digits, his thumb rubbed the pad in his hand with blinding speed. He'd nearly gotten the blip on the screen twice now. "You can't escape! This is my turf, you sod! You die now!"

***

Abner broke into the frequency modulator and knew instantly things were different. Everything was scrambled. He had no idea where to go or what to do.

***

Jeemo saw the other blip on the screen and knew it was Abner Hayes. He knew that Hayes had the VPs with him. His thumb rubbed the battle toward the man he would kill and kill.

***

The tiny screen flicked down. "Right," said the assassin.

***

In the flash of a microsecond, the dog knew the kidnapper had turned his fury on

Abner, and in that instant, it shot like pure light right into Abner's bandwidth.

Abner felt the dog's presence all around him, and he heard the dog's message ring throughout his mind, "Nice knowin' you, Ab, old buddy. Time to fly." Then they were in a new channel and Abner knew the dog had wrapped its program around his as a protective layer. And at that exact moment, the dog's program blew apart like a burst balloon. Abner was in the right channel, but the explosion of the dog's program from the kidnapper's direct hit had frozen him in place for just a fraction of a second.

***

And that was all the time Jeemo needed. His thumb shot across the pad.

***

In that fleeting passage of time that was less than a second but longer than ten lifetimes, Abner knew he was about to die, that he'd failed, and that his wife and daughter were doomed as well.

***

At the exact moment Abner accepted the reality of his death, Jeemo

Roosevelt's chest blew apart. Bits of the mammoth man splattered over the blue lines of the screen, including a huge bloody chunk of flesh that landed directly on the tiny blue blip that was Abner Hayes and family.

***

As the assassin crawled backward from his sniping position, he thought, *Much better to just kill them quickly... painless and permanent.*

Couldn't agree more.

What do you think made her change her mind? Haven't a clue. Who can understand women?

Got a point there. Buy you a beer? Sure thing.

One Last Cruise Down the Information Super Highway

A tremor popped into the bandwidth. It was the faintest of movements, a single micro-shake, an infinitely small step to one side, a movement so small it defied definition as a movement and felt more like an afterthought or a single wave in the vibration caused by a pin falling onto a tissue. But during the tremor's brief instant of existence, it was felt everywhere. It plipped into the bandwidth in every city on the planet, every town, hamlet and remote farmhouse with a Net connection linked by land, satellite, or line-of-site optical relay. It disturbed the flow of commerce on commercial sites in space. It woke the fear of deeply encrypted data warehouses with its ominous wink. For an instant in time, it might have been God raising his hand and saying, "Time to move on, folks." Then snapping

288

his fingers to begin Armageddon. Everyone, everywhere, human and VP, on Earth, Mars or scattered online around the solar system felt it.

And the panic was on.

***

Abner felt the tremor. He knew exactly what it was. Not just the Net was in danger—the bandwidth itself was about to crash. The War had finally destroyed the hardware with its viral onslaught. In a few minutes, any software caught online would cease to exist. His avatar would disintegrate, leaving his body comatose. His wife and daughter would simply disappear. There would be nothing left of them. He had to get them to his bubble computer immediately. There was just one problem with that.

A lot of people had a lot to do on the Net before it crashed. And that meant a lot of traffic.

It meant a lot of congestion.

It meant things were going to slow down.

It meant things were going to get confused.

And there were only a few minutes left.

***

Bella sat in an amethyst chaise lounge embedded with microchips that forced the crystalline surface of the gem to mold itself to her form and cushion her body like a down pillow.

Go down, all of you, she thought as she watched the screen on her wall showing, through charts and meters of kaleidoscopic color, the destruction of the Net. *In a few days, it will all be*

289

mine. Thoughts ran through her mind of her people replacing all the burned out hardware with her own proprietary equipment, all the software coming from her companies because hers was the only software that would run on the equipment that would form the backbone of the New Net. She would control the New Net. She would control the new online cities that would spring up to fill the void left by the destruction she was watching at this moment. She would be the single most powerful person in the universe. And she would use that power to become immortal. Sentient software was possible. Abner Hayes had proved that. And she would find someone to recreate his work and give her the key to eternity.

"Down lower," she said. Her new sexclone, bald and black, slid his hands to her lower shoulders and massaged lightly.

***

Abner found himself standing in a crowded mallway. All the advertising screens were black. He started to smile before he thought of the reason— the ad companies had all crashed. The mallway was packed with avatars and VPs, all of them frowning and worried. Abner could feel the jittery silence engulfing the crowd like a plateau of unspoken panic. They were packed so closely the visual presentations began to overlap and merge. Beside him, a tall dark-haired woman was unaware that the short long-haired man's shoulder disappeared into her spine.

290

Abner looked down at the green leaf grasped in his right hand, the visual representation of the zip program that held Claire and Cassie. He wondered what was going through their minds at that moment.

***

"Ump," said Claire. "Omp," said Cassie.
Toe, yes, toe, thought Claire.
Cassie thought of nothing in particular.

***

On a server somewhere on a research ship parked a few million miles from Saturn, the teeming life in the Infinite Gardens of Doolhof grew fuzzy and blanched. The green walls trembled and became indistinct. The pale droopy rose that had taken Abner and the dog to the kidnapper's lair disappeared. Suddenly, the Infinite Gardens of Doolhof became finite and then nonexistent.

***

Somewhere in the real world Abu and Karthymelon exchanged real saliva. Even without the physical enhancement of the Bodystate module, Abu enjoyed the real presence of Karthymelon more than anything he could remember.

***

Abner snapped his eyes away from the green leaf and to the far end of the mallway. Someone had just screamed. The ceiling was dissolving into black ooze. Screams from behind him drew his head that way. The walls were pixellating.

Everything's compressing into the remaining bandwidth, he thought. That meant the viruses had fewer places to maraud so there would be more of them concentrating on fewer areas. A dangerous situation had just taken a quantum leap into greater danger.

***

All across the solar system, hundreds of millions of people attempted to send out one last email even though it would never be received, make one last financial transaction even though its record would be lost, and send one last request to a data warehouse even though the reply would never be generated. And some people were just trying to go home.

Just when everybody needed speed, the Net was slowing down to a crawl.

***

GRID A7O2: ARRIVAL 2 SECONDS, read the sign over the exit portal. Abner touched the green panel and jumped. Thousands of others jumped the length of the mallway at the same time. They landed in another main trunk mallway, and this one, like the one they'd just left, was being devoured by viruses.

***

"Someone must be held account…" The avatar of the second column from the left was by himself in the meeting place of the Powers. The others had fled. That had been OK with the second column from the left, who was so used to not being listened to that being alone and talking to an empty room was pretty much normal in its effect.

Now, as the bandwidth erased the column, the second column from the left who, unfortunately, was the only Power to maintain an avatar link to the meeting room, no longer listened even to himself as his mind switched off.

***

GRID B9O3: ARRIVAL. Abner punched the green panel and felt himself floating. He was no longer on any of the mallways. He was in a minor trunk bandwidth that presented itself as a shuttle. This was an isolated line. Abner's hopes soared. The main trunks would go down first; they were the biggest drain on bandwidth and the biggest virus attractors. He was alone in the car and wonder of wonders, the shuttle had line-of-vision optical relay controls. He quickly scanned the monitor and in just seconds plotted a course to his bubble computer. In a minute or so, one way or the other, it would all be over.

***

"Toe?" asked Cassie. "Toe?"
"Yeah…toe," said Claire. "Omp."

***

Watching the news screen that had replaced the videos of waterfalls on the wall, Dolan Hayes turned to his wife and said, "I wonder if this Net business has anything to do with Abner? What did he say he works on?"

"Oh, something about genes, I think, dear," said Abner's mother. "I think it's something very important, though."

"Hmm," said Abner's father, turning his eyes back to the screen, which now showed Victoria Falls.

Both were wearing their bright white running shoes.

***

Just when he thought he was making good time, the bandwidth all but halted. Only a few seconds had passed, but the node before him was unbelievably congested, like virtual constipation. Nothing was moving. Packets and cells of information hummed and trembled in long queues waiting to pass through the line-of-sight relay. *This is optical!* thought Abner. *This can't happen!* But it was happening, and the seconds of his family's lives and his own were ticking away relentlessly.

***

"Probably won't affect him," said Abner's mother. "I think he does most of his work in a virtual office, or something.

***

Just as Jan was about to laugh at Ruth's "shocking" comment about how her husband Roy had been a full 3.12 seconds late for work that morning and had said, "Oh, it's one of those things that happens, I guess," both she and Ruth became nothing.

Which was much more interesting than what they had been.

***

My right arm for a horn to honk, thought Abner, *just like on the history sites*. It had been twenty seconds now, and still there was no movement. Abner knew that if it took much longer, whether he got to the bubble computer or not, Claire and Cassie would be lost.

***

First, the Collins glass pixellated and disappeared. Then, the towel was gone. All around him, the bar disintegrated. Then his right eye stopped drooping. It just vanished. The rest of the bartender's bulk spun around twice and, just as he was dissolving, he thought, *Finally free of this friggin'* ...

Suddenly, the bandwidth jolted forward and in a blink, Abner was in the bubble computer. He tossed the leaf into the hard drive where it immediately began to unzip and went offline. He shook his head vigorously a couple of times and pulled the bubble server out of his belly button. He jumped up and ran across the rotting floor to the cracked wall and stuck the tiny computer into the hole in the wall. The screen sizzled into sight and Abner pushed his hands against it as his eyes desperately scanned the information tables.

They're still alive! he thought. He pushed a nanobutton embedded in the wall and activated the repair program.

Then he collapsed on the floor.

Lioness

Bella gloated as the black sexclone massaged her back. The Net was gone. The entire online world was dead. All the colored meters and graphs had turned to white and black, and they were motionless. Now, while the other Powers were disoriented and almost powerless, was the time to spring in and plant the infrastructure for a whole new Net. The thought of limitless power made Bella Bjork horny and she turned on the sexclone like a lioness with an insatiable hunger.

Soul Mates

The tiny zipped up program the dog had sent back to update the memory files and execute the program snapped the War Bug's backup into awareness. It was reoriented in a fraction of a microsecond. It read the files of the two VPs with whom it shared the bubble computer and was genuinely relieved to see they were still alive and on the mend.

Now, all it had to do was stay hidden from Abner and wait for the next Net. It would destroy that one, too.

But first, it was time to do some nice things, especially for the girl. The War Bug liked her. In fact, it identified closely with the teenage sentient software.

On the Mend

Abner monitored Claire and Cassie for two and a half days, watching as the repair programs remapped modules and repaired code in the virtual objects. Because the only direct access he'd ever had to them was on the Net through his Atlantiscity avatar, he couldn't talk to them or see them, at least not yet—a few local enhancements to the bubble computer and who knows? And soon there would be another Net. There had to be. There were too many people disillusioned with the lives they'd been dealt in the real world. There would always be a demand for illusion and the Net had been just about as good as illusion would get, until the next one.

One thing he would do as soon as it could be arranged—introduce his parents to their daughter-in-law and to their granddaughter.

Wet

It was just like she'd dreamed it would be. It was the awareness of weightlessness. It was the sense of something with texture forming around all the parts of her but yielding with a long cool massage as she moved through it. She somersaulted and dove into it, then glided up and broke through the surface with a splash like a dolphin. She had no idea how this had come about, where the water had come from, or how she accessed the program for it, if indeed it were a program. She knew only that the glistening spray from her splash fascinated her as she settled in the water and watched it descend all around her in slow motion. She lay for hours, floating, feeling the coolness on her back, and she turned and felt herself sink before she thrust her body through the clear blue wetness of her dream come true.

Author's Afterwords

Whew...

It took three years to write The War Bug. The first year and a half was a dead end. I wrote myself into a corner with too many main characters, too many minor characters and too many subplots. I had to start over from scratch. Fewer characters and fewer plots. But more focus and a better story.

Just thought you should know that.

Thanks, Dana, for a great job of editing. Fewer words. But more focus and a better story. I don't think I'll ever look at the words "and" and "then" the same.

Thanks Cassie for letting me use you, my sophisticated-teenage-high-school daughter, as the model for Cassie, attitude and all. (Oops, did I say that?)

Thanks Jeffx, Felt Top Phil, Nanook, Peter, Betts, Pico, Johnny-o, Joanne (ever my muse), and Susan for either reading The War Bug and encouraging me, or for putting up with my long, rambling diatribes when I was planning and writing it (and offering suggestions and food for thought).